FURIA

FURIA

YAMILE SAIED MÉNDEZ

Algonquin 2020

Published by Algonquin Young Readers
an imprint of Algonquin Books of Chapel Hill
Post Office Box 2225
Chapel Hill, North Carolina 27515-2225

a division of Workman Publishing
225 Varick Street
New York, New York 10014

Library of Congress Cataloging-in-Publication Data
Names: Méndez, Yamile Saied, author.
Title: Furia / Yamile Saied Méndez.
Description: Chapel Hill, North Carolina :
Algonquin Young Readers, 2020. |
Audience: Ages 12 and up. | Audience: Grades 7–9. |
Summary: Seventeen-year-old Camila Hassan, a rising soccer star in
Rosario, Argentina, dreams of playing professionally, in defiance of
her father's wishes and at the risk of her budding romance with Diego.
Identifiers: LCCN 2020020758 | ISBN 9781616209919 (hardcover) |
ISBN 9781643751207 (ebook)
Subjects: CYAC: Soccer—Fiction. |
Dating (Social customs)—Fiction. | Sexism—Fiction. |
Family life—Argentina—Fiction. | Argentina—Fiction.
Classification: LCC PZ7.1.M4713 Fur 2020 | DDC [Fic]—dc23
LC record available at https://lccn.loc.gov/2020020758

10 9 8 7 6 5 4 3 2 1

First Edition

For my daughters, Magalí and Areli,
For my sister, María Belén Saied,
For the little girl I once was,
For all las Incorregibles and las Furias of the world.

But a mermaid has no tears, and therefore she suffers so much more.

—HANS CHRISTIAN ANDERSEN,
"THE LITTLE MERMAID"

FURIA

LIES HAVE SHORT LEGS. I LEARNED THIS PROVERB BEFORE I
could speak. I never knew exactly where it came from.
Maybe the saying followed my family across the Atlantic,
all the way to Rosario, the second-largest city in Argentina,
at the end of the world.

My Russian great-grandmother, Isabel, embroidered
it on a pillow after her first love broke her heart and
married her sister. My Palestinian grandfather, Ahmed,
whispered it to me every time my mom found his hidden
stash of wine bottles. My Andalusian grandmother, Elena,
repeated it like a mantra until her memories and regrets
called her to the next life. Maybe it came from Matilde,
the woman who chased freedom to Las Pampas all the

way from Brazil, but of her, this Black woman whose blood roared in my veins, we hardly ever spoke. Her last name got lost, but my grandma's grandma still showed up so many generations later in the way my brown hair curled, the shape of my nose, and my stubbornness—ay, Dios mío, my stubbornness. Like her, if family folklore was to be trusted, I had never learned to shut up or do as I was told.

But perhaps the words sprouted from this land that the conquistadores thought was encrusted with silver, the only inheritance I'd ever receive from the indigenous branch of my family tree. In any case, when my mom said them to me as I was getting ready to leave the house that afternoon, I brushed her off.

"I'm not lying," I insisted, fighting with the tangled laces of my sneakers—*real* Nikes that Pablo, my brother, had given me for Christmas after he got his first footballer paycheck. "I told you, I'll be at Roxana's."

My mom put down her sewing—a sequined skirt for a quinceañera—and stared at me. "Be back by seven. The whole family will be over to celebrate the season opener."

The whole family.

As if.

For all their talk of family unity, my parents weren't on speaking terms with any of their siblings or cousins. But my dad's friends and Pablo's girlfriend would be here eating and gossiping and laughing until who knew when.

"You know Pablo, Ma. I'm sure he has plans with the team."

"He specifically asked me to make pizzas," she said with a smirk. "Now, *you* be on time, and don't do anything stupid."

"Stupid like what?" My words came out too harsh, but I had stellar grades. I didn't do drugs. I didn't sleep around. Hell, I was seventeen and *not* pregnant, unlike every other woman in my family. You would've thought she'd give me some credit, be on my side, but no. Nothing I did was enough. *I* was not enough. "It's not like I can go to El Gigante. I don't have money for a ticket."

She flung the fabric aside. "Mirá, Camila, how many times have I told you that a fútbol stadium's no place for a decent señorita? That girl who turned up in a ditch? If she hadn't been hanging out with the wrong crowd, she'd still be alive."

There was a little bit of truth in what she said. But just a little. *That* girl, Gimena Márquez, had gone missing after a game last year, but she had been killed by her boyfriend, el Paco. He and Pope Francisco shared a name, but el Paco was no saint.

Everyone knew that, just as everyone knew he used every woman in his life as a punching bag, starting with his mother. If I pointed this out, though, my mom would start ranting about the Ni Una Menos movement, how it was all feminist propaganda, and I'd miss my bus. My championship game, the one my mom couldn't know about, was at four, the same time as Central's league opener. At least they were at opposite ends of the city.

"Vieja," I said, instantly regretting calling her old. She wasn't even forty yet. "We live in the twenty-first century in a free-ish country. If I wanted to go to the stadium, I could. You could, too, Mami. Pablo would want to see you there. You know that, right?"

Her face hardened. The last time she'd been to the stadium, Central had lost, and my dad had joked that she'd been la yeta, bad luck. My mom was a never-forgive, never-forget kind of person and would remember his words until her last breath. Because what if he was right? What if she had been the reason Pablo's team had lost?

Throwing my last card, I let just enough of the truth spill out (I *was* going to Roxana's after my game) to quench her fears. "At Roxana's I can hear what happens in the stadium, Mama. Just give me this, please. What am I supposed to do here all day?"

She tugged at a stubborn thread. "It's *Mamá*, Camila—don't talk like a country girl. If my sister Graciela heard you speak like this . . ." Her eyes swept over me, up and down. "And why are you wearing those baggy pants, hija? If you'd let me make you a few dresses . . ."

I almost laughed. If she was picking on how I talked

and how I dressed, I'd won this battle. But then she said, "You're hiding something, and it worries me."

My heart softened.

I'd been hiding that something for an entire year, since Coach Alicia had discovered Roxana and me playing in a night league and recruited us to her team.

Pobre Mamá.

I wished I could share my secret with her. But in spite of what my parents believed, I had learned my lessons. When I was twelve, my dad found me playing fútbol in the neighborhood potrero with a bunch of boys. I'd been having the time of my life . . . until he started bellowing at me in front of the whole barrio that he wasn't raising a marimacho, that fútbol was for men. I took it all in silence, ready to cry at my mom's feet, but she sided with him. I hadn't talked to her about fútbol since.

"Chau, Ma." I pecked her cheek and dashed for the door and freedom. "I'll tell Mrs. Fong you said hi."

"Answer your phone when I call you!"

My cheap phone was inside my backpack, safely out of credit. But she didn't know that. "Chau, te quiero!" I threw her a kiss and ran out before she could stop me.

I paused for half a second by the closed metal door of our apartment, but she didn't say te quiero back.

The neighbor's music, "Mi Gente," set a reggaeton rhythm for my pounding feet. I took every shortcut between the cinder block buildings and shacks in 7 de Septiembre, our barrio. By the time I made it to the bus stop, I couldn't hear the music anymore, but the *pam-pam* beat still resonated inside me.

The 142 bus turned the corner just after I checked my watch. Two forty.

"You're on time!" I gave the driver a grateful smile as I scanned my student card on the reader, and when it beeped, I thanked la Virgencita. I couldn't really afford to spend money on the fare, but the game field in Parque Yrigoyen was too far away to walk.

"Well, you're lucky," the driver said. "This is the emergency services bus for Central's opener. Most Scoundrels are already at El Gigante, but I'm supporting from here." He smiled, showing me the blue-and-yellow jersey peeking out from under his worn blue button-up. "You heading there?"

I didn't want to give him an excuse to get too friendly, so I shrugged and found a seat. The shiny black leather was cracked with yellowish stuffing peeking out, but it was far enough from both the middle-aged couple making out in the back and the man leering at me on the right.

The bus gathered speed and left el barrio. The drone of the engine and the warmth of the heater lulled me as I gazed out the window at the still-naked August trees and the flocks of birds who hadn't made the flight north for warmer weather.

After a brief stop on Circunvalación, I felt something touch my leg—a card with a picture of La Difunta Correa, the patron saint of impossible things. The paper was yellowing, and a corner was bent. I looked up to see the flash of a young boy's crooked smile as he walked the length of the bus giving out estampitas, saint cards, hoping for small donations.

In spite of attending a Catholic school since third grade, I'd never been particularly religious, but I recognized La Difunta. The image of a dead mother still breastfeeding her baby in a beam of divine sunshine had always mesmerized me. Sometime during the chaotic postcolonial years in the mid-1800s, the army had taken La Difunta's husband to fatten up its ranks. Heartbroken, she'd carried their infant son and followed her husband through the sierras and the desert until she died of thirst. When two drovers found her body, her child was still alive, suckling from her breast. Ever since, miracles have been attributed to her. She isn't officially a saint, but shrines to La Difunta dot Argentina's roads, encircled by bottles of water, the offering and payment for her favors.

My conscience reminded me of all my lies, of the miracle my team would need to win the championship today. The sadness in the boy's hunched shoulders pricked my heart. I rummaged in my pocket for some money. There wasn't much he could get with fifty pesos, but it was all I had.

"Gracias," he said, "May La Difunta bless you."

I held up the estampita and asked, "Will this really work?"

He shrugged, but when he smiled, a dimple pocked his cheek. "What can you lose, eh?" He couldn't have been more than ten, but he was already old.

No one else took an estampita or gave him money, and he sent me another smile before he stepped off the bus.

The engine's roar couldn't drown out the frantic muttering in my head: today might be the last day I played with my team. No legs would be fast enough to give us victory. We needed a miracle.

I glanced down at the estampita and sent La Difunta a silent prayer for a future in which I could play fútbol and be free. What could I lose, eh?

THE BUS ARRIVED IN BARRIO GENERAL JOSÉ DE SAN MARTÍN just as my watch pointed at three fifteen. I was late. I ran the rest of the way to Parque Yrigoyen field. Central Córdoba's stadium loomed right behind it, but our girls' league had no access there.

When I arrived, a referee in antiquated black—a guy— was checking my team's shin guards.

Roxana, our goalie and my best friend, sent me a killer glare as I peeled out of my sweatpants and sweater to reveal the blue and silver of my uniform. I took the last place in line and knocked on my shins to prove I was protected.

The rest of the girls dispersed, and I laced my boots, Pablo's hand-me-downs, which were falling apart and smelled like an animal had died and decomposed in them.

"You're late, Hassan," Coach said. A lifetime of squinting and playing tough in a man's world had left a map of lines on her face, which said I'd better apologize or I wouldn't like my destination.

"I'm sorry." I didn't promise it wouldn't happen again. I could lie to my mom, but to Coach Alicia? Absolutely not.

On the opposite side of the field, the Royals in purple and gold warmed up, doing jumping jacks and stretches.

"Today is a big day," Coach Alicia muttered like she was talking to herself, but I recognized the hope blazing in her words. If we won, we'd go to the Sudamericano women's tournament in December, and that would bring us all kinds of things that were impossible right now. Exposure. Opportunities. Respect.

I was a dreamer, but Coach Alicia was one of the most ambitious people I knew. She wanted so much for us.

"If we win, a pro team might finally notice you . . . I had hoped Gabi would be here today, but in December? By then there'll be no hiding your talents, Hassan."

Coach's sister, Gabi, worked with a super successful team somewhere up north. The rebellious futboleras like us couldn't go pro in Argentina. In the States, though, it was a different story. Every time Coach talked about some of us girls going pro, I wanted to believe her. But to hide my ridiculous dreams, I laughed dismissively.

Coach Alicia pierced me with her falcon eyes. "Don't laugh. You might not be playing at El Gigante yet, but you have more talent than your brother. You'll go further than he will. Mark my words."

Pablo would be richer for sure. I only wanted the chance to play, but even that was like wishing for the moon.

Coach Alicia half smiled. "You have something Pablo doesn't."

"What?"

"Freedom from society's expectations."

"Thanks, I guess."

"Now, don't give me that look." She placed an arm over my shoulder in an almost-hug. "Pablo's a professional now. If he doesn't perform, the press slays him. You don't have that pressure, except from me. I want nothing but the best from you today. ¿Está claro?"

"Like water," I replied, still wounded.

She winked at me and handed me a captain band. She walked away before I could explain that she was asking too much, that I was just a girl with strong legs and a stubborn streak.

There was no time for drama, though. I wrapped the band around my arm and did a quick warm-up on my own. Too soon, Coach called us in for a huddle.

Sandwiched between Roxana and Cintia, I gazed at my teammates' faces as Coach Alicia urged us to leave everything we had on the pitch.

Cintia was the oldest player at nineteen. Lucrecia, la Flaca, was the youngest at fifteen, and her confidence had bloomed in the last few months. Sofía and Yesica had never played before trying out for Coach Alicia, and now they were the best two defenders in our league. Mabel and Evelin were unstoppable in the middle. Mía had played in the United States as a kid before her family came back to Argentina, and what she lacked in skill she made up for in determination. Abril, Yael, and Gisela joined us after their barrio's futsal team disbanded. Absent from the huddle was Marisa, our best striker. Marisa's two-year-old daughter, Micaela, was our unofficial team mascot. I'd miss her tiny voice cheering for us today.

"We've all made sacrifices to be here," Coach Alicia said. "Remember that your families support you. Fight for your compañeras, especially the ones who aren't here today, and treat the ball with the respect it deserves."

Without Marisa, there was only one sub, but after Coach's words, there was no room for fear.

We cheered, "Eva María!"

It sounded like an invocation.

The ref blew the whistle for the captains to join him in the middle of the field. Roxana clapped her gloved hands and trotted to my side. Even with a thick headband on, Roxana's hair was too fine to stay put. Tiny wisps stuck out from the black braid dangling down her back.

"Hard time getting out today?" she asked. "I was afraid you wouldn't make it. With Marisa gone . . ." She shuddered. The possibility of having two missing players was too horrific to consider.

"Nothing I couldn't handle. Tell your mom my mom says hi."

Roxana laughed. "Tell her yourself. She's over there with the whole family."

Her large extended family occupied the sidelines; the Fongs never missed a game. Some had been born in China, some in Argentina, and all of them were fútbol obsessed. My friend was rich in ways that went beyond the supermarkets and clothing stores her father owned.

"They look so excited to be here," I said, laughing to hide my jealousy.

"Hurry up, señoritas," the ref called.

When he finished going over the fair play blah-blah-blah, I curtsied like a señorita.

"Watch it, number seven," he warned me. "You don't want to provoke me."

Apparently encouraged by his attitude, the other team's captains laughed. I looked them up and down: a chemical-blond girl and a chubby one with pretty green eyes.

"We're going to kick your ass," the blonde said.

The chubby girl giggled. Her eyes didn't look pretty anymore. "We'll stomp that smirk off your face, Hassan."

As soon as the words were out of her mouth, a familiar

fizzing sensation made my vision go sharp and blurry at the same time. I took a step in the girl's direction.

Roxana pulled me back by the shirt.

"Save it for later," she hissed in my ear. She was right. I couldn't lose my temper and our chance to win with it.

The ref blew the whistle, signaling the start of the game. Already high on adrenaline, I unleashed the part of me that came alive only on the pitch.

I ran back to my position in the midfield just in time to land Cintia's cross.

"Adelante, Camila!" Mrs. Fong's faith in me propelled my feet forward as I weaved through the line of defenders blocking my way to victory. The Royals' number three tackled me right before the box. I tasted dirt, but the ref didn't call a foul.

A rain of protests pelted him, but he wouldn't change his mind. Refs never did.

The Royals goalie kicked. La Flaca blocked the ball with her chest, cutting its arc through the air.

"What a lucky ball to land there!" a boy yelled from the sidelines. Some people laughed, and I saw red, but I couldn't waste attention on vermin.

Instead, I ran to catch the ball a Royal had wrestled from Evelin. I hooked it with the side of my foot and stole it back for my team.

Cintia waited, unguarded, for a chance to score, and I sent the ball straight to her foot. The Royals' goalie was tall but insecure. Her feet were glued to the dirt of her box. Cintia kicked with the precision of a tattoo artist. Even the wind held its breath, not daring to interfere with the play.

The ball hit the crossbar, but I was in a perfect spot, right in front of the goal, waiting for the rebound. Without time to think, I jumped into the air and scissor kicked. I fell hard on my hip, but the pain didn't even register as the net waved like a sail.

"Goooooooalllllll!" I screamed. I pushed myself up and ran with my fingers pointed to heaven. La Difunta had earned her water.

Just as my team jumped on me to celebrate, a cry of victory came from the houses across the pitch, followed by firecrackers. Someone had scored at El Gigante, and I wondered who, but only for a second. I couldn't be distracted from *my* game.

During the second half, the Royals' number four and I battled for a high ball right in the box. Pain shook my teeth and sent me to the ground, and when I heard the shrill whistle, I registered that the girl had elbowed me in the mouth.

While the Royals and my team swarmed around the ref, I recovered, taking deep breaths, making sure my teeth were still firmly attached.

"Are you okay?" Yael asked.

I swallowed the taste of blood and wiped my mouth with the back of my hand, hoping none of it had dripped on my uniform. I didn't have a spare jersey. But when I glanced down to check, it was clean. La Difunta's blessing was still protecting me.

My knees were a little wobbly as I stood up, but the nerves stayed on the dirt. "I'm fine."

The Royals didn't reach Roxana's kingdom until near the end of the game, when the ref gave them a free kick dangerously close to the box. With only minutes left, there was no way we could let them close the gap. Two to zero is the most dangerous score of all. I joined the defense to make a protective wall in front of Roxana as the blond Royal captain got ready to shoot. She glanced over at her coach, then at me. At one meter and fifty-five centimeters, I was the shortest person on my team. She'd try to send it over my head. I was her only opening. So I jumped, and the ball hit me right in the face.

Stars exploded in my eyes as I fell hard on the ground, where I stayed, catching my breath.

"Hassan, do you need a sub?" Coach Alicia called from the sidelines.

I pretended not to hear her. Mía had already left with a painful ankle. We didn't have another sub. No way in hell would I have left the field before the final whistle.

Taking my sweet time, I climbed back to my feet.

"One more minute," the ref called.

Mabel, our number five, kicked the ball back and forth

with Cintia, then back to Roxana, the expert in letting time slip by.

The Royals fans shrieked, enraged.

At last, the ref blew the final whistle. Before the sound was swallowed by the roar of the crowd, our team was running to Coach Alicia.

The Fongs and our other fans broke onto the field, kicking up dust that mixed with firecracker smoke.

It smelled of miracles.

"Camila! You were a furia!" Mrs. Fong's voice was hoarse as she baptized me with a new name.

"Furia! Furia!" my team chanted like a spell.

The part of me that had been set free during the game stretched her wings and howled at the sun.

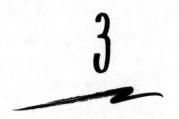

YAEL AND YESICA TRIED TO LIFT ME UP ON THEIR shoulders, but we fell down and laughed like little girls. Between someone's dirt-streaked legs, I caught a glimpse of the chubby, pretty Royal crying in the arms of a tall boy in a Newell's Old Boys shirt while a woman—her mom?—patted her shoulder.

What would it be like to have my mom come watch my games, comfort me if I lost, celebrate my victories?

Now, *that* was wishing for the moon, and before I let sadness ruin the sweetness of this moment, I joined my teammates in jumping and singing around our coach.

"Vení, vení, cantá conmigo, que una amiga vas a encontrar. Que de la mano de Coach Alicia, todas la vuelta vamos a dar!"

We did our Olympic run around the field, trailing behind Coach Alicia, waving our tattered flag.

No one wanted to stop celebrating.

Once we left the field, it would be back to regular life. Back to being ordinary. Here, we were the Rosarina Ladies' League champions, and the feeling was more intoxicating than a cup of forbidden beer on a hot summer night.

Finally, Coach Alicia reminded us about the prize ceremony. We walked shoulder to shoulder toward a table set up in the middle of the field. Two lines of trophies shone gold in the late-afternoon sun. The biggest, with FIRST PLACE engraved on the front, stood on the ground, where a couple of Roxana's cousins guarded it as if it were an imperial treasure. One of them, Alejandro, winked at me, but I pretended not to see.

The ref stood next to a balding guy with greasy hair, who held a megaphone up to his face. "Ladies and gentlemen," he said, his voice reverberating, "the champions, Eva María Fútbol Club, led by Camila Hassan, sister of none other than the Stallion, Pablo Hassan."

In an instant, the phantom presence of my brother and his accomplishments eclipsed my win, my team's efforts, and Coach Alicia's never-ending work. I stood, stubbornly rooted in place, but Coach Alicia motioned for me to step forward and accept the trophy.

"Vamos, Furia!" someone yelled, invoking my braver self.

And just like that, the newly born part of me took over.

All of a sudden, I was raising the trophy as if it were the head of a vanquished enemy. The metal held the warmth of the yellow sunshine. Carried by the euphoria, we sang our battle song and together lifted Coach Alicia in the air like the hero she was. My teeth were gritty with dirt and blood, but still I smiled for the group picture.

The friends, families, and neighbors who'd joined our celebration sang along.

"Put that away!" someone yelled. "Don't bring politics into the game! Not when there are reporters here."

I scanned the crowd and saw a woman waving the green handkerchief of the feminist movement. Then I noticed a guy nearby with a TV camera aimed in my direction. Had he been recording the whole time?

Roxana and I locked eyes. She had a green handkerchief in her backpack, and in that moment, I was grateful she hadn't pulled it out or, worse, asked me to wave it around like a victory flag. If anyone from school even thought we supported the movement's pro-choice politics, we'd be expelled without consideration. Sister Esther had been clear on that.

But if my parents saw me on TV, being expelled would be the least of my problems.

"Capitana, give us a few words." The reporter with the cameraman, a beautiful brunette with a beauty mark next to her red-painted lips, didn't wait to start peppering me with questions. "How do you feel right now, number seven? First place in the Rosarina Ladies' League. How did you learn to play like that? What are your plans for the future? What does your family think?"

Trapped into answering, I deflected the spotlight. "This was a collective effort. If anything, Coach Alicia's the one who should be answering all these questions. She's been working for years to take a team to the Sudamericano. I just do what she says."

The reporter's forehead creased with determination. "Of course, but from what I saw today, you're pretty amazing. You have a flair that's uncommon, especially for a girl. What does your brother, the Stallion, Pablo Hassan"—she flashed a smile at the camera as if she was hoping to charm him with the sound of his name—"say about how good you are?"

My teammates laughed. They all had a thing for Pablo, the fools.

Unnerved by my silence, the reporter pressed on. "Well, what does he say?" Her eyes swept over the crowd.

"My brother loves it," I said, making soft eyes at the camera because what the hell? I was already in the dance, so I danced. "He taught me *everything* I know."

The reporter's voice lowered in pitch, and she asked, "Furia, do you have a message for your family? For the federation? Do you think this win is a turning point for women's rights?"

She had seen the green handkerchief in the crowd, too. Frantically, I looked around, begging someone to rescue me from this woman and her dangerous questions.

"My family is very supportive, and . . . to the federation, I just want to say thank you for making this space for us girls."

We'd made the space. *We'd* filled in the cracks of the system and made room for ourselves where there was none. No one had given us anything. *We* had taken it. But no one wanted to hear the truth. Most importantly, this wasn't the time or the place for that conversation.

The crowd clapped enthusiastically. Finally, the reporter turned her attention to Roxana, and I wiggled my way out of trouble. The sun was low on the horizon, and now that the adrenaline from the game had left me, the evening breeze gave me chills. The sound of chanting from El Gigante squeaked from a phone speaker, and I tried to find its owner, who might have news from Central. It was the ref. A bulging sports bag rested at his feet.

"Did Central just score?" I asked, trying to sound friendly.

Instead of saying anything, even a simple *yes*, he gave a one-shouldered shrug and turned his back on me.

"Hurry up!" the camera guy yelled. "We can still make the second half! I can't believe we're stuck here at this game no one cares about." He struggled to put his equipment away. Even in daylight, only fools displayed that kind of expensive camera traveling around this kind of barrio. "We gotta go *now*!" he yelled to the reporter.

The reporter seemed unfazed by his rudeness, but there was a stiffness in the way she held her shoulders. Instead of running like he obviously wanted her to, she turned her attention back to me. My body froze. But the woman just approached me with her arm outstretched for a handshake. "Thanks for your time . . . Furia, right?"

The camera guy fumed behind her.

I nodded, and she said, "Good luck with the Sudamericano. I'll be cheering for you, and if you ever need anything, let me know."

"Thank you," I said, but what could I ever need from her?

"Luisana! We need to go!" The camera guy was advancing on us, stomping, on the verge of a temper tantrum.

Luisana inhaled deeply, as if praying for patience.

He grabbed her arm. "My contact at Channel Five said el Titán's in the stands."

She shrugged his hand off, and without another word, they ran toward their car. They were gone in a whirl of screeching tires and smoke.

El Titán, Diego, was in town.

"LET'S GO, HASSAN," ROXANA SAID, HER MEDAL SHOWING through her shirt. "My parents want to make it home before the game's over and the street gets blocked."

Although I hated when she called me by my last name, I ran to her side, bursting to tell her that Diego was at the stadium. Diego Ferrari was Pablo's best friend, Rosario's golden boy, an international sensation. The press called him el Titán because the names God and Messiah were already taken by Maradona and Messi. They said that on the pitch, Diego had more presence than royalty.

He was one of those rare talents that comes along only once in a generation. Last year, Juventus had swooped in and signed him for their first team before he had the chance to debut for Central.

He'd been my first crush, had given me my first kiss, and like millions of people around the world, I was obsessed with him.

I stopped my words just in time.

Roxana didn't like him. But then, she didn't like any male fútbol players. She claimed they were all narcissistic jerks, and considering my father and brother, I couldn't really disagree.

Diego was different, though. But I hadn't seen him in a year. A person could change a lot in that time. I had. Who knew how fame had changed him?

The temptation to try and catch a peek at him was too strong. Chances were, he'd go to the bar right across the street from Roxana's and wait to celebrate with the guys if Central won or commiserate if they lost.

My team should've been heading out to celebrate, but unlike the professional players, most of us were broke. The girls trickled off the field, each one going her separate way.

"Chau, Furia," Cintia said.

Mía and Lucrecia echoed, "Chau, Furia."

Coach Alicia was packing the equipment into her car: balls, nets, and corner posts. At the sound of my new nickname, she looked up and winked at me. "No days off, team!" she reminded us.

I waved at Coach and the girls. And without owning up to my ulterior motives, I followed Roxana to her dad's car.

The roads around the stadium were all closed. Even when Mr. Fong explained that he lived on the next block, the young traffic officer wouldn't budge.

The song blaring from thousands of throats in the stadium swallowed Mr. Fong's protests.

Un amor como el guerrero, no debe morir jamás...

"Drop us here, and we'll walk," Roxana said to her dad. "I'm dying to go to the bathroom."

Her parents argued back and forth until Mrs. Fong said, "It's fine, Gustavo. Let's drop them off. I need to check something at the store in Avellaneda anyway."

"In that case, this is your stop, girls."

"Just be careful, chicas," Mrs. Fong called after us as we got out of the car.

"I love your parents," I told Roxana. "My dad would've fought me even if he'd wanted me to walk home to begin with."

Roxana shrugged, but her cheeks turned a little pink. "I guess they're all right."

The men's game was over, and people trickled out of El Gigante, their faces glowing with glory. They swung yellow-and-blue-striped jerseys and flags in the air, chanting our Sunday hymns, happy because Central had won and nothing else mattered.

Fútbol could do that—make people forget about the

price of the dollar, the upcoming elections, even their love lives. For a few hours, life was beautiful.

We stood at the corner of Cordiviola and Juan B. Justo behind a group of guys singing and jumping in place, waiting for an ambulance to drive away. The scent of charred chorizos from the choripán vendor made my stomach growl. A line of officers made a roadblock across the street. Before we could continue toward the house, a rumble of excitement erupted from the singing guys.

A girl in their group ran to the barrier of disgruntled guards.

"She just saw el Titán," a boy announced. "Diego Ferrari."

Like the rest of the people in the street, I turned my face toward the bar like a sunflower chasing the dawn. Right then, Diego walked out, and the street exploded into applause and cheers.

In a distressed but obviously new leather jacket and a white T-shirt with the image of Lionel Messi as the Sacred Heart, Diego looked like the superstar he was. His brown hair was gelled back, but it still curled around his ears. He wore studs. *Diamond* studs that glinted when he moved. The reporters swarmed around him while he signed everything people put in front of him: paper, jerseys, an arm, a baby's blanket.

Roxana rounded on me. "Did you know he was here?"

I didn't even have the chance to deny it.

"Amore mío, fai l'amore con me!" a woman in her twenties yelled from behind me, startling us. Roxana started laughing. Even though I was about to die of embarrassment on the woman's behalf, I couldn't help laughing, too.

A couple of years ago, Roxana became obsessed with the book and the movie *A Tres Metros Sobre el Cielo.* It was a classic, but Roxana was all in. She tagged "3MSC" *everywhere.* She even learned Italian to read it in the original, and she made me practice with her. I'd make it fun for myself by repeating silly phrases in Italian, things we'd never dare to say in real life.

This was *my* phrase.

The woman repeated it, and this time, Diego must have heard her. Even from afar, I saw him blush. He waved, biting his lower lip. It made me want to forget everything and run to him.

Just as I was about to tell Roxana we should go home, he looked straight at me. His face broke into a megawatt smile.

Its force knocked me breathless.

"Camila!" he yelled, and waved for me to join him.

But Roxana shielded me with her body. "The cameras!" she warned me, but I had already scurried behind a group of girls fighting over who Diego was calling out for. All of them seemed to be a Camila.

Of course, I was the one he was calling for, and I wanted to go to him. But Roxana was right. This moment could be the end of me. Now that Diego was home from Italy, the news of a team of unknown girls winning the Rosarinian League Cup wouldn't get any airtime. This would give me some time to break the news about the Sudamericano to my parents before the news did it for me. But not if the cameras following Diego turned their attention my way. Then I would have a different kind of trouble at home.

We ran away from the crowd. Once we were out of reach of the cameras, Roxana hooked her arm through mine. Sore from the game, we hobbled our way to her house in charged silence.

"What was he thinking?" Roxana finally said, shaking her head. "Putting you in the spotlight like that . . ."

The chants of the fans hanging from a bus that thundered down the avenue swallowed the rest of her words. But not the thoughts clamoring inside me. Diego had seen me. He had called for me without hesitation.

The first-place medal pressed against my chest, reminding me of the most important thing that had happened today: my team had won. Now I would have to tell my parents.

BY THE TIME I SHOWERED AND CHANGED BACK INTO MY obedient daughter uniform and the buses started running again, my seven o'clock curfew had come and gone. When I actually left Roxana's hours later, night had fallen dark and damp over the city. The bus left me on the corner of José Ingenieros and Colombres. Far from home, but still better than walking by myself through Empalme and Circunvalación.

With only a flicker of starlight to guide me, my mom's warning about the murdered girl didn't seem empty anymore. I quickened my pace. Finally, I saw the light in front of my building, number six, shining bright yellow. It was ten forty-five. The more I delayed, the more trouble I would be in.

With each step I took, I forced my face into a mask, obliterating the vestiges of my rebellious afternoon: the sunshine breaking through the clouds during my victory goal, us picking up Coach Alicia, Diego with his leather jacket and gelled hair. I moved all these images to the back of my mind to revisit in the quiet of my room later.

"Chau, Pablo's sister!" a small boy riding a bicycle shouted at me cheerfully. "Say hi to the Stallion for me!"

"Camila!" I yelled. "My name is Camila!" He didn't turn back, though, and soon the darkness of la placita swallowed him.

In my barrio, most of the people didn't know my name or even that I existed. To them, I was only Pablo's sister, or Andrés and the seamstress's daughter—my mom, too, was nameless. But I was determined to leave my mark. And with the Sudamericano, I would have my chance.

No one in the barrio knew that I'd been reborn as Furia, and I held this luminous secret inside me like a talisman.

As I reached my apartment at the top of four flights of stairs, my father's laughter boomed through the metal door. The hallway light went off, and damp blackness enveloped me. I filled my lungs with wintry night air and went in.

The scene around the table was always the same after a game. My brother, dressed to go clubbing, was sprawled on a rattan chair with Marisol the girlfriend, the permanent ornament, by his side. My father, also ready to go out,

31

was flanked by Tío César and Tío Héctor, his sidekicks. They weren't really my uncles, but they'd all been friends since they were young boys.

The scent of homemade pizza was overwhelming, and my stomach growled loudly.

"Princesa Camila is here!" César exclaimed, and I gifted him with a smile. He always had a kind word for me.

Héctor's eyes scanned me and then lingered on my chest. "Kind of late for a respectable girl to be out and about, don't you think? Come here, negra. Give me a kiss."

I cringed as he planted a wet kiss on my cheek and closed my jacket to hide my chest even though all he could've seen was my black T-shirt. Before I could summon up my snark, my mom asked from the kitchen, "Where have you been, Camila? You were supposed to be here hours ago. Why didn't you answer your phone?"

I weighed what would happen if I blurted out the truth, telling them all I was late because my team had won the championship and I'd celebrated by sneaking a peek at Diego. They would think I was joking. But even so, saying my secrets aloud was too risky.

"Sorry, Ma. The phone ran out of credit." I slid the backpack off my shoulder. I left it next to the dark hallway, where I hoped no one would notice it.

It didn't work.

"What's in the backpack?" My father tried to be casual. César and Héctor kept their eyes glued to the TV, which was airing a replay of the day's games with the volume turned all the way down. In spite of their blank expressions, I knew they were paying attention to each word my dad said. Like me, they knew him too well to miss the signs.

I looked my father in the eye, mustered a courage I didn't really possess, and said, "Math books." I didn't blink. "I was studying."

"Where?"

"At Roxana's."

He smiled like a cat. "Roxana? The pretty chinita from school?"

"What other Roxanas do you know, Papá?"

In the corner of my eye, I saw Pablo, his smile frozen in place, warning me to stop.

Luckily, my father's eyes had already drifted back to the TV and the replay of Pablo's goal.

"Just wait until the national team calls Pali for the U20 World Cup," he said.

"They'll call Diego for sure." César stabbed where it would hurt my father the most. "Two from Rosario is a lot for the Buenos Aires jefes, Andrés. Diego's Juve material now. Pablo can't compete with that."

"Maybe he's in town to meet with AFA?" Héctor said.

"He was right there in the stands. I saw him. Did you, Pablito?"

Pablo shrugged, but he glanced at me like he wanted to make sure I didn't say anything stupid.

As if.

"Who cares that he's in town?" My father's laughter was jarring. "Diego's a fine player, but Pablo will make a better impression. You mark my words. And *then* it will be Europe. No Italy, though. For Pablo it will be Barcelona or Manchester United. Did you hear, Camila? You can help us with the English. Get your bags ready!"

"Don't count on me," I said, glancing at Pablo so he'd remember my fight was with our father, not with him. "I'm not going anywhere with you guys." I'd leave this house the first chance I got, but not by chasing after a boy, including my brother. I'd do it on my own terms, following my own dreams, not someone else's. And most importantly, no one would leech off my sacrifices. No one.

From behind me, my dad continued as if I hadn't said anything. "We'll follow the Stallion to the ends of the world. We'll finally be able to leave this rat hole and live the life we were meant to. Like I would've if that damned Paraguayan hadn't broken my leg."

"Paraguayo hijo de puta," Héctor muttered.

"You were the best one, Andrés. The best one of all." César recited his part.

"Pablo's better," my father said with a melodramatic quiver in his voice that I was immune to. "He'll save us all."

"Yes," Héctor said. "He'll make us rich."

Marisol rolled her eyes at me. If she had a say in all this, no one but her would enjoy Pablo's millions. She'd already dyed her hair platinum blond a la Wanda, the most famous botinera—footballer catcher—of all time.

My brother whispered something in Marisol's ear, and she smiled. This intimate gesture gave me goose bumps. I went to the kitchen to kiss my mom hello.

"Hola, Ma. You're going out?" I already knew the answer.

"At this hour? No, bebé. I still have to finish that dress, if you want to help."

"I can. After I do my accounting homework. I ran out of time."

"So they're calling it accounting homework now?" She sniffed at me. "Where were you? Your jacket stinks."

"A guy was smoking on the bus."

Nico, my dog, saved me from more questions. He whimpered from the laundry on the back balcony, where he was banished when there was company. He shed horribly even in the winter, and now that his coat was getting ready for our short spring and scorching summer, the shedding was out of control.

I escaped to his side. "There you are, mi amor."

Nico wagged his whole back half to make up for his lack of a tail. He licked my face in greeting, and I held my breath. His mouth stank worse than my boots, but he loved me unconditionally.

"I scored two goals, Nico," I whispered in his pointy ear. "We won the championship! And guess what? Diego's here. You should've seen him . . ."

Nico bobbed his head up and down like he understood every word, even those I couldn't say. I tried to kiss his triangular face, but he slunk away from me to greet my brother, who had just joined me.

"Marisol's in the bathroom," Pablo explained. "And I had to get out of there."

I widened my eyes in an exaggerated expression of shock. "Oh? I didn't know she pooped like the rest of us!"

He swatted my shoulder, and I scooted over so he could sit beside me on the floor. After a long exhale, I rested my head on his shoulder. My brother's long black hair was silky under my cheek. Nico sprawled across our legs, pinning us under him so we'd behave.

"Good job on that goal, Pali." I was bursting with pride at how fine his shot had looked on TV.

"I was watching you the whole time in the kitchen, and you weren't even paying attention to the TV."

Roxana and I had dissected every play, but he didn't need to know how obsessively we studied the men's games. "I watched it at Roxana's," I said.

"Roxana? The pretty chinita from school?" He mocked our father's voice. "And your game?" Pablo whispered after a few seconds.

My heart hammered. He'd remembered about my championship.

"We won," was all I said. "I scored."

He ruffled my already-messy hair and said, "Ah, Maradonita! I wish I could come see you someday."

"Maybe next time." I wasn't going to hold my breath.

After his debut on Central's first team two years ago, Pablo's life had become even more complicated than when he was in the youth academy. He never had time to come see me play. Which was for the better, maybe. Ever since the baby leagues, he'd won dozens of international championships. Pablo had never laughed at me for wanting to be a futbolera. He had always encouraged me behind our parents' backs, but he didn't really know the hunger I had. He thought fútbol was something I did for fun. Maybe it was time I trusted him more.

"I'll tell you the rest later," I said.

He nodded, but his face darkened as he cleared his throat.

"What's going on?"

"Diego thought he saw you outside the bar. Were you roaming around the stadium hoping to see him?"

"Stop it!" I said, and slapped Pablo's leg.

Nico whined.

Pablo pulled away from me and looked into my face until I finally met his eyes. "Mirá, nena, you're my little sister, and I have to protect you." He sounded so much like our mom that I rolled my eyes. "I don't like you going out all alone, coming back late, and doing who knows what." He smiled but drilled me with one of his stares, the kind he'd inherited from our father. "Remember what I said last time?"

"What, Pablo? What did you say?"

"That you're going to get hurt," he said as if he were an ancient wise man. "Stay away from him. Trust me."

Pablo was so full of it.

When I didn't reply, he asked, "You haven't been talking to him behind my back, have you?"

Last year, Pablo had given me the talk, a tirade about not being like the other girls and wanting a piece of Diego just because he was going to be famous. What Diego and I had wasn't like that at all, but the words had burrowed deep inside of me.

"What are you now? My dad?" I asked, slapping his leg again.

"He's only here for a week, you know? Then he'll go back to his fame and fortune and glamorous life." There was a sharp edge to his voice that made the hairs at the back of my neck prickle. What had happened between them?

"I haven't talked to him. Happy now?"

Pablo's eyes flickered away from mine, as if he knew way more than he pretended to. Had Diego told him anything? I was dying to ask, but my pride was greater than my curiosity.

"I saw how you two looked at each other the night he left," Pablo said. "I'm a guy, too, Camila—"

"How did we look at each other? That was a whole year ago. And now, what? I'm not even supposed to look at him because he's famous?" Now it was Pablo's turn to roll his eyes, and I continued, "It's not like that, Pablo. Not at all. We're just friends, or we were. We haven't talked much since he left. Besides, I'm too busy with school, and . . . planning for med school."

Héctor's laughter echoed from the kitchen, followed by César's and my father's. Pablo and I listened.

The night before Diego had left, there had been more than charged looks between us. A lot more. But ignorance was bliss, and I intended to keep my brother in the dark. What was the point in fighting? For all I knew, Diego was over our . . . fling.

I patted my brother's shoulder and changed the subject. "In any case, I'm sure he was amazed to see you play. You guys flattened Talleres, honestly."

Pablo laughed. "It was good to see him there," he said with a crooked smile. "But I want *you* to come watch one day. When was the last time you came to the stadium?"

Two years. When Pablo had debuted on the first team.

"I'll come see you one day," I said. "Stallion."

The nickname was perfect for him. Tall and dark. He could run forever and never stop smiling. How many girls had lost themselves over that grin?

"Pali!" Marisol's musical voice called from the dining room.

Like an obedient lapdog, Pablo jumped to his feet and ran to her.

Pali?

Pali was just for family, and Marisol wasn't that. God willing, she would never be. She had never given Pablo the time of day until Diego had left. But if I ever even hinted at this, I'd make an enemy out of my brother. I could deal with anything but losing Pablo.

BACK IN THE DINING ROOM, CÉSAR AND HÉCTOR THANKED my mom for the delicious fugazza con queso. She hid her smile behind a paper napkin, but her eyes sparkled. Her gaze, so full of longing, flitted to my father every few seconds. She was still hoping, waiting, for . . . I didn't know what. They'd been together since they were sixteen. If he hadn't changed by now . . .

My mom grabbed a bit of crust from a plate and nibbled on it.

My father dropped one of his bombs. "You're eating pizza, Isabel? I thought you were staying off carbs to look amazing. Like me." His hand swiped over his lean body, and then he winked at her, as if the gesture could erase the damage to her heart.

I grabbed a slice of pizza and took a bite. My taste buds exploded in pleasure. "Oh, Mami! This is the food of the gods!"

"You say that now," my dad said with a mocking expression. "Just wait until your thirties, when even the air you breathe accumulates on your thighs. Right, Isabel?"

Mami's smile vanished, and her luminous copper skin turned ashy, as if she'd been struck by a curse.

Pablo put a hand on Mami's shoulder. "No, Mama. You're beautiful just the way you are."

She didn't tell Pablo off for speaking like a country boy, but the endearment wasn't enough to bring the color back to her face. She gathered the plates and took them to the sink.

Pablo and I locked eyes, and when I turned around, I saw Héctor and César having their own silent conversation. But no one said anything. My father excused himself to the bathroom. César walked out for a cigarette, since my mom didn't let him smoke inside the house. I should have escaped to my room then, but the TV caught my attention. It was the reporter who'd been at my game, Luisana. I was about to turn the volume up when Héctor said, "Don't. It's that woman commentator, and I can't stand listening to her burradas."

I hesitated, debating whether I should obey him or turn it all the way up out of spite. But they were showing footage of Diego waving at his fans. I had to see if there was any trace of me on the sidewalk, staring at him like a zombified fool. I stood in front of the TV for a few minutes, but the whole time, I saw Héctor out of the corner of my eye. He shifted from side to side and looked at me like he wanted to say something. When I turned to face him, he opened his mouth to speak once or twice, but in the end, he just sighed and went back to checking his phone.

"¡Vamos!" My father called to him, and walked out, completely ignoring me.

Héctor looked at me sadly. Before following my father, he said, "Careful, Camila. You're too pretty to be out on your own."

Now it was my turn to struggle for words. It was as if a fish bone were stuck in my throat. Was he threatening me, or was he genuinely worried about me?

Soon after, Pablo and Marisol left, too. Usually they didn't go clubbing on Sunday nights—she was in fifth year, the last, just like I was—but tomorrow was a holiday. The memory of Pablo whispering in her ear and Marisol's sly smile flashed through my mind again, and I shuddered.

The news went back to reporting about Gimena Márquez and a march organized in her honor, demanding justice for her murder. I turned up the volume.

People marched, chanting, "¡Ni una menos!" Then the demands for an end to the violence got overshadowed by a fight between a group with pro-choice green handkerchiefs and another with pro-life light blue ones. No amount of insults was going to bring Gimena back. People could fight over handkerchief colors until the sun bleached them all to the same shade of gray, and in the meantime, girls would continue to die.

The anchor cut in with news of another missing girl, a twelve-year-old this time.

My mom sighed heavily behind me. I turned to look at her. She stared disapprovingly at me, as if *I* were responsible for these girls and had failed to protect them.

Or as if my own carelessness meant I'd be next.

I grabbed my backpack and a plate with more pizza and escaped to my room. Maluma smiled at me from the poster on the wall next to the only picture I had of Abuelo Ahmed—the one with a love letter to a woman who wasn't my grandmother scribbled on the back. In sepia, he looked like an old-fashioned movie star.

I unpacked my bag and hid my medal under the mattress. Cliché, but there wasn't any other place to hide it. Maybe it would infuse my sleep with strength and feed my hunger for more. I placed la estampita of La Difunta Correa on my nightstand, leaning against a tottering pile of books, mostly TOEFL prep manuals and *The Shadow of the Wind*, which Diego had lent me before he left. All I had for La Difunta's ofrenda was a half-empty water bottle, and I set it next to the card.

After plugging in my phone, I played one of my mom's old Vilma Palma e Vampiros CDs on my ancient boom box.

When I lay down on my bed, my sore muscles complained, but not loudly enough to drown out all the voices in my head blaring about homework, my brother and Marisol, my father, the money I'd need for the tournament, the *permission* I'd need for the tournament, and Diego.

Especially Diego. Why did he have to show up now?

Uninvited, a memory of the last time we were together weaved its way into my mind. The loud music of the club booming, Diego's soft lips on mine. My right hand on his chest, feeling his heart beating through his unbuttoned shirt, my left hand holding a yellow lollipop he'd traded for my pink one.

I still had the yellow lollipop in my trove of treasures under the mattress.

That night, a future together seemed magical and possible. And then life got in the way.

For the first weeks after he left, we chatted constantly. He even called me a couple of times. But then the time difference and his schedule and my unreliable internet connection and having to hide it all from my family took a toll. The emails and chats became shorter, colder, stiffer, until finally, they stopped.

We hadn't spoken since November.

I scoured the internet, looking for signs that he'd made up with his ex-girlfriend, that he'd been playing with me, just like Pablo had warned. But all I found were brief reports of a prodigious boy from Rosario who lived only for the ball and the white-and-black jersey of his new club. I was too proud to ask him if his feelings had changed.

Still, I wished I could tell him about my games and my dreams and ask him about his new life. When I went on long runs past his building, I carried on imaginary conversations, recycling words he'd once said to me.

Eventually, I forgot the sound of his laughter. Coach Alicia's promises that I could have a life playing fútbol replaced fantasies of a future where I was a spectator, witnessing Diego's transformation from a boy into a titan. Even if I loved him.

It was true what the songs said—no one dies of a wounded heart—and I believed mine had healed. But the sound of my name on Diego's lips had tugged at the scar, unraveling feelings I'd ignored all these months.

The shrill ringing of the house phone pierced through the music and my memories. My mom's voice reverberated through the walls.

"Hola, Dieguito, mi amoooooor." She stretched that *o* to an impossible length. "I can't believe you're back and that you remember your old friends."

I tried breathing deeply to calm myself, but it didn't work.

"No, nene. Pablo left," she said. "I thought he was going to meet you."

El Pájaro kept singing in the background. I ran to turn the music off.

"Since when do you ask permission to come visit?"
There was a pause, and then Mamá added, "Tonight? This
is your home." She laughed. "I'll tell her you're on your
way, then."

She hung up the phone but didn't come to my room to
tell me Diego had called.

Diegui was coming here. My phone was dead, so I
couldn't even call Roxana. I had no time, anyway. Ana,
Diego's adoptive mom, lived only a couple of blocks from
us. He'd be here in minutes.

I told myself he was just the same Diego as always.
No big deal. But it was midnight, and I looked terrible. I
peeled off my T-shirt. It reeked of cigarette smoke from
the bus. When I undid my braid, my hair puffed up into
a halo of frizz around my head, but there was nothing I
could do.

The slamming of a car door brought me back to my
room. As I listened, someone whistled the melody of
Central's anthem. *Un amor como el guerrero, no debe morir
jamás* . . . The melody came closer and closer.

I was paralyzed.

Nico's booming barks preceded the doorbell. I counted
the seconds.

One . . . two . . .

"Quiet!" my mom snapped at the dog. The door
opened, and in a softer, more civilized voice, she added,
"Diego! Come in. I'm so proud of you, hijo. I see you on

TV, but you look so grown up in person! Say something in Italian for me."

Diego said something I didn't catch. She laughed like a young girl, and the sound spurred me into action.

My hands moved lightning fast as I put on a clean T-shirt. My mom's footsteps approached my door, and I jumped back onto my bed and grabbed a book. A second later, she opened without knocking.

"Camila?"

"What, Ma?" I looked at her, but I avoided her eyes, pretending I'd been reading.

"Diego's here." The glow on her face was back. My heart went into triple time, as if I were sprinting to the goal line.

We stared at each other for a couple of seconds until I whispered, "What's he doing here?"

She shrugged. "He wanted to come see Pablo, but your brother's gone. I told him you were the only one home."

I scrambled off the bed, and when I put the book back on the nightstand, the rest of the pile tottered and collapsed, knocking down the bottle of water that was La Difunta's offering.

My mom hurried to help me pick up the mess. "What's this?" she asked, studying la estampita.

"La Difunta Correa, Ma."

"Where did you get it?"

"From a little boy on the bus. He looked hungry."

Mami sighed, the kind of sigh that took my soul into one of her specialties—the guilt trip. "What have I told you, Camila? Those kids never get to keep their money. There's always an adult exploiting them."

She placed the estampita on the nightstand and the bottle beside it. "Make sure you go to a shrine and leave the offering. La Difunta is a strict cobradora. She never forgets who owes her." Her voice was so serious. "I hope whatever you asked for was worth it."

I'd already asked for so many things . . .

"Diego's waiting," I said.

She stared at me for a few long seconds. Finally, her finger raised for emphasis, she said, "Don't keep him too long. That boy must have places to go."

ROXANA DIDN'T LIKE DIEGO, BUT SHE'D GIVE ME GRIEF
when she found out I'd let him see me looking like hell.
She'd say that I could have at least put on some lipstick or
perfume to impress him. I was supposed to be over him,
after all. But it was too late for all that.

Diego's footsteps moved from the dining room to the
laundry. "There you are, old boy," he whispered as he let
Nico out.

The dog's nails *click-clack*ed on the kitchen floor, and
from the darkened hallway, I saw him lick Diego's face
with such tenderness that even my prickly heart was
moved. Then Nico whined and ran to the door that led to
the front balcony, looking at Diego with urgency. Diego

laughed and opened the door. My dog lunged from the apartment.

I could only see Diego's outline illuminated by the pale silver moonlight, unguarded and forlorn.

The times Diego and I had talked on the phone, he'd told me stories about the places he'd visited and what life was like having roommates from all over the world. His tales had sounded like adventures right out of Harry Potter, boys training to be wizards. I'd had to squash my envy—Diego was living a life that I could only dream of, no matter how much I loved fútbol, no matter how great an athlete I might be.

And now he was here.

As if he felt my eyes on him, Diego turned around and looked straight into the hallway where I stood. He looked at *me*. He saw *me*. Not the Stallion's sister. Not Andrés and the seamstress's daughter. Me, Camila Beatriz Hassan.

The fútbol star replaced the forlorn boy. He took a step in my direction.

"Camila."

Now that there were no cameras or adoring fans, I stepped into his open arms. He hugged me tightly and picked me up a little, but I refused to let my tippy-toes come unglued from the floor. He smelled like the cologne they sold at the expensive shops in the Alto Rosario Mall, and his leather jacket was buttery soft against my cheek. When I moved my head, my lips brushed the tender skin of his neck. I wanted to kiss my way to his mouth and pick up where we'd left off.

I resisted.

"I missed you." His voice tickled my ear.

I pulled away from his embrace and looked up at him. From this short distance, I saw the gold flecks in his light brown eyes. His eyes were galaxies I could lose myself in, but the cold floor brought me back to earth. I was a barefoot schoolgirl in my barrio apartment; he was a star flashing past us all, and the glow would disappear with him when he left again. In spite of our shared childhood, we now lived worlds apart. As much as he might say he missed me, it hadn't been enough for him to stay in touch.

"How long are you here for?" I asked, stepping away from him and crossing my arms like a shield.

"A week. It's a FIFA date, and everyone else is with their national teams."

"Héctor and César said you'll get called up next time, Titán."

There was a fire in his eyes. "They said that?"

I nodded.

Diego brushed his hand through his hair and said, "We have so much to talk about. Will you invite me for some *mates*?"

An enemy wouldn't be refused this request, much less Diego.

"I'm shocked you're still drinking *mate*, Titán." If I

used this name, I wouldn't forget that he wasn't my Diegui anymore.

He followed me to the kitchen. "Of course! I always have the Central thermos you gave me. But you haven't watched my stories or liked my posts or been online at all in forever. You disappeared."

"At least I have an excuse," I said, trying not to sound like a rejected telenovela heroine and totally failing.

He didn't seem to notice the ice in my voice. "What happened?"

"Got my phone stolen a couple of months ago. The one I have now is from the nineteen-hundreds." I laughed like it wasn't a big deal, but I shivered at the memory of the two young boys, no older than twelve, pointing a gun at me. Diego didn't need to know the details.

He hugged me one-armed and said, "We'll have to fix that, then. Come, I'm dying to tell you everything." He paused for a second, and then said, "I thought I saw you at the stadium today, wearing a gray jersey. What team was that?"

"Wasn't me," I said, and changed the subject. "And *you* didn't come for pizza with the family. Pali didn't invite you?"

He shrugged and continued filling up the kettle. "He did, but I went to the stadium straight from the airport and hadn't seen Mamana yet. After the game I took her out, just the two of us."

I filled my favorite *mate* cup with the herbs (yerba and peppermint) and just a pinch of sugar, but then I remembered he was a world-class athlete. "Is this okay?"

He narrowed his eyes and let out a long sigh. "Okay, but just a little, because if the boss finds out . . ." With a tiny smile, I added just a little more, and he whispered, "Temptress."

I didn't shake the *mate* to settle the dust or do any of the theatrics some people fell for. The secret to the perfect *mate* was in the temperature of the water and the hand of the server. And my touch was magical. Even my father had complimented me once or twice.

I looked up to see Diego staring at me, leaning against the Formica countertop. He looked so out of place here. I had to make an effort not to stare back. He seemed taller, his smile brighter. Had he had his smile whitened and his chipped tooth fixed? Absentmindedly, I brushed my tongue over my own teeth; my gums were still sore from when the ball had hit me. His skin was clearer, too, as if it shone from the inside.

The water started humming; a few seconds, and it would be ready. Just so I had something to do besides gape at him, I pulled my hair into a ponytail. My T-shirt crept up, exposing my belly. His eyes followed it.

"What?" I asked, blushing. His eyebrows were perfectly shaped, way better than mine, and when he moved, the diamond studs in his ears cast sparkles of light all around us.

The kettle sang. I turned off the stove and picked it up. "What?" I asked again.

"So . . ." He swallowed. "I was walking up the stairs, and I looked up at your window, and . . . nena! You were wearing just your bra!'"

I had to put the kettle down so I wouldn't drop it. My face felt hotter than the water, and I feared steam was coming out of my ears.

"I didn't notice the shutters were open," I whisper-shouted.

I wanted to die.

"Be more careful next time, then." There was concern in his voice. "Don't encourage the creeps. What if someone other than me saw you? If your dad finds out, he'll lock you up in the tallest tower, and you'll have to wait for me to come rescue you."

"I'll rescue myself," I said, a couple of seconds too late. "And don't worry. No one will ever lock me up in a tower."

"I'd like to see someone try." He was standing so close I felt the heat of his body. Or maybe it was just me burning up. "I heard about Gimena." His face was unreadable, but his voice was so sad. "She was in my class in elementary school. She dropped out in seventh grade, and Pablo was devastated. He had a crush on her, remember? Back when he liked brunettes."

If she hadn't been hanging out with the wrong crowd, she'd still be alive . . .

"Every day there's a new girl."

"If anyone ever bothers you, you tell me, and I'll kick his ass. I'll make him swallow his teeth. Just say the word."

But what could Diego really do? He didn't even live here anymore.

I patted his hand and then pulled away so quickly I almost knocked the *mate* over. "Ay," I muttered, pushing back the swear words I would've said if he hadn't been here. "Like I said, I can take care of myself. Don't worry." Then, trying to change the subject, I added, "Do you want some pizza to go with el *mate*, or crackers? Or my mom made pastafrola yesterday. Maybe there's still some left." I looked inside the fridge, and yes, the quince pie was still there.

Diego's eyes flared with desire. For the cake. He had a sweet tooth. "Just a little."

"Come sit here." I led him to the table, taking my regular spot in front of the window, and he sat across from me, as he'd done a million times before.

"I . . . I see you on TV. I mean, we watch the games." I poured water in the *mate*. "My mom and me. She says the black and white looks good on you, bianconero."

My eyes wandered over him, caressing his bashful face, which was so closely shaved I could almost feel the softness of his skin against my fingertips. I took a sip of *mate* and almost scalded my tongue.

"You watch the games?"

I swallowed quickly so I could reply. "Whenever we can. Sometimes we listen on the radio, and when we watch, it's online. Because the pay-per-view costs an egg and a half."

He laughed. "Always so delicate."

He swallowed a bite of pie. Crumbs clung to his lips, and ay, Dios mío, my insides twisted, but I went back to the *mate* and pretended to be cool.

"Oh, you meant *chicken* eggs," he said.

"Of course! What kind of impure thoughts are you having, Ferrari?"

He licked his lower lip and bit it before he said dramatically, "All of them, Hassan."

My mind exploded with indecent images. I laughed, lowering my eyes to my napkin. I had shredded it.

Another uncomfortable silence enveloped us. Smothered us. Frantically looking for a way to shatter the awkwardness, I remembered I still had his book. "I have something for you." I sprang out of my seat to get *The Shadow of the Wind* from my room. When I returned to the kitchen, he was still nursing el *mate* in his hands. "I'm sorry I kept it for so long." I laughed. "Your house is too far to return it."

The lamp in the corner cast a feeble light that didn't reach me, and I hoped he couldn't see that I was blushing again. Avoiding his eyes, I handed him the book. When he took it, our fingers brushed. I balled my hands into tight fists and crossed my arms so he couldn't see I was shaking.

"What did you think?" he asked. When I didn't answer, he went on, "I mean, if you still remember the story. It's been so long."

"I read it more than once. I just don't know where to start."

His face glowed with surprise. "Oh, you liked it, then."

"Yes, I loved it. The translation is great. It reads just like in Castellano." He looked at me with a small smile, and I continued, "Barcelona! What else can I say?" I picked my words carefully to avoid mentioning the romance at the heart of the story. "I loved the bit about leaving a part of ourselves in every book we read. How we collect the fragmented souls of those who found the story first. That's beautiful." Put like this, reading a borrowed book sounded like an extremely intimate experience. "And you? What's your favorite part?"

Diego blinked and stared into the darkness of the kitchen. "That sometimes we're cursed, and we can't break free without the help of those who love us." He took my hand in his, and this time I didn't snatch it away. "I've been to Els Quatre Gats and all the other places Daniel and Fermín go. In the old city, I even thought I saw Julián and Penélope once or twice."

Diego had strolled through those crooked alleyways and la Puerta del Ángel, had gone down Las Ramblas and through el Barrio Gótico to the Mediterranean Sea, which I'd only seen online.

"And you found the Cemetery of Forgotten Books?"

His eyes flashed with an emotion I couldn't decipher. "Not yet, Cami. Not yet."

The quiet laughter coming from the TV in my mom's room clashed with the intimate mood in the living room. The *mate* was lavado, but I didn't want to change the yerba. I didn't want to ruin the moment. I didn't want Diego to let go of my hand.

"How did the test go?" Diego asked.

"The test?"

He studied my face, and I realized he was talking about the exam I'd taken last month. I was studying and doing prep tests when he left. He was stuck on old news.

"Oh! I *aced* the TOEFL and the SAT." Before he could say anything, I added, "Not only that, but you're now speaking to a licenciada in the English language."

"You're still planning on going to school in Norteamérica, then?"

When he said it like that, it sounded so simple: because I had aced the tests, all the doors would be open to me.

"No," I said, and sipped my *mate*. "It's impossible."

All my life, I had wanted to go to college in the United States, because there I could play fútbol while I got an education. But school in the States was irrationally expensive. With the exchange rate from peso to dollar, I wouldn't be able to attend if I saved for a million years, not even with scholarships.

But the Sudamericano would be a window of opportunity for a team to discover me. I could put college on hold and keep playing fútbol. I'd start small on a Buenos Aires team like Urquiza. Their men's team wasn't even in the first division, but the women had been to Copa Libertadores de América.

Maybe in a few years, I'd climb my way up to the North American national league, the best women's league in the world. *Then* my English would serve me well.

"Nothing's impossible, Camila. I assure you, the people who knew me when I was nine never imagined that one day I'd be playing in Italy."

He was right. Diego's was a Cinderella story, which inspired me. It really did. After all, Rosario exported players to all corners of the world. Male players.

"Anyway, look at you! A licenciada!" he said. That smile again. "You should've told me!"

I retied my hair. "Well, you've been busy, haven't you?" I hesitated, but if not now, when? "Besides, it's not like we've been talking. You stopped calling me and never wrote me back."

The glow on his face dimmed. "Ay," he said, placing a hand over his heart.

"Ay," I echoed.

Diego bit his lower lip. "I'm sorry . . . things got . . ."

"Complicated?"

He nodded and grabbed my hand again. "Camila, you don't know . . . I almost quit so many times. I missed you. I was homesick, lonely, confused . . . The mister said I wasn't playing with my heart and asked if I wanted to come home."

"What did you say?"

"That I wanted to stay in Turín. What else? Being there was my dream, and the possibility of them sending me back was terrifying. I focused all my energy on doing my best one day at a time. Before I knew it, weeks had passed, and then I didn't know how to explain . . ." He exhaled like he had just dropped the heaviest burden. "Forgive me?"

In my imaginary conversations with Diego, I always confronted him without hesitation, stating that we could still be friends, that we could pretend the kiss and the heartbreak were blips we could jump over and move on. But a part of me had always worried that we could never go back to the way things were before that night at the club. I didn't want to lose him.

I'd never expected an apology. I wasn't ready for it, and

now I was disarmed. It would've been so much easier to hold a grudge forever.

His explanation made sense. In his place, I would've done the same thing. The time apart had taught me I could live without him. Perhaps what my heart needed was closure, and his being here explaining, apologizing, was enough.

Diego looked at me like a man waiting for his sentence.

Finally, I said, "I'm glad you stayed in Turín. I really am, Titán."

"I'm glad you have your degree. People need English for everything," he said. "Are you making any extra money with it?"

I laughed. "*Extra* money? I don't have *any* money." I shifted in the chair. My foot was falling asleep. I had the terrible habit of putting my leg under my bum to make up for my height. It messed up my ankle, and if Coach had seen me, she'd've had my head on a platter. "I went to the new mall to apply for this job at a clothing store. They asked for English speakers."

"And?" He motioned with his hand for me to continue.

"Marisol came along, and after I completed her application and pretty much coached her through the whole interview, I didn't get called back, but she did! No, don't laugh. I speak English fluently and know accounting and tons of other things, and they hired *her*. She worked for two days and quit. They *still* didn't call me."

By this time, I was kneeling on my chair, leaning over the table, both hands in the air, Evita Perón–style. All that was missing was the cry, *¡Pueblo Argentino . . . !* Diego laughed, and slowly, I sat back down and crossed my arms. "I have strong suspicions about why they hired her and not me."

"Which are?" he asked.

"Really? She's like a fragile anime fairy, batting her eyelashes and pretending to be dumb so people will like her. And then look at me." I waved my hand in front of my body. "Employers don't look beyond appearances."

The intensity in his eyes made every inch of my skin prickle. "I don't understand what you mean, Cami."

"Never mind," I said, cursing myself for walking into that trap. "Money. I need to earn some. Do you have any jobs for me, Titán?"

His eyes narrowed, and his mouth quirked. I'd thought I knew all his gestures and expressions, but this fancy new Diego was a mystery. "Actually, I might."

"What?"

"Did you see in the news that the church of El Buen Pastor opened up again?"

"The abandoned church where they had the jail?"

"Jail?"

"The asylum for disobedient women?"

Diego looked like he had no idea what I was talking about. But then, not a lot of people knew its history.

"The one all the way in the Zona Sur?"

"Yeah, that one," Diego said.

"Roxana showed me an article from *La Capital* about this asylum. Back in the day, families sent their disobedient daughters to El Buen Pastor."

"They did?"

"Yes, and also their sisters, wives, even employees, sometimes. It was like a depository for unwanted women. Some orphan girls raised there became rich families' free maids."

"I had no idea," he said.

"The girls were called 'Las Incorregibles.' Roxana said I was lucky it closed down or I may have ended up there."

"Ay, that's not why I brought it up." Diego grimaced and added, "It is a beautiful building to go to waste, and now it will be a place of healing . . . hopefully."

Maybe that would shoo away the ghosts that surely still haunted it. "I thought there was a nursing home there now."

"A section is, but the rest was vacant. Father Hugo has set up workshops for woodworking, sewing, gardening, and a comedor for the kids to get their afternoon merienda. He wants to start a new program for the kids in the group home to keep them off the streets. He can't pay much, but a group of Argentines from the United States is funding some of it. Father Hugo wants someone, preferably a woman"—Diego's eyes flickered—"or a girl, or . . .

whatever, to teach them English." He swallowed. "Would you be interested?"

"It might work." I said. "I'm a *whatever*, after all, and I do have a degree."

He had the good sense to duck his head sheepishly. "Okay, *woman*. Licenciada."

"Good," I said. Honestly, this sounded like a great opportunity, and I needed money. But sneaking out for practice was already hard enough. How could I get away for this, too?

"What's the matter, bambina?" Diego reached across the table and pushed my chin up with his index finger.

Trying not to shiver at his touch, I said, "You know . . . my dad."

"What about him? You look like Rapunzel when Mother Gothel tells her she can't go see the lights in the sky."

I laughed. We must have watched *Tangled* a thousand times when we were little. "I am *not* Rapunzel. And Titán, what will your fans say when they find out you still watch animated movies? *Princess* movies?"

His smile faltered. "Don't call me Titán. I'm just Diego, Mama."

No boy I cared for had ever called me Mama before.

Mama is such a complicated word. It's what we call our mothers. What we call a friend, a cute little girl that plays in the park.

What a man calls his woman.

Diego cleared his throat and said, "Tomorrow's a holiday. After lunch, I'll pick you up here and take you to Father Hugo's."

"I don't want to sneak out." I said, shaking my head. "He's going to be here all day. He'll find out. He'll drive by the church and see us. I'll meet someone he knows, or we'll have an accident—"

Diego trapped both of my hands in his. "I'm not telling you to sneak. I'm asking you . . ." He hesitated. "I'm asking you out. Last time, everything happened so quickly—the kiss, saying goodbye like that. I've never taken you out. Just you and me."

His words sucked the air out of the room.

"Let's go catch a show at the planetarium. I've seen so many amazing places in Europe, but there's still so much I don't know about Rosario. Sad, right? I want to see it all so I can remember it when I'm away. I want to go with *you*. On the way back, we'll stop and talk to Father Hugo."

Diego had always loved Rosario irrationally. Our industrial city could never compare to Italy, or even Buenos Aires, but Diego had never wanted to leave. He'd only left because *no one* said no to Juventus FC.

I thought for a few heartbeats. I needed a job, and a real date with him was irresistible. When I finally smiled, he beamed as if he'd scored a goal.

A metallic sound startled us, and we both jumped.

"What's that?" he asked.

Someone, or something, was scratching the door. I glanced at the clock.

One in the morning. Time to go back to reality.

"Oh!" I laughed when I recognized the whining. "It's only Nico."

I hurried to open the door, and Nico trotted toward my room. I, on the other hand, walked out onto the balcony, welcoming the cold south wind, which blew on my face and cleared my thoughts. My lungs expanded, taking in the smell of eucalyptus leaves and quebracho smoke. Diego followed me out and stood next to me, leaning on the balustrade.

Last time we were alone in the dark, he'd found me shaking with cold outside the club, wearing a skimpy dress I'd borrowed from Roxana and high heels I was surprisingly good at walking in. All night long, Diego and I had looked at each other across the dance floor, but neither of us had made a move. At two in the morning, when Roxana said her dad was waiting for us outside, I told her I needed to say goodbye to Diego. But I had lost him in the throngs of people dancing and the girls passing out lollipops for La Semana de la Dulzura.

Outside, I couldn't find Roxana or her dad's car. I couldn't walk home dressed like this. I'd never make it back. Desperation had started to creep in when someone tapped me on the shoulder. I pulled my arm back, ready to punch whoever thought they could play with me.

"Let's swap?" Diego said, holding out a yellow lollipop.

In my hand, I had a pink one. His favorite flavor.

Fate had given me a chance, and I wasn't going to waste it. Diego was flying out in a few hours, and I might never see him again.

"I will for a kiss. Everyone knows the pink lollipop is better than a yellow one."

His eyes sparkled, and he bit his lip deliciously.

We leaned in at the same time. His mouth tasted so sweet, it made me drunk; his arms around me were so warm, I felt myself melt into him. When someone wolf whistled, we broke apart, gasping for air. I started shaking again, and Diego gave me his coat.

"Let's go back inside," he said in my ear, and we spent the next few hours in our own bubble in the club, trying to pretend he wasn't about to leave.

More than a year later, here we were. Both of us shivering again, apparently too confused to put our feelings into words.

There was so much I wanted to tell him. About the championship and my whole double life as a futbolera. About how much I'd missed him. How hurt I'd been when he'd stopped calling me.

There was so much he hadn't told me yet. About Turín, and Luís Felipe, his roommate from Brazil. But it was late, and I didn't trust myself to say anything in case the wrong words came out.

I glanced down at his arm and noticed the tattoo on his wrist. It was kind of hidden by a humble red ribbon meant to ward off the evil eye and a fancy watch that looked nothing like the knockoffs the manteros sold in Plaza Sarmiento. I grabbed his wrist and traced the words: *La Banda del 7*. His pulse hammered under my fingers.

"A tattoo for our barrio?"

I tried to keep my face impassive. I couldn't afford to lose my head. Not now.

He leaned forward and kissed me on the cheek.

His lips lingered on my skin. Before I made up my mind and turned my face that crucial distance, he pulled away.

He turned around and went down the stairs. "Good night, Mama," he said. "See you tomorrow."

NICO WOKE ME UP THE NEXT MORNING, WHINING FOR ME
to let him out of my bedroom. There was music blasting
from the apartment downstairs, a Christian ballad with
awesome drums, and the sun was baking my face. The
clock read 11:30 a.m. I jumped out of bed.

"Ay, por Dios, Nico! Why did you let me sleep so late,
che?"

I opened the door, and he darted outside. I hobbled
back to my room to change for my run. I put on a pair of
long pants, because although the sky through the window
was a perfect blue, the air would be chilly. I tied my shoes
tightly and headed to the kitchen. Every inch of my body
complained about how hard I'd played the day before. I

ignored the weakness screaming in my muscles. The gym was all right for conditioning once in a while, but an outdoor run the day after a game was a must.

Still, I didn't have much time. Diego had said he'd be here at one . . . if he didn't forget or change his mind or get too busy.

My mom was in the kitchen listening to the radio station that played old nineties songs, and she hummed along to Gustavo Cerati, stubbornly ignoring the neighbor's music. It smelled of tomato sauce already, and my stomach rumbled.

"Good morning, Mami." I kissed her on the cheek. She looked up and smiled briefly. She was pale and had dark circles under her eyes. The little freckles on her nose and cheeks popped out. Before Tío César became my father's minion, he and Mamá had been neighbors and friends. He had told me stories of what she was like when she was little. I couldn't imagine her so free.

"I got us facturas," she said, pointing at a plate on the table. The rest of the surface was covered in sequins and crystals. She was supposed to deliver the dress tomorrow so the girl could take pictures before her quinces party. She was almost finished.

My mouth watered at the pastries, but I stopped myself from taking one. "Later, vieja. I'm going for a run."

"But why, Camila? You're so thin already. I know

summer's coming, but you don't need to look like the skel-etons on *Dancing for a Dream*."

I took a deep breath. I'd never aspired to star in a danc-ing show. She said I was too thin, but the moment I picked up a pastry, she'd tell me to watch my carbs. My goal was to be fast, strong, and unstoppable, and I couldn't be that by starving myself *or* by eating pastries. My mom wouldn't get it.

"I feel better when I run. You should come with me sometime," I said. "Besides, Mami, I need to make room for your amazing food. What are you cooking?"

"Gnocchi," she said with a smile. "You're going to love them. I made some spinach ones so Pablo can get vegeta-bles, you know? I need to sneak them in." She babied him so much. "Roxana said to call her."

My heart went into batucada mode. I had to know what was so urgent that she'd call in the morning, but I couldn't risk using the house phone. My mom had super hearing.

"I'll call her later," I said.

Mamá went back to her embroidering and didn't glance at me as I left.

Earbuds in, I let the energy of Gigi D'Agostino's songs set the tempo of my steps.

A couple of blocks into my run, a German shepherd jumped at me from behind a makeshift chicken wire fence that sagged under the weight of his body. A deep voice called him from inside the house. I didn't look back. I ran and ran, imagining the bite of the dog would shock me at any second. I breathed, chasing my goal, the Sudamericano, a chance at a future in which I was the master of my own fate.

———

The first autumn Diego lived in el barrio, when he was twelve and I was ten, everyone was obsessed with running. An Argentine athlete had won an Olympic medal for racing, and every kid in el barrio was trying to imitate our new idol. Some were good runners. Not me.

When I asked Pablo for help, he said I wasn't built for running. My legs were thin like a tero bird's. Determined to prove him wrong, I raced the girl from downstairs, Analía, the monoblock's best runner after my brother.

I tried to keep up with her, but as I watched her reach the finish line, I tripped on the uneven pavement and fell. Blood bloomed from my knee and ran down my leg, seeping into my white knee-high sock. My mom was furious when she saw how I'd ruined my school clothes.

I was crying on the balcony when I heard Diego, whistling as he climbed the stairs. I would have climbed up onto the roof if I'd known how, but there was no way to escape.

Diego saw me. The melody died on his puckered-up lips. "What happened?" he asked. "Did someone hurt you?" His voice was so gentle.

I shook my head. I didn't want him to be angry, not even at Analía. When boys and men became angry, they tried to fix the world by breaking it down with their fists. I tried to speak, but I burst into tears instead.

In hushed whispers, I told him everything. He listened, and when I was done crying, he wiped my face with the inside of his Pokémon T-shirt.

Unable to find words to express my gratitude, I wrapped my arms around his neck.

Diego's skin smelled of sunshine and sweat.

In the tone my teacher at school used when telling a story, he said, "The other day, Ana told me the legend of a warrior princess who had your name."

I couldn't help but look up at his face. Was he making fun of me? No Disney princesses—the only ones I knew—had my name.

"Camila? Like me? She was a warrior?"

He nodded. "And not only that, she was a great runner. She ran so fast that when she ran across the sea, her feet didn't even get wet."

I peered down at my ugly black shoes and saw the blood stain on my sock getting darker and bigger as it spread through the cotton fibers. "Can you teach me how to run like that?"

His eyes flickered in the direction of my brother's window before returning to me. "Abuelo isn't home, is he?

You know he'd teach you like he taught Pablo. He'd do anything for you."

"He's out."

Diego hesitated, but then he said, "Let's go to the road behind the sports center. I can teach you there. I'll tell your mom where we're going."

But I shook my head. Even then, I'd known there were things she didn't want to hear.

While we walked under the naked paradise trees that lined the street, Diego told me more stories about the other Camila, the warrior princess who fought in the great Trojan War. The sunlight painted intricate designs on the ground. The dust swirled on the shimmering air before it settled on my dry lips.

"I'll hold your hand and run," he said. "You hold on tight and raise those knees. Don't look down."

I bit my lip and nodded.

"Ready?" he asked.

I looked ahead at the curving road that went on forever. We could run to the end of the world.

"Ready," I said.

Our feet hit the compacted dirt hard, raising a cloud of dust around us. Diego's hand was sweating in mine. He picked up speed, and for a second, I panicked. I imagined myself falling, bringing him down with me. I pulled his arm back to slow him down.

"Don't give up," he yelled.

I willed my legs to keep up. We ran and ran until he let go of my hand. "Race you to the willows!"

We were both flying. I was the first to reach the line of trees by the Ludueña River.

We threw ourselves on the soft, fragrant clover, breathing in the greenness around us. The fat white clouds flew above us. We were in heaven.

"Remember I said Abuelo would do anything for you?" Diego asked, propping himself on his elbow.

"Yes." Somehow I was holding his hand again.

I saw my reflection in his honey-brown eyes.

"So would I. I'd do anything for you," Diego said, and kissed me on the cheek.

———

There were no clover fields anymore. The little kids Diego and I once were would hate the chain-link fences around the new soy crops. But what would they think of the people we had become?

As I headed back home, sweat trickled down the sides of my face and my back and in between my breasts, which were squashed under two running bras two sizes too small.

I crossed the street to avoid the Jehovah's Witnesses waiting with their pamphlets. I didn't try to avoid the golden-haired North American Mormons, because even though they always smiled, they didn't talk to girls in the street, not even when I tried to practice my English. I was pretty sure they changed those guys regularly, but they all looked the same to me.

When I turned the corner of Schweitzer and Sánchez de Loria, finishing my loop, I saw kids wearing Juventus jerseys huddled around a fancy black car.

It could only belong to one person. Diego was early, and I was doomed.

"Franco!" I called to my downstairs neighbor. He was about nine years old and lived with his grandma. His brown hair gleamed like polished ebony, and his blue eyes brimmed with joy, as if he had seen Papá Noel in person.

"Camila! Look at what el Titán brought us!"

Seven or eight boys, all under the age of ten, rushed to show me their treasures.

"Mirá! An authentic Juve jersey! He signed it, too. He signed it!"

Franco's aunt, Paola, barely thirteen, was among the boys. She hugged her own white-and-black jersey, and her blue eyes sparkled just like Franco's.

She ran to me. "He even remembered me, Camila. He said he didn't bring me a Central jersey because, you know, Franco and his dad are Boca fans, but that we could all wear Juve, so that's what he brought us. They're originals, not knock-offs! And look," she whispered, showing me a picture of the whole Juventus FC squad. She turned it over. It was signed by all the players, personalized to Paola. Even the superstars like Buffon and Dybala had signed it.

"Put it in a safe place." I whispered back. "One day, this might be worth a lot of money."

She clutched it against her chest and shook her head. "Diego gave this to me. I'll never sell it. Would you?"

"Maybe?" I taunted her.

"Seriously, Camila," she said, shaking her head. "You're so lucky. He's upstairs waiting for you already, and you're here stinking like a pig. What are you thinking?"

"How do you know he's waiting for me?"

She gave me a smile that was too knowing for thirteen years old. "Because he literally told me, 'I'm here for Camila, Pao.'"

Pretty words and a fancy postcard might have enchanted Paola, but I wasn't thirteen. Diego could spin the sweetest promises, but I knew better than to create fantasies that would leave me brokenhearted when he left again at the end of the week.

I opened the door.

Sitting across from my father at our kitchen table, Diego looked like a model out of those old AXE commercials Roxana and I loved watching on YouTube.

Impeccably pressed black shirt. Worn-out jeans and sleek leather shoes. His outfit probably cost more than what my mom made in a month of straining her eyes, poking her fingers, and hunching over her sewing machine.

When Diego saw me, he flashed that radiant smile of his, but he didn't quite meet my eyes.

"There you are." He stood up while a thousand replies blared in my mind.

Looking great, Titán.

I can't stop thinking about you.

Voglio fare l'amore con te.

Conscious of my father staring at us, I stepped back, put a hand up, and said, "Paola told me I smell like a pig. You might want to stay away until I shower. Give me a few minutes."

And I made my grand escape.

After my shower, I locked my door and stood in front of my armoire. If there was a fairy godmother giving out wardrobes, now would have been a really great time for her to show up.

With Diego's outfit in mind, I settled for jeans and a charcoal sweater. My black combat boots were more fashionable than my Nikes. Abandoning all attempts to tame my long, wet mane of hair, I twisted it into a bun high on my head. I spritzed Impulse into the air and I waved the scent away so it wouldn't be too obvious I was trying. I wished I owned fancy perfume. After some frenzied eye-liner and mascara application, I dabbed on some lip gloss and grabbed my purse.

My glance fell on la estampita of La Difunta, but asking her for a favor felt sacrilegious when I hadn't even left her an offering yet.

Wish me luck, pretty boy, I begged my poster of Maluma instead before I headed out to the kitchen.

Quietly, I crossed the hallway on tiptoe. My dad and Diego spoke in hushed tones.

"What did Giusti say about the last game, Diego?" my dad asked. "You played the whole ninety."

Diego shook his head. "He isn't too lavish with praise. He always wants more and better."

My dad laughed. "And right he is. You need to keep your feet on the ground. Don't let your fame go to your head, but it's never too early for your manager to think about the next step, you know? He should be talking about increasing your salary. No, don't make that face. I won't ask. I already know how much you make. But there's always more. What about the national team? I have already started making arrangements to find a better team for Pablo. We all love Central, but we're wasting our time here."

I tried not to scoff. My father acted like he knew better than Diego's manager—the one who represented several first-class players and who already had Diego starting at Juventus FC.

But Diego only said, "I'm sure there are plenty of teams who'll want Pablo."

His gaze flicked to the hallway where I stood eaves-dropping. The way his eyes swept over me made me light up like a bonfire. My dad turned his chair, obviously trying to see for himself what had captured Diego's attention.

My dad looked at me like he had X-ray vision. I took a quick inventory of the things he would find objectionable: my tight jeans, the sweater that tottered on the precipice between modest and provocative, the makeup.

Beads of sweat broke out along the bridge of my nose. My hand itched to wipe it off, but if I did, he would notice how nervous I was.

A heavy hand slapped me on the shoulder, and I yelped.

"Pablo!" I said, turning around and pounding my brother's bare chest.

Pablo roared with laughter, clutching his abs with one hand and pointing at me with the other. "I had to! You should've seen how high you jumped!"

My dad laughed, too, but my mom said, "Leave her alone, Pali. Put a shirt on before you sit at the table, please."

I was too embarrassed to look at Diego.

"At least you have some color in your face, Camila." Pablo defended himself, putting on the shirt that had been tucked in his back pocket. "You were pale as clay." He and Diego kissed on the cheek and embraced. "And why are you wearing lipstick?" Pablo asked, looking at me over Diego's shoulder. "Are you going out with a friend?"

"She's going out with me," Diego said.

My ears rang.

Pablo clenched his teeth. "Cutting right to the chase, Titán?"

I couldn't believe he'd said that.

"Ay, Pablo. ¡Qué boludo!" I rolled my eyes. "Why don't you shut up?"

Diego shook his head and whispered something I didn't catch.

"Camila, what a potty mouth!" my mom exclaimed. "And in front of Diego, too." If saying "boludo" was having a potty mouth, then there wasn't a single clean-mouthed person in our country, not even my mother. "Diego, you should've told me last night that you were going to come back today. I would've made sure Pablo was up."

"You came over last night?" Pablo's words were directed at Diego, but he looked at me and shook his head as if I'd disappointed him.

"Mamá," I said, trying to stop her from making this a bigger mess than it already was.

"Are you sure you don't want Pablo and Marisol to go along?" she asked Diego.

Pablo and Marisol? Like *chaperones*?

Luckily, Diego shook his head. "We can't wait for this vago to get ready. He'll take hours."

Pablo grimaced. "And I don't do double dates with my sister. We'll hang out later, no, Diegui?"

My dad had been too quiet, but I knew the scheming look on his face. "What ever happened to that girlfriend you had, Diego?" he asked, narrowing his eyes. "Won't she be jealous that you're spending your free time with little Camila?"

Little Camila?

"She has no business being jealous." Diego's ears were flaming red. "I haven't seen her . . . I haven't even talked to her."

"That's too bad," my dad continued, as if he hadn't noticed we were halfway out the door. "She was a bon-bon. But you were smart to break up with her. In Europe, you can find a proper woman. None of the villeritas, the botineras wanting to suck you dry in every way, you know what I mean?" He chuckled.

My mom looked from my dad to me, but she didn't say anything. She just straightened out a crooked corner of the tablecloth. Even Pablo's face was scrunched with disgust, but he'd started this.

In response, Diego walked to the door, opened it, and turned to look at me. I followed him. I had to get out of there.

From the stairs, I heard Pablo call out, "Take care of my little sister, Titán."

"Oh, don't worry. I will."

He closed the door. I didn't even want to imagine the reaction on the other side.

DIEGO'S CAR WAS A MASTERPIECE. I SAT ON MY HANDS TO stop myself from touching the spaceship-like controls on the dashboard. The light gray leather was smooth under my fingers.

"Is this the famous new car smell I've heard about?" I asked to break the awkwardness that had enveloped Diego and me as we made our way downstairs.

He bit his lower lip as if trying not to smile and shrugged. "Just got it from the dealer this morning. They were holding it for me."

"But you're going back to Turín next week."

"Renting a car each time I come back would be more expensive than owning one, to be honest." I wasn't going to ask when he'd be coming back. Not after the scene with Pablo and my dad. But if he'd bought a car, maybe he'd buy a house or an apartment in one of the brand-new buildings in Puerto Norte.

"Where are you parking it?" I asked. "When you return, you won't find even a thread of the leather seats."

"I'm driving it to Buenos Aires. This guy has a parking garage for players' cars."

"Genius," I said. The guy who owned that garage must have been raking it in with shovels.

The BMW barely rocked on the narrow streets of el barrio, pockmarked by too much rain and too little maintenance. The seat automatically adjusted around my body and cushioned me from the minimal jostling.

"Cool, huh?" Diego asked, noting my surprise.

"Just like the 142," I said, and looked out the window. From the safety of the car, I didn't mind the wild dogs sprawled on the sidewalks, sleeping off the adventures of the previous night.

Once we were outside el barrio, Diego rolled down his window. The wind that tangled his hair carried the scent of burning leaves. The sound of the popcorn seller's handcart bell just barely reached my ears—a whisper, and then it was gone.

"You look beautiful," Diego said softly.

I turned to see if he was joking, but he was looking at the road ahead, his hands clenching the steering wheel.

He was beautiful.

"I need to call Roxana. Can I borrow your phone?"

"Now?"

"Now. It's urgent, and mine's dead."

The corner of his mouth twitched, but he took a slick phone from his jacket pocket and handed it to me. Pablo had a much older iPhone, and I hesitated because I didn't know how to unlock this one.

"Here," he said, taking the phone back, lifting the screen to his face for just a second, and then passing it back to me in a swift movement.

He rolled the window back up, and I dialed Roxana's number, once, twice, three times. She didn't pick up. She probably didn't recognize the number. Finally, I texted her.

Answer the phone. It's Camila.

Diego drove on, and I held the phone in my sweaty hand, praying for Roxana to call and rescue me. No matter how long I stared at the screen, she didn't reply. Carefully, I put the phone on the center console. Diego glanced at me and then at it but didn't say a word.

The tension between us was oppressive.

This wasn't a normal first date. It wasn't like I could ask him basic question to break the ice. I already knew all his trivia. He was an Aquarius. His favorite colors were blue and yellow, but he preferred pink candy. His favorite number was ten—duh—and his favorite superhero was Spider-Man, the same as mine.

Still, even if his favorite colors and superheroes hadn't changed, *he* had changed. I'd known the pre-Juventus Diego. Who was he now?

"Last night we didn't get to talk about Turín," I finally said. "What is it like to play on that kind of team? How is it being back home?" I sounded like the reporter who'd pelted me with questions after the championship.

He sighed with relief, the awkwardness gone. "Sometimes it feels like I never left Rosario." He gave me that crooked smile. "Everything's the same. The kids play in the parking lot, and the popcorn seller stands on the corner; there's pasta on holidays, and wild dogs scratch their flea bites on the sidewalk. But this morning, it took me a second to remember where I was. I miss my apartment and my own bed."

"Everything must be beautiful in Turín."

Diego shrugged. "Yes, but the price of living there is too steep, and I'm not talking about euros."

"You miss Rosario?"

"So much it hurts." He rubbed his chest. "I'm doing what I love, but I miss Rosario in a way I never expected. Luís Felipe calls it saudade."

The Portuguese word filled me with longing for something I hadn't lost yet. My saudade had more to do with not getting to experience what he had: a life playing fútbol without having to hide.

"Tell me about Luís Felipe?" I'd seen Diego's room-mate in some of the Snapchats Roxana had shown me. Luís Felipe was gorgeous. His face looked chiseled by Michelangelo. Judging by how much Diego laughed when he was with him, he seemed like a great friend to live with. His girlfriend, Flávia, a model, was his childhood sweetheart, and they were trying the long-distance thing.

Diego laughed. "That guy is Carnaval personified! 'Tudo bem, tudo bem,' he says, and then he scores like a beast after partying all night with girls. He . . . he's a char-acter, that's for sure."

My mouth went dry as I pictured Flávia at home, think-ing her long-distance relationship was working while her boyfriend was out partying all night with other women. Did she know? Did she care? And what about Diego? Did he party all night long with them?

I turned toward the window. We were driving past the municipal cemetery, La Piedad. A legion of stone angels watched over its expanse. Abuelo Ahmed was there. I'd never visited his grave, not even to help Pablo and my mom repaint it yellow and blue last spring. I looked away when we drove past the marble entrance, but I still felt its chill through the car window like icy fingers.

After a turn on 27 de Febrero, we drove through a neighborhood of freshly painted two-story houses with iron bars on the windows and satellite dishes on the interconnected roofs. There was litter on the side of the road—cigarette butts and beer cans. Vagabond dogs sprawled everywhere. Kids of all sizes and ages walked, played, and worked. Runny-nosed little ones stood at the traffic lights, doing magic tricks or cleaning windshields for a few coins. Trapitos, people called them—Little Rags.

Diego's face was grave when we stopped at a light. He lowered his window and handed a boy of about five a hundred-peso bill. There wasn't much the boy could buy with that, not even a McDonald's Happy Meal. Diego had been gone too long to keep up with inflation.

"Pobrecito." Diego sighed.

I turned in my seat to see the little boy running toward a girl not much older than he was. Their joined silhouettes became a speck in the distance.

Diego's expression was stony. Before Ana had found him, he'd been that boy at a traffic light, juggling a fútbol for spare coins. I didn't know what to say, so I placed a hand on his arm, and he flexed instinctively.

"You're jacked!" I exclaimed half jokingly. He'd always been athletic, of course, but training in Europe had turned him into a sculpture.

Diego smiled, shaking his head, the sheen of sadness gone from his eyes.

After a couple of blocks, we pulled up in front of a magnificent sanctuary of red brick and sand-colored stucco.

Arched Gothic windows ran along the walls on both sides of the church's entrance.

"We're going here first?"

Diego smiled sheepishly. "Work first, and then we . . . we can have some fun."

I got out before Diego could open the door for me. Flustered, we crossed the street. Once on the sidewalk, I realized Eva María's practice field was just around the block at Parque Yrigoyen. I must have passed this church hundreds of times, but I'd never noticed it.

Rosario showed a different face depending on how you looked at her. She changed when you saw her from a bus, or a luxury car, or your own feet.

The main entrance to the church was chained shut, but we went through a smaller side door. A metal plaque read INSTITUTO DEL BUEN PASTOR. FUNDADO 1896." I thought of the girls imprisoned here for fighting for the right to vote, or demanding not to be beaten by their fathers or husbands, or for wanting to earn a decent salary. Las Incorregibles. These walls had witnessed so much pain and despair, and I wondered if the ghosts of those girls still haunted them. Eighteen ninety-six was so long ago, but so many things remained the same.

We followed a hallway, the characteristic sounds of childhood—laughter, chatter, shrieking—inviting us in. A baby cried nearby.

We ended up in an inner courtyard dotted with white statues, some of saints I didn't know and one of Jesus carrying a lamb on his shoulders. A broken fountain was covered in dead leaves.

A tall, dark-skinned man walked in. His hair was speckled with white, and his eyes were framed by webs of wrinkles. I'd known about Father Hugo for as long as I'd known Diego, but I'd never met him in person.

"Padre!" Diego called.

"Dieguito! You're here!" The joy in his voice made me smile.

The priest placed his hands on Diego's shoulders and looked into his eyes. "The kids saw you on TV celebrating in the stands with the rest of the barra, and the kitchen exploded. I thought they were witnessing the Lord's second coming. But that was nothing compared to when they saw you start for la Juve."

Diego's laughter bounced off the crumbling stucco walls that surrounded the courtyard, and the priest beamed at him.

"This is Camila, Father."

"Camila, of course." He shook my hand. "Diego has spoken so much about you. For years now, it has been Camila this, Camila that—"

"Now, Father," Diego said, blushing, "don't go revealing my secrets. Camila's here for the English tutoring job."

Father Hugo looked at me. His eyes were almost black, but there was no darkness in them.

"I'll go play some ball with the kids while you two talk, okay?" Diego asked.

"Don't make them wild. That's all I ask."

"I'll do my best." Diego ran to meet his admirers.

I couldn't take my eyes off Diego and the little boys running after him.

The priest cleared his throat. "Now, Camila, Diego tells me you taught yourself English, and that you got your licenciatura before you finished high school. That's impressive!"

"Thank you, Father," I said, unused to the praise.

"What motivated you to learn?"

"Honestly, all my life I've wanted to attend school in the United States."

I might as well have said I wanted to be an astronaut. "The United States? People from all over the continent and even the world come to Argentina for a free first-class education. Why do you want to leave?"

"I want an education," I said, "but I also wanted to play fútbol. The U.S. teams are multi-world, multi-Olympic champions. And it's because their college programs are incredible." My heart pounded, and a sheen of sweat broke out on my nose as if I were at confession. I'd never had a normal conversation with a priest before.

"I see . . . Playing for a school there would be a little like getting a contract with la Juve, right?"

I laughed, shaking my head. Nothing was further from the truth. "Minus all the millions. College players make no money, actually. But playing for a college would open doors that don't even exist here. Their female league is professional."

His eyes widened.

"But there aren't many scholarships for international students, so I'll aim for the National Women's Soccer League. Getting there is difficult but not impossible. Even if that goal is too far-fetched, who knows where the journey will take me." It felt so good to open up to him.

"Every year, multitudes travel to my native India to find enlightenment," Father Hugo said. "When I was eighteen, I left to seek *myself*. I, too, wanted to know what I could do, and never in a million years did I dream I'd end up in Rosario. Now this is my home. These are my people."

It wasn't until he mentioned he was from India that I noticed his slight accent. Behind me, a little kid squealed in delight, and I turned to see Diego in the middle of the courtyard, buried in a pile of dry leaves. His hair looked like a nest. There was no trace of el Titán.

If he'd been a jerk, drunk on fame and glory, it would've been so easy to turn away from him. But seeing him like this disarmed me.

Before I could hide my feelings, I noticed Father Hugo studying my face. "So, fútbol is your dream?"

"It is," I said.

Father Hugo smiled and opened his hands. "In the

meantime, you need a job, and I need an English teacher for the kids."

I nodded, waiting to hear what he had to say. He continued, "Do you have experience teaching?"

"I've tutored kids for end-of-the-year tests, but not in a classroom setting. I like children, though, and I'm a fast learner."

"I see . . . but before you commit to something you're not ready for, I want to make sure you know exactly what you'll encounter here."

The church's turret cast a long shadow over the courtyard. Trying not to shiver from nerves or cold, I crossed my arms over my chest.

"A lot of the children here have gone through things most of us can't imagine." Father Hugo's intense gaze accentuated the seriousness of his words. "The kids here aren't like the kids at the American institute downtown, but in God's eyes, they're equally treasured. Other than the help from international charities, we have no support. The work the Sisters and I do here is like running on a hamster wheel. We run, we tire, but we don't go anywhere. We repeat the same motions the next day and the one after that. Every day. And maybe there will be one or two like Diego. Or like you. A little one with dreams too big and amazing to ignore. When they go for those dreams, all the effort and failure are worth it."

"Sounds to me like this is a big job," I said, squaring my shoulders. "You and the Sisters can't do it all by yourselves. There might be others like Diego waiting for someone to give them a hand."

"That's true. But you have to understand that Diego is an exception to the rule. He's among the precious few children I've met through the years not to end up in jail or living under a bridge. Most of the kids who seek refuge here, Camila, have families. They come here or else they don't eat. They come because children still have that divine spark intact in them, and they instinctually gravitate to a place where there is order, warmth, and love.

"It's only when they grow, or when they get hurt by those who should protect them, that the spark in them dies. That death, that loss of innocence and hope, is something many volunteers can't endure. And they give up. If you agree to teach here, will you pledge to keep working no matter how little progress we make?"

Oddly at ease with this stranger of the strong will and soft eyes, I said, "I know it won't be easy, Father. I won't promise I'll always be in high spirits, but I'll never lose heart. Now, what do you need me to do?"

He regarded me in silence, and then his face broke into a generous smile. "You can come after school to help me give the kids their afternoon snack and help with their schoolwork. There are a couple at risk of repeating the year, and I think we can get them excited if, as a reward for passing, they get to learn the English. They want to be involved on the YouTube and Instagram. What do you think?"

"I think I can manage that." Practices were at eight, so the schedule worked perfectly for me. My mind was already whirring with ideas for how to start teaching them "the" English.

"The pay is not great."

"No, no, don't worry about that." I needed every single peso I could scrape together, but could I really take it from these kids, who needed it even more?

"But I do worry about that," Father Hugo interjected. "It's a meager salary, but you need to take it. This is a job, not a volunteer position." He said it with such firmness that I didn't dare contradict him.

"Okay, I'll take it."

"Of course you will. Two thousand pesos a week—a pittance." He shook his head.

Two thousand pesos a week was eight thousand a month, more money than I'd ever had at once, so for me, it wasn't a pittance. If I saved for a whole year, it would be about fifteen hundred U.S. dollars. A fortune.

"Believe me, it's okay," I said.

He took both my hands in his own warm and calloused ones and led me to the center of the cobblestone courtyard. "Let's go join the children now that all's settled."

The children, Diego included, played under the supervision of one of the Sisters.

Peter and the Lost Boys. I prayed they all reached their dreams like Diego had reached his. But more than that, I prayed that I might reach mine, and that nothing and no one—not even me—would get in the way.

"EVERYTHING WENT WELL?" DIEGO ASKED.

"Yes, I think the job's going to be fun." My heart was pounding, and not because of the kids or Father Hugo. It was only three thirty, and the promise of spending the rest of the day with Diego, just the two of us, made my body thrill.

"The kids already love you." His smile was blazing, and then his eyes got bashful. "And how can I blame them?"

"Stop it," I said, slapping his arm but really wanting to slap myself.

It didn't take much more than a charged look for my fantasies to grow like a wildfire. I didn't know what to do or say.

"What's wrong?" He must have felt my anxiety.

A dry leaf was lodged in his hair, and I reached out my hand to pluck it. My fingers lingered on his soft curls for a second, and when I brushed the back of his neck, his skin broke into goosebumps.

"Your hands are cold," he said, grabbing my wrist and kissing my palm.

Softly I pulled my hand away and crossed my arms.

In a few days, he'd be back in Turín. Was I really going to do this again? Fall for him even though he was leaving? I didn't want to have him and then lose him again.

Diego turned the engine on. "Do you still want to go out with me, Mama?"

"Do you?"

Chamuyo and histeriqueo: the Argentine national arts of sweet-talking, teasing, and flirting. I didn't want to play this game with Diego, but I couldn't stop myself.

"I've been dreaming about taking you to the river forever. And look, the weather's perfect. We couldn't have asked for a better day."

"I thought we were going to the planetarium."

"It's closed until December. They're renovating it. Next time I'm taking you for sure."

"Let's go, then." I sat back, relishing the warm caress of the sun on my face. Diego turned the radio on and pushed some buttons on the dashboard before he landed on FM Vida.

"You still listen to this station?" I asked, tapping my

foot to a Gustavo Cerati song I'd never heard before. His voice and the guitar were unmistakable.

"All the time. On the app," he said. "The guys on the team love my music."

A car behind us honked and passed us on the right.

"You're driving too slowly, Titán," I said. "Are you scared?"

Diego shrugged but kept his eyes glued to the road ahead. He sped up, honking at every intersection, even when he had the right of way, just like all the other cars around us. "I've driven in Paris and Rome, but driving in Rosario requires a sixth sense, you know?"

"No, I actually don't, seeing as I've never driven before," I said, worried for the delivery girl with giant headphones zigzagging through the traffic on a motorcycle.

Diego glanced at me. "Do you want to learn?"

"Sure!" I laughed. "But how? My dad's never going to let me touch his Peugeot. Not even my mom knows where he hides the car keys."

"Let's do it, then," Diego said, turning sharply on Chacabuco toward Parque Urquiza.

"What?" I asked, sounding panicky. "What if I crash into a tree, or a person?"

"It's not like jumping out of an airplane, Cami. You'll see how easy it is."

Too soon, the planetarium dome peeked through the naked tree branches and palm trees. The park was teeming with activity. A group of elderly people practiced tai chi on the lawn, apparently oblivious to the teenagers playing fútbol next to them. On the other side of the sidewalk, older men in berets and knitted cardigans threw bocce balls with the same concentration I saw on my mom's face when she embroidered dresses. A young father jogged next to a little girl pedaling furiously on her tiny pink bicycle. His hand hovered behind her when her bike wobbled, but she didn't fall.

Diego slowed down and finally stopped at an empty parking lot behind an abandoned supermarket. "Now get out."

"I can't," I said, grabbing on to my seat.

Diego got out, came around the car, and opened my door. "Let's do it, nena," he said, taking my hand and gently pulling me out.

"What if you get hurt?" I tried to take my hand back, but he didn't budge. He tugged me to the driver's side, leaving me in front of the door. "¿Estás loco?"

He turned around and held my gaze as if daring me to read the answer in his eyes. He stepped forward, and I stepped back like we were in a tango duel. The car pressed against my back. I had no escape.

"Nothing bad is going to happen," he said. "Don't be scared."

The scent of his cologne went to my head, and before I did something stupider than driving a car that cost more than my life, I stomped my foot and said, "Fine!" I got in the driver's seat, fuming.

Diego laughed and got in the passenger seat. He turned the music off. "So you can focus."

As if his presence wasn't the biggest distraction of them all.

I rolled down the window so the breeze would help me stay cool.

"First, put your seat belt on." He waited for me to comply, and I could tell he enjoyed being in charge. "Next, press the brake and shift to drive. The *D*." He put his hand over mine as I fumbled with the gear shift. "Let go of the brake, and give the car a little bit of juice. Yes, accelerate like that. Softly and slowly. You're doing perfect. Go straight. Confident."

I was trying to focus, but my mind twisted around every single double meaning of his words.

He sat back, looking as relaxed as if he were sunning at La Florida beach. "Eyes on the road."

My hands were sweaty, but I didn't dare let go of the steering wheel to wipe them on my jeans. But after a few seconds, my heartbeat went back to normal, and my thoughts cleared. I took a few deep breaths. I wanted to show Diego I was strong and could do anything he challenged me to do.

"Now, ease up on the gas and brake with your right foot. Like that."

The car lurched forward when I slammed on the pedal. "Ay! Sorry."

So much for impressing him.

"Your seat's too far out, shorty," he said calmly, and reached across me to adjust the seat with the controls on the driver's side door.

Every one of my nerve endings became hyperaware of his whole body pressing against mine.

"Stop it! I'll do it," I said, gently pushing him off me.

He laughed as I moved my seat forward and up until I could reach the pedals comfortably.

My armpits prickled, and I hoped I smelled okay.

"What do I do with my left foot?" I asked, trying to get control of the situation.

"Just relax it on the footrest. Give it a break. The car's automatic."

That explained a lot. Last year, Roxana had tried to drive her dad's truck to practice, but our adventure had almost ended in disaster when she hadn't known how to reverse out of the carport.

If Roxana saw me now, she'd chew me out.

"Let's go around the block. Careful with the kids," Diego said, pointing at a group of tweens riding rented electric scooters.

My every sense focusing on not running over anyone, ruining this car, the price of which I couldn't even fathom, or hurting Diego, who had just renewed his contract with Juventus, I drove around the block.

"Again," he said.

Now that I knew how to steer and control the speed, I became aware of how sensitive the controls were. The car felt like an extension of my body, like it knew what I was about to do a millisecond before I did it. A part of me wanted to see how fast I could go, but I kept my foot steady, turning carefully at the corners. I finally smiled.

"Now I'm ruined for life," I said, heading toward the parking lot where we'd started.

"What do you mean?"

"After driving this car, anything else will be a letdown."

He laughed.

I stopped behind the supermarket. "Ta-da!" I said, beaming at him.

The sun shone behind him so I couldn't see his features. "You're a natural," he said with a smile in his voice. "Before we know it, you'll be zooming down the streets of Turín in my Jeep."

"You have a Jeep?"

"Yes. Jeep's one of the team's sponsors, so the players drive the newest model to show it off. Mine's white with the darkest windows I was allowed to get."

My mind buzzed, trying to make sense of him owning not one but two luxury cars, and this one would just sit in a garage in Buenos Aires most of the year. This was easier to think about than what he'd said about me driving in Turín.

"We're not finished yet." Diego took my hand from

the steering wheel and placed it on the gear shift again. "Now switch it to park. This button turns off the engine."

The car stopped rumbling, but at his touch, my heart started galloping again.

"This was fun," I said, avoiding his eyes. My hand was still on the ignition. "Thank you."

"Anything for you," he said, sweeping his hair back from his face. "Now let's go get some sunshine."

─────

We headed toward the river, walking so close our hands brushed every few seconds.

"I hope the car's still here when we come back," I said, looking at it over my shoulder. It was the only luxury car in the parking lot. It might as well have had a neon sign on it that said TAKE ME.

"Nothing will go wrong today," he promised, like he'd peeked into the future and seen nothing but good fortune.

It was so easy to believe him.

Maybe it was relief that I hadn't hurt anyone or embarrassed myself with my driving. Maybe it was the adrenaline. But in that moment, everything around us looked beautiful. The sun shone bright and warm for August, the sky a vivid blue that seemed straight out of a postcard. Ahead of us, the river glinted a golden brown, lapping against the concrete causeway. My heart soared as I looked at the expanse of sky and water, Diego by my side.

Before we crossed Avenida Belgrano, he grabbed my hand.

I looked at him.

He shrugged. "I don't want to lose you."

Instead of digging for a lame comeback, I rolled my eyes, and he smiled. He didn't let go when we reached the other side, and I didn't pull my hand away, either.

Like in Parque Urquiza, the green spaces along Avenida Belgrano were teeming with people trying to squeeze every bit of pleasure out of the three-day weekend. La Costanera— the pedestrian way that went from the Flag Memorial through Parque España all the way to Rosario Central Stadium and beyond—was lined with food vendors, artisans, and entertainers.

No one looked twice at Diego.

We could've been an ordinary couple. Us. A couple.

"I've missed the smell of the river," he said, taking a deep breath. "Blending in. Enjoying the day."

A guy in his twenties pushing a food cart whistled, and Diego said, "Let's get something to eat. I'm famished."

The man sold torta asada, and in his cart he had a fire grill. My mouth watered at the scent.

"Here," Diego said, and he broke off half a flatbread and handed it to me. He bit the torta, closed his eyes, and groaned. "This is the most delicious thing I've ever tasted in my life."

"We should've brought los *mates*," I said.

Diego tilted his head back, looked at the sky, and sighed. "Why didn't I think of that?"

"Shoddy planning, Titán."

He clicked his tongue. "We can buy a *mate* listo and hot water in the kiosco later."

"They charge a fortune," I said.

"I exchanged some euros at the car dealership. We're rich." He patted his pocket, and I laughed.

A boy on a skateboard stopped in the middle of the trail and exclaimed, "Look!"

Diego and I turned toward the river, where the boy was pointing. I first saw the yellow-and-red kite, hanging low above the waves. I followed its line to the man in a black wet suit jumping over the water with his board, his arms tense as he held on to the surf kite. When he jumped about three meters and then smacked back down on the water, the audience that had gathered along the rail clapped.

After a few minutes, most of the crowd dispersed, but Diego leaned against the brick wall that separated the sidewalk from the barranca, still gazing at the surfer. He draped his arm around my waist and drew me against him. My first instinct was to shrug out of his embrace, but instead, I leaned in.

He placed his chin on my head, and in silence we watched the river, the man and his kite, and the blue swallows that seemed like enchanted, chirping origami.

"My abs hurt just looking at him," Diego said.

The man had to have incredible core strength to maneuver the board while trying to control the kite so he wouldn't crash every time the wind carried him too close to the edge of the river. I watched his strained face in fascination.

"Next time we can try that," Diego said.

"There are so many things you want to do next time . . ."

"There are so many things I want to do now."

I turned toward him. "Like what?"

Diego didn't answer. He glanced down at my mouth, and I placed my hand on the wall to steady myself.

The boy with the skateboard stepped right in front of us, staring at Diego. His eyes widened. "Diego Ferrari?" he whispered.

Diego nodded. A silent request to keep his identity secret flashed over his face.

"Can I get a selfie with you, please, genio?" The boy took out a phone from his pocket. "To show my little brother. He adores you. He won't believe you were here."

"Of course," Diego said.

The kid smiled from ear to ear as he stood next to Diego and took the picture. He checked the screen, then clapped Diego on the shoulder. "Thank you, maestro."

Maestro, genio. This was Diego's life now.

The boy zoomed toward the Flag Memorial on his skateboard, and Diego took my hand and led me in the opposite direction. We dodged a dog walker and his pack of huskies, chihuahuas, and mestizos, wending through the artisans' stands and food vendors until we came across a group of people blocking the path.

"What's happening?" I asked, standing on my tiptoes.

I caught a glimpse of girls doing Zumba in clothes too skimpy for the season.

Diego never let go of my hand as we skirted around them. His eyes never strayed toward the girls, either. In spite of all the people around us, I was aware of his breath, the way he looked at me, the scent of his cologne and his leather jacket.

We talked the whole way.

"Basically, when I'm not training, all I do is play FIFA, read, and sleep."

I shook my head. "Stop trying to pretend your life is totally unglamorous."

He laughed. "It is. Well, most times. I'm a simple guy. I want a simple life, or as simple as it can be in my position, you know?"

By then we'd reached the red-brick stairs in Parque España.

"I'll race you, simple guy," I said, climbing the steps two at a time.

"¡Tramposa!" Diego called from behind me, laughing. He caught up with me in no time. By the time we reached the top, I was gasping for air. I had never understood how I could run for miles without a problem, but climbing stairs always left me breathless.

"I win!" I said, jumping up and down.

"*I* win."

I leaned against the wall. "I beat you by like two seconds. How did you win?"

"I had the best view," he said, standing next to me.

It was golden hour, the sun hovering over the horizon like it didn't want this afternoon to end, either.

"It looks beautiful," Diego said. From here, we could see the whole esplanade. "It's changed so much in just a year. I didn't know they'd put up a fair and a carousel."

"I didn't know, either," I said. It was like I, too, was seeing Rosario after a long absence.

"I love it."

"As much as you love Turín? Do you love la Juve as much as you lo—"

"—as I love Central?" Although he guessed my question, he didn't answer right away.

"Well . . . do you?"

He sighed, and his Adam's apple bobbed.

Finally, he answered, "I never knew the heart could expand to love different places and clubs so much." He looked at me then, and his eyes were sparkly like the diamonds in his ears. "Central will be my first love forever— my home, the catapult I needed to become el Titán, you know? And La Juve? Ay, Camila! That place is magical.

The people there are sick with futbolitis. The passion . . . when I do something on the field and the stadium explodes . . . I don't know how to describe it. It's like a fever."

"Yes, I know," I said.

Diego was claimed by la Vecchia Signora, a demanding mistress. I could never compete with her.

"La Juve is the most winning team in Italy," he continued. "The weight on my shoulders when I put the jersey on . . ." He shivered. "It's something indescribable . . . like I'm possessed by one thing and one thing only: the need to be the best."

I wanted what he had. I needed to play on a team like that, to feel the love of the fans. I needed the chance to do something impossible and amazing. To be great.

I wanted Diego's life. But I wanted to live it, not watch it from the sidelines.

We looked at the river in silence, and after a few seconds, he asked. "Do you want to head back to the car? We can go eat dinner."

"Don't they feed you in Turín?" I asked. "You never stop eating."

Diego laughed, and two girls jogging past us glanced at him. One of them did a double take and said something to her friend.

"Come," I told him, and grabbed his hand. "Let's go before your fans attack you again."

We made our way back through the fair. About half-way there, we found a stage where a group was singing a cumbia song to a dancing audience. As if to prove his point about wanting a simple life, Diego stepped in front of me and said, "Dance with me."

I almost accused him of playing with me. I took his hand and followed him to the center of the square.

When I turned fifteen, I hadn't had a quinceañera, but since my father was out of town, my mom had let me go dancing with Pablo and his friends. Diego dancing cumbia had plagued my dreams ever since.

Now he expertly led me and sang softly in my ear. I lifted my arms to hook them around his neck. His fingertips brushed my waist where my sweater crept up. He twirled me elegantly, then stepped behind me, pressing me close to his chest.

The steps were so familiar, I didn't even have to think to fall into the next one. I leaned my head back, and he dipped his face and kissed my neck. I looked at the stars, which were just starting to come out.

The song slowed, and when I turned around, we were face-to-face, just a breath apart.

"What are we doing?"

"We're dancing, Mami."

"Señor," a girl's voice said. "A flower for your girl?"

We both looked to the side to see a girl of about thirteen with a handful of individually wrapped roses.

"How much?" he asked.

"Fifty each."

Diego took most of the colorful bills from his wallet and handed them to the girl. "I'll take all of them."

Her face lit up in a joyful smile. She brushed her dark brown hair away from her face, nodded at me, and said, "Good for you," handing me the roses.

When I took them, a thorn pricked me. "Ay!"

Diego took the flowers and looked at my hand. A drop of blood was blooming on the tender skin where the thumb meets the index finger. Without hesitation, he lifted my hand to his mouth and licked the blood away, making me burst into fire.

"Sana, sana, colita de rana," he whispered.

The band started playing another song. A girl with a boy in a rugby jersey watched me from next to the stage. I recognized her green eyes and hostile expression from yesterday's game—the Royals' captain.

Diego handed me back the flowers. "Flowers for my girl."

My heart thundered in my ears. Me. His girl.

Stunned, bewitched, I took the flowers and placed them in the crook of my arm like a beauty pageant winner. He held my other hand, and slowly we walked back to his car.

"¡Gracias a Dios!" we said in unison when we arrived

at the parking lot and saw his car, safe and sound under the one streetlamp.

When we got in, I placed the flowers on my lap. The tips of the petals had already wilted. The clock on the console read eight.

"I know you need to go back home," he said. "But we have the rest of the week."

Today had been perfect, and I didn't know how I'd ever go back to my normal life when he left.

"Diego," I said, placing my hand on his arm.

"I love how you say my name."

He never let my hand go as he drove along the scenic route, doubling back the way we'd come, passing Parque España, the multicolored silos, and the stadium. A giant sign announced its World Cup class status: *Estadio Mundialista Gigante de Arroyito.*

We both softly sang, *"Un amor como el guerrero . . ."*

"I promised the guys from the team I'd go out with them tonight. And tomorrow morning I have a meeting at the Central headquarters with the AFA bosses, but in the afternoon, I'll come get you."

"Tomorrow I'm teaching the kids," I said, "And then I have—"

His phone rang, and when he looked down at the console, his eyes widened. He pressed the red ignore button.

The phone rang again. This time, I saw the name flashing on the screen. *Giusti*. His manager.

"Answer it," I said.

He shook his head. "He's in Buenos Aires. I'll call him later."

If I had a manager, I would never ignore a call from them. I pushed the button on the console, and Giusti's voice blared through the speakers. "Diego, come stai?"

Diego winked at me. He and Giusti spoke more Italian than Spanish, but the sound of Italian on Diego's lips was like music. Soon we were at the barrio's boundaries.

For as long as I could remember, there had been a gaggle of boys smoking and talking on the corner of Colombres and Schweitzer. It's like they signed a contract when they reached a certain age.

Diego honked at them. Cries of recognition and teasing and the smell of their cigarettes followed us like streamers.

When we arrived in the parking lot in front of my building, I waited for him to hang up. I didn't want this day to end, but the seconds swished away.

"Guarda con la comida, Diego," Giusti said.

Diego flinched when his manager reminded him to eat well, hunching his shoulders like a scolded little boy.

Doña Rosa from apartment 2D stopped on the side-walk, shopping bag in hand, and stared at the car. Alberto from across the street joined her and actually pointed at us.

"Giusti, I'll call you back in two minutes," Diego said when he noticed we had attracted an audience. I had to get out of the car before the neighbors started rumors about us.

"I have to—"

He stopped my words with a kiss that extinguished the world around us.

Like when we'd danced, my lips knew how to follow the beat of the music made of our galloping hearts and the sighs escaping our mouths.

I wrapped my arms around his neck, pulling him against me, my fingers raking through his tangled hair. His eyelashes fluttered against mine, butterfly kisses that made me gasp with longing for more.

"I'll see you tomorrow," he whispered, his hand cupping my face.

"Tomorrow," I said, breathless.

The tug of real life pulled at me, but I still floated in a daze as I made my way upstairs and watched him drive away.

NO ONE BUT NICO WAS HOME WHEN I ARRIVED, AND I
thanked whichever guardian angel was on duty for this
small grace. My dog did his happy dance while I filled
a vase and put my flowers in it, hoping they would live
forever, but a shower of petals dropped when I took the
cellophane off.

Eventually I'd have to tell my family about Diego, but
for now, I wanted to hold on to the golden glow of the
afternoon and keep it sacred in my heart. I wished I could
stash the memories of us dancing and the warmth of his
lips on mine under my mattress with the yellow lollipop.

Being with Diego was like stepping into a parallel
world where I was beautiful. Important. When he'd shivered at my touch, I'd felt powerful and unstoppable. As the

minutes passed, the afternoon began to feel like it had happened to another person in another lifetime. Now, back in reality, I was crashing.

A little note in my mom's handwriting sat by the phone as if we lived in 1999. *Call Roxana.* Once again, guilt squirmed inside me. After I tried calling her on Diego's cell, I'd forgotten about her. But I couldn't talk to anyone yet. I'd see her at school tomorrow.

I gazed at the estampita on my nightstand. La Difunta Correa had died trying to save her husband, and although her sacrifice had cost her own life, she'd become immortal. But her journey didn't speak to me. If I followed Diego, where would I end up? What doors were closing with each decision that I made?

The emotions from the last few days caught up with me, and I climbed into bed, intending to close my eyes for only a few minutes. Hours later, I woke to the sound of my doorknob turning.

"Camila, open." My father's voice sent me into high alert. "I want to speak with you."

Nico stretched in the bed beside me and looked at me as if asking what was going on.

"Open the door," my father's voice boomed.

Outside my window, even the crickets went quiet with terror. The door handle jiggled until it finally broke with a crack. My dog growled and jumped from the bed before I could stop him.

I froze. I couldn't even call Nico back.

Once when I was in kindergarten and I was still perfect and beloved because my body hadn't changed yet, my dad and I had walked to school hand in hand. He'd pointed at a baby sparrow dying on the sidewalk. It had fallen from the nest before it even had the chance to open its eyes and see the world. It was exposed to the biting wind; ants crawled out of its mouth.

Now, standing in front of my father, wearing only a long T-shirt and underwear, I felt like that doomed bird.

He lifted a hand, and like a child, I cowered. Nico barked twice, the sound piercing my ears.

"¿Qué te pasa? Why do you do this?" my father asked, as if I were the one who had just broken into a room and breached someone else's defenses. "What's gotten into you, Camila?"

Nico barked again.

"Perro de mierda, shut up!" My father turned on Nico and struck him with the back of his hand. Nico squealed in pain and streaked out of the room.

"Leave him alone!" I yelled. "What are *you* doing?"

Across the hallway, sitting on her bed, my mom warned, "Camila."

Pablo's door remained closed, but I felt his presence, quailing as he waited for each word to drop like a hammer. I was on my own.

"Why did you hit him?"

My father hissed, "Lower your voice. We don't want the neighbors to talk about us more than they already do."

"What?" I asked.

"It's all online," he scoffed. "How Diego's in town and all the women, including *you*"—he pointed his finger at me—"are throwing themselves at him, wanting to be a new Wanda or Antonela."

I had never wanted to be like Icardi's wife or Messi's. Not that there was anything wrong with them, but I wasn't looking for that. It wasn't like that. I knew people would talk about Diego and me. I just hadn't imagined the word would spread this fast.

I crossed my arms and squeezed them against my body.

"Listen," my father said. "I see the way you look at Diego." In a low whisper that couldn't possibly carry to my mom, he added, "All this time, your mom thought you kept sneaking out to be with a boy, but I didn't think you were into boys, to be honest." My blood roared in my ears. He continued in a louder voice, "To my surprise, your mother and I noticed how *he* looks at *you*, too. We've been talking . . ."

The magic of my afternoon with Diego dimmed and then flickered. I tried to hold on to the thrill of his hand on mine as he taught me how to drive, how the wind had tangled his hair by the river, that look in his eyes when he'd called me his girl and given me the flowers. But the images curdled, stained by my father's implications.

I implored La Difunta for her protection again, but I had done nothing for her. Why would she listen to me now? My dad's words soaked everything they touched with tar.

"I mean, you were acting like a cat in heat, Camila. What did you think that was going to lead to?"

"Andrés," my mom warned from her room, but he ignored her.

"You need to play your cards smart. He has a lot of money and an amazing career ahead of him. Imagine where he'll be five years from now. Your life could turn into a fairy tale if you're as smart as you pretend to be. Yours and ours, because of course you'll help your family when fortune smiles on you."

My tongue knotted, and the air in my lungs turned into steam. I took in the words in silence, but later, I'd purge them from my body. I'd vomit them up and shit them out and stomp on them until they were forgotten. But for now, I stood.

"Well . . ." he urged with a hand motion. "Say something."

"It's not like that," I whispered.

My father showed me his hands, palms up. "The devil knows more for being old than for being the devil, negrita." He sounded just like a loving father. "And I just want the best for you, mi amor. Haven't I cared for you and your education and future?" For him, my whole childhood had been a business investment. "I mean, you go to that private school with the nuns, and you've had English lessons. You have your licenciatura, which you haven't used, but you have it. You have a home, and although we don't have luxuries, you've never gone hungry. The only thing I ask in return is that you don't throw away the opportunities that life sends your way. Today life offered you a silver platter, and you have only to pick what's best for you and your family."

"I don't know what you mean, Papá." If he was going to ask me to do this, I wanted him to say it. He couldn't dance around it.

He laughed, and his voice boomed off the walls.

"You want me to be blunt? To spell it out for you? Well, then, don't give *it* out for free."

It.

"If you still have something going on with another boy, don't tell Diego about it. I mean, Diego's a good boy. I wouldn't let him inside the house if I suspected he was a druggie or a maricón, but he has a dark past. Who knows what happened? People abandon babies all the time, but to abandon an eight-year-old boy? Now, that's coldhearted. He's nice-looking, blanquito, with his light brown hair and those greenish eyes, but he's damaged goods. In any case, now that he's famous, none of that matters."

There was so much wrong with what my father had just said that I didn't know where to start arguing with him. Besides, the words wouldn't come. He reached out and brushed my hair from my eyes. I forced myself not to flinch.

"Things might not work out in the long run, but make the most of it, if you know what I mean. Once men taste the forbidden fruit, they lose interest. And as soon as Diego goes back to Europe and becomes more famous . . . because he will, oh, he will. I know good fútbol when I see it." He clapped his hands, and this time I did flinch. "Techniques can be learned, but not that flair. You can't teach it. I mean, look at your brother! How many times have I tried to teach him? Pablo is a nice player, but if he doesn't shape up, he'll be forgotten in a couple of years. Now, Diego . . . Diego's the real deal. He really is."

He swallowed. His hands were shaking.

He wasn't really speaking to me. He was working things out in his mind. All he wanted was a bite of what Diego had.

I was his way in. He didn't even know that I had that flair, too. For him, I was just a tool to get what he wanted. But I wouldn't help him get Diego's money and glory, and as hell was my witness, he wouldn't get any of mine, either. He'd be the last person to know I played fútbol, and when he tried to take credit for my success, I'd squash him like a cockroach.

By then adrenaline was coursing through my body, and I started shaking. My father stared at me, squinting, as if he was wondering what I was doing here in my room. "Go to bed," he said. "We'll talk more tomorrow."

My mom and I locked eyes from across the hallway before he shut their door in my face.

My lock was broken.

It couldn't protect me anymore. It never could.

Nico was waiting at the end of the dark hallway. I couldn't even say anything to him. Tentatively, he walked back to my room and sat next to me as I dragged my dresser in front of the broken door, conscious that I was scratching the floor, that I was probably waking up the neighbors. But it was the heaviest thing I had.

THROUGHOUT THE NIGHT, MY FATHER'S WORDS BUR-
rowed into every crevice of my mind like vermin. By the
morning, the pain they had inflicted was a dull echo. Not
only was my future at stake, but so was Diego's. I would
not be the vulture feeding off his fame.

Love can be a burden and a curse. I wasn't going to be
that for Diego.

I had a secret card to play, and I had to be smart about
it. I couldn't tell my mom about the tournament. She
hadn't stood up for me when I was little or last night, so
why would she support me now?

As I got ready for school, I carefully packed my practice clothes in my backpack.

Nico, my loyal honor guard, walked me to the kitchen.

"Buenos días." My mom sat at the little table against the window in a single beam of morning sunshine. Her index finger was hooked around a piece of ivory silk, as if she'd been trying to feel the shape the fabric wanted to take. I kissed her cheek. Before I pulled away, she grabbed my wrist softly and whispered, "Papi didn't mean it, negrita. You don't have to do anything with *any* boy to save us."

She let go of me and motioned to the chair in front of her. On the table, a café con leche was steaming. She put her fabric aside and made my favorite breakfast: toast with butter and tomato marmalade.

"I'd like to know how your date with Diego went yesterday." She spoke in a low voice, glancing back at the hallway every few seconds. "Or will that be another secret?"

"Mami, I don't have any secrets. It's impossible to have a secret in this house. Please—"

"You don't need to hide your feelings from me. I'm your mother. I just want you to know"—she licked her lips and swallowed before continuing—"that you can tell me *anything*."

For a second, part of me leaned into the warmth of her offer. I wished I could confide in her.

And then she said, "I was a girl like you once, and I got pregnant with Pablo in my last year of high school."

A cold dread fell over me; I didn't need to be a math genius to understand that there had only been six months between my parents' wedding and Pablo's birth. Still, I'd never been reckless enough to mention it, and no one in our family had ever confirmed it.

"I was so afraid of telling my mom," she continued. "My dad had died the year before. He had never liked your father. I thought it was because my dad was a Newell's fan."

Fútbol was woven into every family story, even the telenovela versions. *Especially* the telenovela versions. We were such a stereotype. What if I told her I was a futbolera and that I had been born with the kind of talent my father was obsessed with? She'd turn and run to him with my secret as if she'd found a precious stone. He would forbid me to play or, worse, use me like he used Pablo, like he wanted to use Diego.

My mom's face quirked in a tentative smile.

"My dad was the odd Leproso in Arroyito," she said, "but he didn't mind the rabid Central fans and players who teased him relentlessly. But he *hated* your dad. My mom, on the other hand, adored Andrés. He can be charming when he wants to, and he *was* to my mom. When my dad died, I leaned on him. I depended on him for everything. He was handsome and famous, and every other girl envied my good luck. He'd chosen me."

Ay, Mamá . . .

But then, hadn't I glowed with joy when Diego had called me his girl? He and my dad were different men, but I couldn't ignore their similarities. Both were handsome professional players any girl would lose her head for.

My mom continued, "He had a great future ahead, and if it hadn't been for the—"

"—Paraguayo de mierda," I said automatically.

She sent me a warning look. It was ironic that we could be talking about fornication, lies, and betrayals, but swearing wasn't allowed, but I didn't say anything.

"The thing is, had my father been alive, I wouldn't have dated your father. Or if fate had brought us together and I had ended up pregnant, my father wouldn't have made me marry Andrés."

"Why?" Never before had she said so plainly that marrying my dad had been the biggest mistake of her life. What did this make Pablo and me?

"Because my father *loved* me, and he knew the kind of man your father would become."

Or the man he's always been, which you didn't want to see.

I drank my café con leche.

"My father would've been disappointed that I had to drop out of school—the nuns wouldn't let me finish." Her eyes filled with tears, and her hands trembled as she wiped them with a kitchen towel. "But he wouldn't have made things worse by shackling me to a boy who really didn't—doesn't—love me."

While my father would jump at the chance to squeeze everything out of Diego's love for me until all that was left was ruin and sorrow.

Whether I liked it not, I had to acknowledge that my

mother and I had a lot in common. We weren't as different as I liked to think. I wasn't better than her.

Our family was stuck in a cosmic hamster wheel of toxic love, making the same mistakes, saying the same words, being hurt in the same ways generation after generation. I didn't want to keep playing a role in this tragedy of errors.

I was la Furia, after all. I'd be the one to break the wheel.

But I didn't know how to help my mom.

"Papá loves you, Mami." I patted her hand, and she flinched.

I didn't know if I had just lied to her or not. After all, my father had stayed with her. As far as I knew, he'd never even hinted at leaving. They pretended things were all right even when every sign pointed toward problems that would have sent normal people running in opposite directions.

She dried her eyes again. "I'm sorry for crying like this. I must be starting the menopause, you know?"

I couldn't help it—I laughed. "In Hollywood, people your age are just starting to have babies. Look at Jennifer López. She's older than you, Mami."

She smiled sadly. "I don't look anything like her. Look at me! Compared to her, I'm a cow." She motioned to her body. She wore jeans and a black blouse. Her curves were impossible to hide, even with dark colors.

"If you put makeup on and had a personal stylist like she does, you'd look even better than J. Lo, Mama."

She beamed at me, her eyes sparkly with tears, and didn't even nag me for talking like a country girl. Then she asked, "How are the med school studies going?"

It took me a fraction of a second to get my bearings. She thought I was studying for the MIU, the college prep classes everyone took in February, but I recovered quickly. "Perfect. By the way, I'm going to Roxana's to study after school. I'll be late."

"Why don't you ever come study here, hija? You're always at her house."

"She has Wi-Fi, Mama."

Her ears were trained to detect any kind of lie, but her heart was trained to ignore the things she couldn't deal with. She nodded and patted my hand. "Be safe, please, hija. I'm so proud of you. The first one to graduate high school and go to the university. I wanted to be a doctor, too, you know, before . . . everything. Doctora Camila sounds good, doesn't it? Pablo never had the chance to study, but you do."

"Doctora Camila sounds good, Mami." I kissed her cheek again, grabbed my things, and left.

———

At the bus stop, posters of missing girls watched me as I stood in line, shivering. As soon as the bus turned the corner and headed in our direction, the crowd waiting in various degrees of sleepiness perked up. The driver hit the brakes, and people scurried to secure seats.

"After you, señorita." A gruff masculine voice startled me.

A young guy dressed in blue factory clothes stepped to the side to let me through.

Miraculously, there were a few empty seats, including one in the single-person row on the right. I took one near the front, and the factory guy made his way to the back of the bus. Perfect—I didn't want to have to talk to him just because of his chivalry. My unfinished accounting home-work was burning in my backpack. I might not have been aiming to become a doctor like my mom believed, but I still needed to graduate. I was behind in several subjects.

By the time we left el barrio, I was immersed in num-bers, and the bus was full way beyond capacity. Passengers pressed against one another, stepped on freshly polished office shoes, and hung from the door, defying several laws of physics.

"I don't know what those nuns are teaching nowa-days!" a woman said. "There she sits like a queen while this poor girl stands right in front of her, full of baby. In my days, the front-row seats were only for the disabled and the elderly, not for good-for-nothing, selfish teenag-ers. And that green handkerchief! The feminazis like her are murderers in the making . . ."

I saw the corner of Roxana's green handkerchief peeking out of the backpack at my feet. I looked up at the pregnant woman. She glared at me. She was a girl, really, maybe even younger than me. She looked too thin to be growing a life inside her.

There was nothing else for me to do. I crammed my accounting homework into my backpack and stood up. The pregnant girl puffed at my attempt to switch places with her and didn't meet my gaze when I told her how sorry I was for not noticing her.

I made my way through the throng of people all the way to the back door, where the factory guy reappeared.

"St. Francis?" he asked.

He leaned against the back seat with a smirk on his face. His eyes swept over my uniform—the red tartan skirt, white shirt, and knee-high socks, a pervert's fantasy. I had the urge to send him to hell, but he looked familiar and somehow harmless. He was younger than I'd first thought.

I shrugged. "And you? La Valeria?"

La Valeria was the spice processing factory on Circunvalación, which the bus had passed long ago. When he smiled, the corners of his eyes wrinkled in lines premature for his young face. "First year," he said. "My uncle knows the manager. I'm heading to a medical appointment first."

And then I recognized him.

"Luciano Durand?" The name came to me through a fog of memories. I hoped he couldn't hear the pity in my voice. He used to play with Pablo and Diego. He'd been Central's most promising player until he tore his meniscus. It ended his career in an instant.

Luciano just nodded, then looked out the window. "I saw my cousin Yael last night." He winked at me like we shared a secret. And we did. "Good luck in the Sudamericano. Bring that trophy to el barrio, Camila." He rang the bell and stepped off the bus.

El Mago, the press used to call him.

His magic couldn't heal his shredded ligaments.

The former Scoundrel limped away.

I replayed Luciano's last words: *Bring that trophy to el barrio.* Who else knew my secret? Who else was talking about us?

I DIDN'T NOTICE ROXANA WAITING FOR ME UNTIL SHE
pretty much jumped me at the front door.

"Chill, Roxana! You almost gave me a heart attack,"
I said.

"Diego posted a picture of you, and you dropped off
the face of the earth. I'm the one who's been apoplectic,"
Roxana hissed as she followed me inside.

At the blank look on my face, she clamped a hand on
my shoulder and said, "Wait, you haven't seen? What happened this weekend?"

A flock of small elementary school girls ran ahead of
us, and Roxana glared at them. "Watch it! You're going to
give her a heart attack!"

What had I ever done to deserve her? Nothing.

Before I even asked, she showed me Diego's Instagram. I dropped my backpack on the floor and grabbed her phone.

It was a picture from when we were eleven and thirteen, which he'd captioned with the word AMIGOS. I wore a blue one-piece swimsuit, and he had on a pair of old Central shorts. We were both tanned dark already, though it wasn't even real summer yet. Skinny like lizards, we sat in a tree eating nísperos, smiles big as the blue sky. I remembered that day clearly. Pablo had taken the photo with his first phone.

I covered my mouth with my hand to stop myself from swearing in front of the innocent elementary school girls.

What had Diego been thinking? He had no right to post about me, but at the same time, I couldn't help the rush of tenderness that swept over me for those two little kids who had no idea what was in store for them. Where would we be now if Diego had never left for Turín? What would our lives be like?

"Can you delete it?" I asked, knowing perfectly well that the answer was no.

Roxana rolled her eyes.

"He has to take it down," I said.

I hooked my hand through the crook of her elbow as we walked to class.

"Everyone, and I mean everyone, is talking about it,"

Roxana said. "It's only a matter of time before the reporters find out who you are. Then what will you do?"

The only thing I knew was that Saturday, the day Diego was supposed to leave, couldn't come fast enough. Even as I wished for it, a part of me still grieved. At least I had Roxana in my life. I thanked the universe for her, because Deolinda couldn't take any credit for it.

I'd found Roxana long before La Difunta Deolinda Correa had come into my life. Maybe if Deolinda had had a friend as good as Roxana, she wouldn't have died of thirst in the desert. Maybe she'd have waited at her friend's house for her husband's safe return. Or maybe I should've stopped having sacrilegious thoughts.

"I called your house probably ten million times," Roxana said. "You need to put some credit on your phone, woman!"

"I called you from Diego's phone, and you didn't answer. I even texted you."

"Yeah, and when I called back, you weren't there, and I had to awkwardly ask about Italy before I hung up."

"You talked to him?"

The hall monitor, a girl named Antonia who had joined the convent last year after graduating, looked at us from the middle of the courtyard. Her early-morning voice blared, "Fong! Shirt tucked in!"

Roxana glared, but she tucked her shirt in. "Who does she think she is? The traitorous bi—"

"Do you want me to tell you about the weekend or not?" I cut her off, because Antonia had supersonic hearing. I couldn't risk getting a detention.

"Tell me everything right now," Roxana demanded.

I didn't even have time to start.

A small group of girls from the commercial track were chatting by the preschool playground. As soon as they saw me, they started pelting me with questions.

"Are you really moving to Italy?"

"Is it true he gave you diamond earrings?"

"How come you didn't tell us you were dating him?"

When I didn't give them any answers, their words turned venomous.

"Some have all the luck in the world, and they don't even know it," Vanina said as her friends nodded in agreement. "In her position, I wouldn't have even come to school today."

"Dios le da pan al que no tiene dientes," Pilar added. "She didn't even like his post."

"Don't you have anything better to do than talk about me?" I said, rushing at her. A surge of pleasure went through me when she scrambled away too quickly and fell backward.

Roxana pulled me by the arm, and Pilar's friends helped her up. If the bell hadn't rung, I don't know what I would've done.

But after that, the gossipers left me alone.

Throughout the morning, I updated Roxana in bits and pieces, ignoring the teachers and the forty girls around us. I didn't mention we'd gone out on a *real* date, though. And of course I didn't even hint at the kiss.

"I don't understand," she said through clenched teeth. "He said 'I'm here for Camila?' Who does he think he is? As if you're gonna jump into his arms and let him take you to Italy!"

Turning my body to the side so the teacher wouldn't see me talking, I said, "I don't know, Roxana. I, like . . . avoided the topic in the car. I don't think he wants me to leave with him. He got me a job, actually, at El Buen Pastor."

"The old women's prison?"

"Yeah. He wouldn't have done that if he wanted to whisk me away."

"You're a futbolera, not a botinera. Did you tell him that?"

"I wanted to, but there was too much going on. I can't drag Diego into my mess."

She shook her phone in front of my face. "It seems to me like he's dragging himself in of his own free will. And when he posted that photo, *he* dragged *you* into a greater mess."

"Once he leaves, everyone will stop talking about that

post." I didn't know how I expected Roxana to believe me when I didn't even believe myself.

"And you?" she asked. "Will you be hung up on this for a year like you were obsessed about that kiss?"

I couldn't meet her gaze. I'd told her it had been just one kiss. If she knew about yesterday . . .

"Camila, be careful."

It was more than Diego's kisses that tormented me. We had so much shared history that every memory was wound around him.

But we were both sick with this incurable fútbol illness. It was bigger than everything else in our lives. Diego was my first love. Seeing him again had proven that in spite of the silence, the time, and the distance between us, he felt the same for me. But to get to the next level, we had to follow our own paths.

We were running in different directions.

Roxana pressed my hand. "I know it must hurt, but I'm proud of you. We're going to the Sudamericano. What else could you want from life?"

"Winning the Sudamericano," I said. I didn't say: *the freedom that would come with winning. The freedom not to answer to my father or even my mother for every choice I make.*

Roxana's face lit up. "You never asked me why I called," she said over the sound of the bell that ended class.

"You should've told me first thing, che," I teased her.

All around us, people relaxed, taking their phones out, snacking, getting caught up on gossip. We had five minutes between accounting and history.

Roxana closed her eyes and shook her head, like she was resetting her brain. "Do you know about the team meeting tomorrow night?"

"No practice today?" My body ached to be back on the pitch.

Roxana handed me her phone again. Her background was the photo of our team raising the cup. With the vintage filter, it seemed like it had happened a lifetime ago and not last weekend.

"Call Coach Alicia," she said. "She texted me last night that she needs to talk with you and couldn't get hold of you, either."

I hesitated. I hoped Coach wasn't mad at me.

"Call her now, before Sister Brígida gets here," Roxana insisted.

I wasted no time. Coach Alicia picked up on the first ring. "Roxana?"

My hand prickled with sweat at the sound of her voice. "It's Camila," I hurried to explain. "My phone doesn't work, Coach. Sorry I never saw your message."

Coach got straight to the point. "Listen carefully. Tomorrow we have a meeting in preparation for the Sudamericano. My sister Gabi is making a flash stop in

Rosario before she heads back to the States. I want you to meet her so that when I gush about you, she can put a face to the name. You *have* to make it. ¿Está claro?"

She hung up just as the teacher walked in, but in any case, I was speechless.

The moment I'd been praying for all my life was just about here.

The rest of the morning, Roxana and I obsessed over the meeting.

"What do you think Coach wants to talk about?" I asked her.

"Money. That tournament's not free."

"How much do you think the fees will be?"

She whistled. "We're going to have to do some serious fundraising."

Diego went unmentioned, but he remained a ghost between us.

Right after the noon Angelus bells, though, when Sister Clara made us stand to recite the mystery of the Word becoming flesh, Roxana took her phone out of her blazer pocket. Her eyes widened, and she looked back at me. "A message for you," she mouthed.

"Coach?" I asked, my heart jumping into my throat.

"No, Diego." She passed me her phone. Sister Clara cleared her voice mid-prayer, and I put the phone in my jacket pocket.

The seconds until I could look at the message stretched

out forever, and by the time the Angelus was over, I was hyperventilating.

> Hey, Ro, can you pass this on to Camila?
> Her phone must be dead.

> Cami! Best of luck today with the kids. I'm
> free later in the afternoon. Can I drive you?
> It's up to you. Let me know, Mami. <3

"Mami?" Roxana asked pointedly. "Heart emoji?"

If Roxana was getting this riled up about an innocent message, I didn't even want to imagine what she'd think of my date with Diego or the kiss. She could never know about it, but it was only a matter of time before she found out.

"Listen, Ro. Can I take your phone for a minute? I need to call him."

She shook her head. "What for? You're not going to fall for his pretty words, are you? Yesterday he almost made me like him. He's dangerous."

Ay, Roxana . . .

"If I text him, he'll call me anyway," I said, pressing her arm. "He's my friend, too, Ro. It's not that simple."

She closed her eyes and exhaled, and when she looked at me again, she said, "Be strong. Remember you're la Furia."

"I will. I am."

Sister Clara wasn't too happy when I told her I needed to go to the bathroom, but she had no choice but to let me go.

When I closed the stall door behind me, my heart was pounding, and not because of the run. A part of me wanted to get this over with, and another screamed that I was going to regret turning my back on Diego now.

Before I gave in to the second voice, I dialed his number.

He picked up on the first ring. "Hola," he said.

The words I was about to say tried to choke me. I swallowed, and they scraped my throat like fish bones. This was for his own good.

"Hola, Diego." I heard him inhale at the sound of my cold, cold voice.

"What happened?"

"It's just that I can't go out with you today. Yesterday was . . . magical, but I have a lot of things going on, and anyway, you're going back to Turín on Saturday—"

"Thursday," he said. "Giusti changed my flight. He wants me at practice on Monday."

I had no right to be disappointed. Maybe this was a miracle La Difunta Correa had performed for me, even though I didn't deserve her grace. But still, my determination to keep Diego away wavered.

"This is for the best, then."

"But why?"

I shook my head, trying to dispel the images of heart-break his voice painted in my mind. It didn't work. "I need some space," I said.

"But Camila, I lo—"

"I said I need some space," I snapped. The words echoed off the tile walls. "Please, don't make this harder for me, okay? This hurts me, too, but I can't let it go further."

There was silence on the other end of the line. Before he found an argument that would change my mind, I said, "I wish you all the best in life, Diego."

And I hung up.

All my life, I'd known how to hide my sorrows behind a mask. But after the call, I wasn't sure I'd be able to pull it off today. I wanted to sleep for a thousand years so the ache in my heart would go away, but I couldn't fail Father Hugo.

On the way to El Buen Pastor, I got off the bus too early and had to walk three blocks to the church. Finally, I turned the corner that led to the entrance. When I saw that Diego's car wasn't parked by the curb, I breathed easier.

Still, my nerves followed me inside like a stray dog.

On the interior patio, two nuns cleaned a flower bed. When the younger one saw me standing at the entrance, she waved and smiled. The other nun peeked out from behind the naked rosebush she was pruning. Her round face broke into a smile, too.

I waved back at them.

A shadow stretching from behind me preceded Father Hugo's voice. "There you are, Camila. Right on time, too."

I exhaled. "Hello, Father. Here I am."

"Ready?"

I nodded, and he motioned for me to follow him. In the shabby room he led me to, there was a long wooden table surrounded by chairs in various degrees of disrepair. Sheets of ruled paper lay on the table and the floor, scattered by the breeze blowing through the open window. Five boys looked at me in respectful silence.

"Kids, this is Señorita Camila Hassan. She'll be helping us here from now on," said Father Hugo.

"Hello," I said, intimidated by being called señorita. The boys looked to be about ten years old. Their teeth were too big for their still-childish faces.

"Camila, these are your students. Miguel, Leandro, Javier, Bautista, and Lautaro . . ." He paused, looking at the group.

I smiled at them, and three of them returned the smile feebly. One just stared, but Lautaro beamed at me.

A few seconds later, a girl rushed in, breathless.

"I'm sor . . . sor . . . sorry I'm . . . I'm late!" The newcomer took a spot at the table opposite the boys, who leaned away as if she were infested with cooties. The priest and the girl ignored them, and I assumed this behavior wasn't out of the ordinary.

"Welcome, Karen," Father Hugo said. "Señorita Camila will help you with your schoolwork from now on. Please, let's treat her with the respect she deserves." He scanned the whole room when he said this, but Karen's cheeks flushed bright red as if the warning had been directed mostly at her.

Then Father Hugo left me alone with my students. Karen looked me up and down, taking stock of me, deciding how much respect I deserved. My soul was instantly attracted to her.

A smattering of freckles covered her white skin. Karen was rod thin and tall, and her hands were rubbed raw. Her pale lips were chapped from the cold, but her brown eyes were bright and wise. Finally, she said, "Welcome to El Buen P . . . P . . . welcome, señorita." A wave of protectiveness overtook me when the boys snickered.

"Thank you," I said.

After wiping my sweaty hands on my skirt, I took a seat next to Karen and tried to emulate appropriate teacher behavior. "Do you want to show me what you've been working on?" I asked.

The boys silently challenged each other to be the first. Karen opened her notebook and pushed it in my direction. I browsed through the thin pages. Everything was in English. The neatness of her handwriting, the correctness of her grammar, and the breadth of her vocabulary rendered me speechless. She mistook my silence for lack of understanding, and with badly concealed pride, she explained, "I am . . . am . . . am writing a translation of Alfonsina Storni, la po . . . la poetisa? Her po-poems. She lived in Rosario when she was very young. Did you know that?"

Karen's eyes shone. She had an infection, *the hunger.* I knew that the only cure was to feed it, and I hoped that I could help Karen like Coach Alicia had helped me.

Miguel groaned. "Not again with la poetisa!"

"La seño might n-not know," Karen shot back.

"They always fight about this," Lautaro told me with a shrug.

"La seño won't care about your stupid poems, Caca," Javier said.

The change in Karen's face was instantaneous. The brave, spunky girl was consumed by a shadow. She moved her lips like she wanted to speak, but no words came out.

I rounded on Javier and snapped, "What did you call her?"

Javier's dark face was mottled with embarrassment, and I exhaled to calm myself down. The last thing these kids needed was another person who yelled, who put them down. I placed my hand on his arm, but he snatched it away as if my touch had burned him.

"I'm sorry, Javier," I said, but Javier turned his face away from me.

Lautaro explained, "Karen stutters. That's why some people call her Caca. When she's nervous and she tries to say her name it sounds like *Ka-Ka-Ka!*" The boys tried to stifle their laughter, but Karen's face hardened. The glassy shine in her eyes made my skin break into goose bumps. There was a little fury inside this girl, and I had the impulse to hug her, to tell her everything would be okay, but I had no right to make this promise when her life was already a hundred times harder than mine.

"Listen," I said. "I won't tolerate name-calling of any kind. I can't tell you what to do when I'm not here, but you won't call Karen any names in my presence. Claro?"

"Claro," Lautaro said quickly.

"Gracias," I said, and all the boys' faces softened, even Javier's.

After such a rocky start, the class felt uncomfortably tense. Karen worked in silence, shielding her writing with her arm. There was no need, though. None of the boys were on her level.

An hour in, I went over a pronunciation guide with them, and they all repeated the words with care. All except for Karen, who seemed to listen with her whole body, staring down at the worn table, moving her lips soundlessly.

Finally, the clock on the wall announced it was five.

"It's merienda time. Will you stay with us, Seño? Today is pan casero day," asked Miguel.

My stomach rumbled embarrassingly loudly. The boys laughed as if I had just told the funniest joke in the world.

"I guess that's a yes," Lautaro said with a little smirk on his face.

Karen glanced at me and gathered her notebook and pencil as if they were the most precious things in the world. I waited for her to finish. Her thin shoulders were folded in on themselves, a glorious butterfly hiding her colors.

My students and I walked out to the courtyard, where there was a round brick-and-mud oven. White smoke leaked from the metal door that hid the pan casero cooking over coals. Lured by the mouthwatering smell of fresh bread baking, streams of little ones came out of several doors that lined the courtyard and joined me and my class.

We all waited in line behind Sister Cruz, the round-faced nun, who served *mate* cocido, ladling the steaming tea into metal mugs. When Sister Cristina opened the oven, the kids cheered. With perfect coordination, the nuns passed a cup and a slice of bread, fragrant and warm from the oven, to each of the children waiting patiently.

"Chau, Karen. See you tomorrow," Sister Cruz called after she placed a slice of bread in my open hand.

I turned to say goodbye, too. On Karen's shoulders, a shopping bag hung as if it were a backpack. The front

cover of her notebook showed through the semitranspar-
ent plastic.

"You aren't staying for your snack?" I asked.

When she turned in my direction, I noticed the
grease-stained paper-wrapped package in her hands. Karen
blushed bright red, and her feet fidgeted like they itched to
be somewhere else. She shook her head and turned to go.

In a little voice, Bautista filled me in. "She's wanted
back home. Her little ones get hungry at this time of the
day."

"Her little ones?" My eyes lingered on her vanishing
figure.

"Her siblings."

Mad at myself for not being more observant or more
tactful, I ran to her. "Karen, take my bread, too."

My arm was outstretched, the warm bread getting cold
in my hand.

"Thanks," she said with a small bow of her head, and
took my offering. She didn't smile, not even out of cour-
tesy, and I admired her so much for it. Without another
word, she walked out of the courtyard and through the
main door.

AFTER A STOP AT THE FERRETERÍA FOR A NEW DOORKNOB
and a chain that ate away at my Sudamericano money, I
arrived home.

Mamá still sat at her worktable, embroidering another
dress, as if she hadn't moved all day. When she saw me, she
set her work down.

"Hola, hija," she said, and I kissed her on the cheek.
"Are you hungry?"

"Always," I said, my stomach roaring for food since I'd
teased it with homemade bread. My appetite didn't understand charity and compassion. "What's in the fridge?"

"Milanesas from lunch. Should I make you a sandwich?"

Tender deep-fried steak sprinkled with lemon juice
was the way to my heart.

"I'll add a fried egg," she said, the pan already sizzling on the burner.

"Temptress." I filled the kettle while Mamá filled the *mate* gourd with herbs.

"How was studying at Roxana's?" she asked. "Will you be okay keeping up with regular school?"

My hand jerked, and I almost burned myself with hot *mate*. I wiped up the spilled drink with a napkin, relieved it was clear. Mamá hated *mate* stains. The green never came out.

"I'll be okay," I said, glancing in her general direction, trying not to make eye contact. I swerved into my confession like a 146 bus merging onto Circunvalación—full throttle. "And actually, I found a job teaching English."

My mom looked at me like she was a judge. "A job on top of prep courses and school? I don't know, Camila." She hesitated. "We're okay for now. I work hard so you don't have to. How did you find this job, anyway? Is it worth it?"

Now it was my turn to hesitate. The image of Karen walking back home with a bundle of food for her siblings flashed into my mind. It was worth it.

"Actually, it's at El Buen Pastor, Mami. Did you know it was reopened? The priest there organizes workshops for the community. A group from the States is funding English lessons for the kids." I was surprised my constricted throat let enough air through for me to speak.

She scoffed. "I wish a group from the States funded your education. We've spent a fortune we don't have on it." She passed me the milanesa sandwich. I chewed slowly to stop myself from talking.

At least she hadn't made a connection between El Buen Pastor, Father Hugo, and Diego.

She passed me the *mate* and said, "I don't know, Camila. Maybe you shouldn't do it. You have me to support you as long as I'm able to work. You need to focus on school."

Gathering strength from somewhere inside me, I made myself look at her. "They pay very well. And I can use this opportunity to build my resumé. Besides, if I don't keep using English, I'll lose it."

The change in her expression was instantaneous.

"In that case, I guess it's a good idea. I worked too hard and spent too much for you to lose it."

She said it as if I hadn't been the one studying till all hours of the night to ace my tests. Before I could remind her, she said, "Make sure to tell your father before he finds out from someone else."

"I will." My voice didn't waver, and my mom's gaze was fixed on the design of her lacy shawl. She pulled it even more tightly around her.

She placed a hand over mine. "Everything okay with Diego?"

Heat rushed to my head. I wanted to tell her everything. But the sound of voices approaching the door from outside shattered the moment. My father and Pablo were arguing. Marisol laughed.

My mom looked at me and groaned. "Don't tell me he brought her again!"

"Mamita," I said, chewing the last bit of my sandwich. "I hate to break it to you, but Pali's in love—"

"No!" she exclaimed. "What he sees in her is beyond me."

Before I could enumerate all the things Pablo saw in Marisol, the door swung open. Nico sprang to his feet and bounced on his hind legs to greet Pablo and my dad and even Marisol, who shooed him away with a wave of her hand. Then he beelined to the person behind them. I should've known why my dog was so excited he had started to cry.

Diego didn't smile when our eyes met. I averted my gaze.

"Good evening," the newcomers said in unison, except for Marisol. She was blocking the door while she brushed dog hair off Diego's shirt, and she whispered something that sounded like, "Perro asqueroso."

"Good evening," my mom said. "Are you all staying for dinner? I need to run to the store for a few things."

My dad and Pablo argued about having Mamá cook versus ordering delivery from the rotisserie on the corner. After Diego told her he didn't mind the dog hair, Marisol excused herself to use the bathroom.

"Hola, Camila," Diego said, hands deep in his pockets, his shoulders hunched. "How are you?"

"Hola," I said.

At that moment, the phone rang, and my mom ran to pick it up, the family's official operator. From the corner of my eye, I saw Diego checking his own phone, pretending he didn't care, but the tips of his ears were bright red.

A second later, my mom's voice rippled through the air. "Hi, Roxana. Yes, Camila's here. Camila!" she shouted as if I were ten blocks away and not next to her.

"Sorry," I said to no one in particular. I took the phone from my mom and left, feeling Diego's eyes following me all the way to my room.

"I'm here," I said into the receiver, leaning against the door and sliding down to sit on the floor.

"Camila?" Roxana sounded like she was crying. My own problems marched into the background. "Marisa quit the team. Her boyfriend won't let her play in the tournament, and . . ." She stopped talking, and although she must have been trying to cover the microphone with her hand, I could hear her muffled sobbing.

My first impulse was to squeeze myself through the phone and help her calm down, then turn around and punch Marisa's boyfriend. But I couldn't do either of those things, so I gave her the only thing I could offer: time.

She blew her nose and spoke again. "She came over with Micaela to give me her uniform and boots. She said she won't need them anymore. She had tried to put makeup on to cover a bruise. When I asked her about it, she said she should learn to shut her mouth. And Cami, the look on her face! Like a beaten dog who thinks she deserves the abuse. How can Marisa do this to herself? To her daughter?"

Marisa and Roxana had been best friends in elementary school, but their friendship hadn't been the same since Marisa got pregnant in second year and didn't confide in Roxana. But given the way Roxana had reacted to the news, I didn't really blame Marisa. Some secrets are too heavy to share.

I let Roxana cry, and when her fury was spent, leaving only disappointment and despondency, she asked, "How do we get her back?"

There wasn't anything we could do, but Roxana wouldn't understand that yet.

"Have you talked to Coach Alicia? What did she say?"

She clicked her tongue. "Coach said not to bother Marisa, that she has enough problems as is and that this is just a game. Can you believe it? Really, how can we do nothing? This tournament could be her way out. She won't have another opportunity like this."

In a way, I understood Marisa's point of view. Roxana had parents who loved each other and doted on her. They worked hard, but they also didn't have to worry about paying the bills every month. Marisa didn't have money or time to spend on things other than her daughter. Not all women could leave abusive relationships. Things weren't that simple.

"Listen, Roxana, the best thing we can do is get a replacement—"

"A replacement for Marisa? Didn't you hear what I just said? She *needs* us."

"She does, Roxana, but I don't know what we can do. Tomorrow we'll see where we stand and if anyone else has dropped out. Then we'll figure out how to help Marisa."

ROXANA'S WORDS AND DIEGO'S WOUNDED EYES HAUNTED me all night long. Worrying about the team was pointless, but the urge to call Diego was torture. I resisted, but only barely.

In the morning, I grabbed my favorite childhood book, *Un Globo de Luz Anda Suelto* by Alma Maritano, and put it in my backpack along with my textbooks and, at the very bottom, my uniform, practice clothes, and cleats. Alfonsina Storni was a national treasure, but at her age, Karen needed light and hope. She needed Alma. There would be time for fury and heartbreak and Alfonsina's poems later.

The day zipped by, and before I had a minute to be nervous about the team meeting, the afternoon bells tolled six. The sun was sinking fast behind the courtyard walls, robing the garden and its statues in a mantle of velvet shadows.

Karen hadn't come to class, but I left Alma's book with Sister Cruz, who told me she would for sure be there for dinner. When I walked outside, Roxana and her father were waiting for me in his ivory Toyota Hilux.

"I could've walked," I said as I got in the back seat, then added quickly, "Thanks for the ride, Papá Fong."

He gave me the thumbs-up but didn't say a word.

Roxana must have seen the worry on my face, because she answered for him. "Don't look all mortified. He just went to the dentist. Root canal. He can't talk." I raised my eyebrows, and she added, "He *can* drive. Don't worry about that."

If he hadn't been completely anti-hug, I would have embraced Mr. Fong for being so amazing. A pat on the shoulder from my spot in the back seat had to suffice.

He looked at me in the rearview mirror, and his dark eyes crinkled into a warm smile. His right cheek was swollen and red.

Then he gave his total attention to the road ahead, driving away from Parque Yrigoyen.

Once again, Roxana guessed my question. "Change of plans."

I sighed. "I'll buy data as soon as I get my first check. I promise." Not being in the loop about the team's business was unforgivable.

"We're going to the Estadio Municipal. Coach sent a message a couple of hours ago. We're meeting there, and then we're playing a scrimmage against a team of North Americans who are touring Argentina. Gabi's team. Rosario is their last stop. Their opponents cancelled, and Coach volunteered us to play instead."

"Gabi's team? For real?"

"For real." Roxana helped me change in the back seat.

The pungent smell of my socks when I unrolled them made Roxana cough. Mr. Fong silently rolled the window down, and I, a little embarrassed, laughed.

"Sorry. I forgot to do laundry on Sunday." The truth was that I hadn't had time to wash my uniform without my mom noticing. In my defense, I hadn't planned on playing today. My practice clothes were clean.

"I'll take them home with me tonight," Roxana said, and handed me a protein drink, the kind I could never afford and that her family bought by the case.

She did so much for me already. So much I should've told her no, but I needed her help more than I was embarrassed to take it. I wasn't too proud to thank her, though. I squeezed Roxana's hand, because I had no words to tell her what she meant to me.

Mr. Fong parked by the curb. A narrow, packed-dirt path flanked by naked liquidambar trees led to the fútbol pitch. Roxana and I dashed out. Seeing the expanse of grass ahead, la Furia stirred inside me.

Under the bright white beams of the floodlights, Coach Alicia stood next to a woman who looked just like her, except somehow even tougher. That had to be Gabi. Mrs. Tapia.

Dogs barked in the distance. The smell of burning leaves made my nose itch, and Nicky Jam's voice blared from one of the houses beyond the trees. Up close, the field looked uneven and full of holes, the white lines almost invisible in the unkept grass.

Roxana and I stood on the sidelines, watching a group of girls jumping in place to warm up. They looked like the Amazon warrior women from Themyscira.

"Ay," was all Roxana said.

I echoed, "Ay."

My team started arriving: Cintia and Lucrecia, Yesica, Sofía, Mabel. Yael, followed by her cousin Luciano, el Mago. He joined the huddle of parents and family waiting at the end of the pitch. Gisela and Mía trickled in.

A few of us watched the Yankee girls stretch and juggle in their professional-looking uniforms. The wind carried a few of the words they exchanged toward us, but I was too intimidated to understand a single one. So much for having a licenciatura.

Next to them, we looked just like what we were: a puzzle made up of mismatched pieces. Yesica and Mía didn't even seem able to look at the girls who were both our competition and our goal. Instead they watched the path, desperate longing in their eyes as we waited. Would we have enough people?

Evelin and Abril joined us, and when a straggler appeared, my heart jumped. I looked up, hoping it would be Marisa. It wasn't her, though. It was the green-eyed Royal, the one I'd seen by the river with her boyfriend. She beelined toward Coach Alicia and stood under her protection while we glared at her and whispered to one another.

"What's she doing here?" Roxana asked.

Coach Alicia kissed the Royal girl on the cheek.

Since when was Coach so familiar with *that* girl? Coach barely nodded when *we* said hi to her. She'd never shown that kind of affection to us, and we'd walk through fire for her.

Together they walked in our direction, followed by Gabi. The American girls practiced shots on goal, kicking with the power of cannons.

Coach Alicia must have thought seeing this team would inspire us, but how were we supposed to compete with them? Without resources, inspiration and effort could only take us so far.

By the time Coach Alicia made her way to us, we were simmering with hostility.

"Ladies," Coach said, and placed a hand on the green-eyed girl's shoulder. "This is Rufina Scalani, and she'll be joining us for the Sudamericano." She paused, but no one would have dreamed of interrupting her in front of Rufina or, more importantly, Gabi, who watched us silently, no doubt ready to judge our reaction. "As you all know, Marisa had to step aside, which was a generous gesture on her part."

"Generous?" Roxana's question was the pebble. Murmurs rippled through the group.

Coach Alicia gave us two seconds to put ourselves together and then continued. "We only have a little more than three months to get ready for the tournament. Marisa has quite a few issues in her personal life, and it *was* generous of her to make this hard decision now and not when finding a replacement would be impossible, like in the middle of the competition."

Understanding fell on me like a bucket of cold water. It splashed onto my teammates, too, who nodded.

"The league is behind us, and we'll leave the rivalry there. Rufina may have played for the Royals last week, but now she's one of us, and you'll treat her as such."

We all nodded again, even though Coach hadn't given us a vote.

"Before we proceed with the scrimmage, let's talk about the Sudamericano."

She motioned for the parents behind us to approach the group. Then she took a stack of photocopied packets from her backpack. She handed half to me and the other half to Roxana. We passed them around to the players and the parents. Mr. Fong smiled at me when I handed him the papers covered in numbers.

"The tournament is taking place the second weekend in December," Coach explained. "Mandatory practices will be twice a week with scrimmages on Saturdays. You must do conditioning on your own every day. We don't have players to spare, and although I'm still aiming for a full roster of eighteen, every one of you is essential."

Roxana and I exchanged a look. Our graduation was the second Saturday in December.

"What if Sofía has to miss a day of the competition?" a mom asked from behind the group. "Her cousin's quinceañera is that weekend."

Coach shrugged. "Then she can't be part of the team. I have to make a FIFA file for each of the players by next week. I won't be able to add anyone after that. This is the real thing, people. We wanted to play seriously, officially, and now here we are."

I looked over my shoulder at the parents whispering amongst themselves. Luciano winked at me, and I smiled. Beyond us, a boy wearing a shirt with the sleeves cut off and a baseball cap practiced shots in a netless goal.

Coach Alicia continued, going over the entrance fees, the practice schedule, and then the Sudamericano format. "There will be three games guaranteed in the first round. Only the best two teams in each group will go on to the knockout stage, then on to the semifinals and the final. Very standard. There will be teams from all of CONMEBOL, the South American Football Confederation, and the lottery will take place in November. We're the only team from Rosario to qualify, and there are three more from Argentina in our age group, which is the oldest." She looked at Lucrecia, our baby at fifteen. "The price will be high, but it's only because the reward could be priceless."

Coach cracked one of her rare smiles and added, "Now, this is my sister, Gabi Tapia. Mrs. Tapia, they call her in the States." Gabi walked up to her. Side by side, the resemblance was uncanny.

She elbowed Coach playfully, and we all laughed. Roxana and I exchanged a look, and she raised her eyebrows.

Coach continued, "Gabi coaches at a club, Wasatch Rage FC, which is a pipeline for colleges and the National Women's Soccer League program."

The air turned electric with anticipation. She might as well have been talking about a secret passage to Narnia.

Gabi took the baton. "This is my U18 team," she said, pointing to the Yankee players. "These girls are heading into their last year of high school, and most of them have been committed to universities for a while. They're multistate cup champions and three-time regional champions. Two of them are with the junior national team right now. We've been touring South America for two weeks, and we're heading back home tomorrow. But I'll be back in

December for the Sudamericano. The current recruiting system—playing in college first—is hindering our professional program, so we're looking for ways to inject younger players into the national league, bypassing university teams.

"Teams from all over the world will be scouting at the Sudamericano, and the national league is sending me. I'll have the chance to offer invitations for discovery slots. You must be eighteen by the time the transfer season opens, but other than that, it'll be down to what the other coaches and I see on the pitch." She gave out another form with NWSL deadlines. Their league started in April.

I'd be eighteen in January.

While we all read the paper, Coach Alicia stepped back in. "There's a Women's World Cup in two years. The Argentine federation is taking a team to qualifiers. The Sudamericano will be a showcase for all of you."

Her words painted visions of glory in my mind. Every girl on my team was picturing herself wearing the Argentine jersey in a World Cup or the colors of a professional team.

It took so little for a spark of faith to ignite a fire. It took so little for that faith to turn into ambition. In that moment, each one of us stood a little taller.

Finally, Coach Alicia clapped her hands, ending our trance, and said, "But now, let's go play. Start warming up. Gabi's girls are ready."

The group, including Rufina, started running. Roxana sent me a pointed look, but Coach Alicia waved me over.

"This is Camila Hassan, *my* discovery from last year," she told her sister. "She speaks perfect English, too. She looked into attending college in the U.S., but you know how it is."

"Impossible," Mrs. Tapia said. Then she turned to me and said in English, "So, you're the unpolished diamond. Alicia sent me a video of the championship game, and I was impressed."

"Thank you," I said, trying to sound confident. I had picked up a few tricks for talking to recruiters from watching Pablo and my father. "That day, we were all magical. Everything went our way." I hoped my American accent impressed Mrs. Tapia.

Alicia's mouth curved in approval. Her sister studied me. After a second, I averted my eyes, worried she'd be put off by my obvious desperation.

A few of the girls from my team slowed down to eavesdrop, and anything I could've said to make myself memorable turned to stones in my mouth. When we played, we were all the same. We were all one. English singled me out in an unwelcome way.

Coach Alicia placed an arm over my shoulder and the other over her sister's and said, "In the beautiful game, words are redundant. Furia, go play, and tell my sister why you deserve a place on a professional team in *our* native language."

I smiled and ran to the field to sing the wordless song of the captive women who roared in my blood. My ancestresses had been waiting to sing for generations.

I was their medium.

16

AS IF SOMEONE HAD FLIPPED A SWITCH, LA FURIA ATE UP her adversaries. Camila took second place. She sat back and observed, cross-armed, a smug smirk on her face.

The American girls complained that the ball was a little deflated and the pitch uneven, and under other circumstances, I might have been embarrassed. Not now. It was time to show them what we could do. La redonda, the ball, obeyed me. She followed me because I treated her well. I cherished her. I treasured her, and most importantly, I let her sing her own song. Energy flowed through my team, and although the game remained scoreless, the North Americans showed signs of fear. Still, I wouldn't be able to play full steam for much longer. My team needed to score fast and then park the bus, play defense until the end.

Knowing I was showing off, I sent a rainbow over their number five in the midfield and muttered *Ole!* so only she could hear me. I ran, feeling her hot breath on the back of my neck, but she never caught me to take her revenge. I was too fast. I passed to Yael, but she was offsides.

The Yankee goalie sent the ball all the way to our half. Mabel was ready to block it with her chest.

I got a break and ran through their line of three defenders. Rufina was standing, unguarded, in the perfect spot. I crossed the ball to her, and with a first touch that belonged in a FIFA video game, she punted it across the goal line.

Rufina bellowed in victory.

My teammates joined with their raw voices in a cry that made the sparrows shoot from the trees.

"Grande, Camila!" Diego yelled from the sidelines.

My trance broke, and la Furia fled like a spooked cat.

I scanned the crowd gathered along the sidelines while I ran to the midfield for kickoff. Looking for Diego.

"Watch out!" Roxana yelled.

Too late. My left foot, the one with the magic touch, landed in a hole I'd been avoiding perfectly well until that moment. My ankle twisted in exquisite pain. As I fell to the ground, my visions of a future full of glory went out like a light.

Gasps and cries of sympathy rose from both teams in a mixture of English and Spanish, curse words and prayers. Then there was a smoldering silence.

Not now, I begged La Difunta. I'd leave her water—blessed water from the sanctuary, even—my heart on a platter, five years of my life for the miracle of not being injured.

Coach Alicia was beside me in seconds. "Don't move your foot," she commanded, rolling down my sock to take a look. Although her fingers were soft, my muscles spasmed with pain.

"I don't think it's broken," she said, but she shook her head. "I'm going to have to take you out."

Quietly, she helped me to the sideline. There wasn't a bench, so I sat on the damp ground. My toe poked out of my busted cleats. I needed a new pair.

The North American players and my teammates regarded me with pity, but the scrimmage resumed. I looked at Roxana protecting the goal but couldn't make out her expression.

Mrs. Tapia and Coach Alicia whispered to each other. I couldn't hear what they said, but the disappointment was palpable.

This had been my chance, and it was ruined.

I looked over my shoulder for Diego, but I couldn't find him.

My team's concentration fractured, the Yankee girls scored once, twice, three times.

La Furia retreated to the depths of my soul. Now I smelled the ammonia scent of my sweat and felt the burns the pitch had left on my skin. Every scratch and kick and elbow to the ribs throbbed. A stitch in my side made it hard to breathe, and when nausea made saliva pool in my mouth, I spat it out unceremoniously. A few minutes later, after another goal by the Yankee team, Coach blew the whistle, and the scrimmage ended.

A few of the North American girls celebrated, but soon the two teams were shaking hands and exchanging kisses on the cheek. Yael and Rufina spoke on the mid-field, and Luciano joined them. The parents gathered their chairs and blankets from the sidelines as Coach Alicia went along, shaking everyone's hands.

I clambered back to my feet, and when I started putting my things in my backpack, I saw Diego looking at me from the corner of the pitch, his brow creased with worry. Tears burned my eyes. I pressed my lips together hard so I wouldn't start crying. The last thing I needed was to fall apart in front of everyone. In front of him.

He started walking in my direction, but at the sound of Coach and her sister approaching, I turned away from him.

"Are you okay, Camila?" Gabi asked. "Everything was going perfectly until that fall."

"You got the goal on video, didn't you?" Coach Alicia asked, standing between us. She sounded angry. I knew she wasn't mad at me, but it was my fault I'd let myself be distracted.

"I got it," she confirmed. "I can't wait to see more of that in December, okay?"

I nodded, because there was no way I could speak without crying.

On the pitch, everyone was talking to each other despite the language barrier. Roxana and the Yankee goalie seemed to be exchanging contact information, and they took a selfie together.

"Let's gather for a group picture!" Coach Alicia said, and a tall, Black American girl, number seven, helped me hobble to the edge of the group. One of the moms grabbed Coach's phone and started snapping pictures. But I couldn't even pretend to smile.

Mrs. Tapia came back over to me. "Sometimes things happen for a reason," she said. "Now you must work to get over this injury."

Coach Alicia handed me a cold Gatorade and placed a hand on my shoulder. "Gabi, la Furia will return stronger than ever if it's the last thing I do."

Her confidence grounded me.

"You have the kind of touch that can't be taught," Gabi said, squinting like she was trying to find the right words. "You have esa picardía . . . there's not a word in English to describe it, but the flair, you know? That cleverness and spontaneity that I hardly ever encounter in the U.S. academies. You played like a female Neymar."

"Neymar?"

At the sight of my wrinkled nose, she added quickly, "Neymar in his Santos years . . . you're too young to remember, but he was magical. I saw some glimpses of that in you."

"We just need you to be healthy," Coach added. "Invincible. Unbreakable."

Even if I were invincible and unbreakable, the world was full of talented players. Chances were that Gabi would meet other girls whose skills would outshine mine. How many times had I heard my father tell Pablo that being talented meant nothing without hard work? I would do everything I could to prove to Coach Alicia that her faith in me wasn't unfounded.

"Thanks for coming to see us," I said after I swallowed.

Gabi nodded solemnly. "It was my pleasure. I'm looking forward to December. Don't lose faith. Now, I think someone's waiting for you." She squinted as if trying to make out who stood behind us. "Is that really . . . ?"

Finally, I looked back.

Diego was surrounded by girls from both teams, who were taking pictures with him and having him sign everything from notebooks to jerseys and even backpacks. Some of the families also approached. He wasn't wearing his fancy clothes, just a pair of Central shorts and a worn-out sweatshirt. His baseball cap couldn't disguise his perfect face. I tried not to stare at his sculpted legs. He was pure muscle and strength. After everyone had a turn to meet him, Mrs. Tapia waved him over.

When he hesitated, Coach Alicia called, "Come chat with your fans, Titán!"

Diego made his way in our direction. If there were ever a time that I wanted the earth to open up and swallow me, it was then.

He had seen *everything*. He knew I played. He had seen me fall.

Mrs. Tapia whispered to herself, "Diego Ferrari, the next Messi, the next Dybala . . ." She sounded like a total fangirl.

"He's better," I said without thinking.

Coach, a rabid Messi fan, shook her head. "Messi already had a Ballon d'Or at nineteen. Diego's just starting out."

Messi had moved to Barcelona when he was thirteen, and at that age, Diego had just been adopted by Ana.

When he reached us, Diego shook Coach Alicia's hand. "An honor to meet you in person, Coach. I've heard so much about what you're doing for girls' fútbol, especially in the barrios." His eyes turned to me. "What an assist, Camila . . . I didn't know you were on this team." He looked at me like he'd never seen me before.

"It was an amazing play," Gabi agreed. "How do you two know each other?"

"Childhood friends, I believe, right?" Coach Alicia gave me a look that made my mouth go dry. Although I had nothing to hide, I looked down at the ground. I couldn't meet her eyes.

"A selfie, Titán?" Gabi asked, and then said, "Come, Alicia! Everyone will freak when they find out I met Diego Ferrari."

While they posed for the picture, I sent Roxana one of the poisonous looks that were usually *her* specialty. She walked over and asked, "Are you okay?"

I knew she wasn't asking only about my foot.

"How did he find me? Did you tell him?"

Roxana placed a hand on her chest, offended. "Never!"

"Then how?"

She shrugged. "Maybe it's fate. Maybe it's for the best. Now he knows why you aren't interested."

"Ay, Roxana . . ." I sighed.

She grabbed my backpack as if we were going to make a run for it right now. On my injured foot. "Do you want to go? My dad's parked right there."

I looked over my shoulder.

Diego was signing a shirt for Gabi, and when he saw me staring, we both blushed.

My heart softened. How could I leave without saying goodbye? Just because I didn't want *a thing* with him didn't mean I had to run away.

"I can't go, Ro. He and I really need to talk," I finally said, taking my backpack.

"Good luck, then." Roxana kissed me goodbye and ran to Diego's side to snap a selfie with him, the traitor. Then she signaled for me to call her later and ran to her dad's truck.

Luciano clapped Diego's shoulder. They hugged, and el Mago whispered something in Diego's ear.

"I'll be in touch," Gabi said to Rufina, who smiled. And then to me, "And you, too, Furia. Take care."

"Thanks for giving her a ride, Titán," Coach Alicia added.

Then everyone left. Coach followed the bus full of North Americans in her beat-up Fiat, and I was alone with Diego.

I turned to face him in all my post-game grime. On TV, he always looked like a superhero after a brutal game. Diego stared at me. His eyes were mirrors. In them, I saw how my hair frizzed out in a cloud around my dismayed face.

And because Deolinda must have decided to collect her debt just then, the nausea came back. I sank to the ground and dry-heaved. Diego was next to me in two strides, holding me up. I started shaking. Stars popped in my eyes, and I inhaled as deeply as I could, but my breath came in ragged gasps. I tried to pull away from him in case I actually threw up, but he wouldn't let go. My leg hurt so much I couldn't stand.

When my head stopped pounding and my heartbeat went back to its normal pace, the shaking slowed. Diego kissed my forehead, and I leaned into him.

"What the hell are you doing here?" I finally asked.

He let go of me, and I looked up at his face.

"Here? This is *my* pitch, *Furia*." From his lips, my new name sounded majestic. "I played here in the baby league. I wanted to practice some shots in my lucky goal before heading back to Turín tomorrow."

"Tomorrow?" When he'd said he was leaving Thursday, it had seemed so far away, but it was just a few hours from now.

He shrugged and looked over at a group of kids playing on the crumbling basketball court next to the pitch. Carefully, I took off my boots. Along with my hamstring, my feet were throbbing.

Although he wore old shorts and a sweatshirt, Diego's silver shoes were slick and futuristic. He rummaged through his backpack and took out a pair of flip-flops. "Put these on," he said, and I slipped my feet into the too-big sandals. The prickly rubber tickled me.

"Too bad I'm injured, or I'd challenge you to some shots."

As if I'd ever be able to beat him.

Diego looked at my legs, and his mouth twitched. "I would challenge you to a best of ten, but I have fresh legs, and you, Furia . . . you have *legs*."

My legs were too muscular and short to be sexy, but Diego stared at me.

"Remember when Pablo called me patas de tero?" I tried to deflect.

"And now they're glorious and fast. Do you remember Princess Camila?"

The glow of that afternoon long ago filled me with light. "Yes, the virgin warrior," I blurted out. The word *virgin* bounced between us for a second too long.

Diego laughed, then took my hand. "Maybe you're dehydrated. You probably need to eat, too. When was the last time—?"

"I had *mates* sometime today, and a protein shake Roxana brought me . . ."

"Warriors, even virgin ones, need to recharge, Furia," he said. In spite of the playful banter, there was something else I'd never heard in a boy's voice before: admiration. "You're tough, but if you don't take care of your body, you're going to keep getting injured. You can't live off *mate*."

Although a part of me swooned at the concern in Diego's voice, the critical side of me recoiled from his words. It wasn't my fault I'd been hurt; it was his for distracting me.

"Let's go get something to eat," he said, my hand still in his. When I resisted, he added, "I have los *mates* in the car. We just need to stop at the bakery."

I closed my eyes, trying to center myself.

"One last time by the river, Camila," he said in a soft voice. "And then I'll be gone."

He had me. He'd had me all along, even if he'd made me fall.

A warrior virgin. What was I thinking?

"One last time," I said, warning myself that this was the end.

I followed him to his car.

THE AIR CONDITIONER BLASTED MY FACE, AND SWEATY AS
I was, I started to shiver.

"Sorry," Diego said, and reached over me to close the vent. He twisted the dial back and forth, but the air didn't stop. I saw the off button on the dashboard, and I reached over. When I did, my whole body pressed against his arm. I hit the button, and the air died like a held sigh.

He fell back in his seat, flustered.

"What's wrong?" I asked, putting my hand on his arm, and I felt him flex automatically.

"It's just that . . . I've been wanting to talk to you. Yesterday I only went to your house because Pablo insisted, but you didn't even want to see me. I'm not a jerk, you know? I can take a no. And now . . ."

If we were going to have *that* conversation, I needed food. "Weren't you going to get me dinner? I'm about to pass out in your brand-new car, Titán." I paused. There was no trace of a superstar in the boy sitting next to me. "Diego." I said his name the same way I'd said it that night when we'd kissed for the first time. Like I did in my imagination when the kiss led to other things. Things I'd never done with a boy before. But my body craved him all the same.

Silently, Diego turned on the engine, and we left.

Time stood still when I played fútbol, but now, like Cinderella at the ball, I felt the clock rushing. Diego was leaving again, and I didn't know how to cope with all my feelings.

He knew my secret now: I was a futbolera. Having someone see *all of me*—besides Roxana—was liberating. No more wearing different faces at home, school, the pitch, with Diego.

I felt naked.

Maluma played softly on the radio, promising a night of fun without contracts or promises. Guys *say* they want that, but they don't. They want all of us, girls, women. All, without leaving us any space to enjoy ourselves. What kind of guy was Diego when he wasn't playing the roles of best friend, superstar, or son?

For once, neither logical Camila nor rash Furia could take the helm. In my mind, there was silence, but it wasn't the calm before the storm; it was the stunning quiet before the unknown.

The car zipped by Ovidio Lagos, all the way downtown to Distinción Bakery. "I'll be right back," he said, and hopped out.

I leaned back into the seat and locked the doors. I closed my eyes for a second that became a minute that became more.

A knock on my window startled me awake. It was Diego.

"Let's go," he said once I'd unlocked the door for him. The smell of fresh bread and powdered sugar made my mouth water. My eyelids fluttered in exhaustion, and when I smiled at him, Diego brushed my hair off my face. "Hey, Furia. If you want to go home, I won't be offended. I've been thinking, and—"

"Call me Camila."

"Camila," he said. "You don't have to come anywhere with me—you know that, right? If you—"

I put a finger on his lips, and he sighed against it. The thrill of knowing what I could do to him with the simplest touch filled my head with bubbles. Maybe it was the magic of the newborn night and the full moon in the sky. Maybe it was the vulnerability of his unmasked face. Maybe I just was tired of fighting against myself. "I want to be here. With you, Diego. What did you have in mind?"

He took my hand and squeezed it softly.

"Take me on one last adventure, Diego, before you go back to Turín."

He looked at me for a second too long. I thought he was going to say something, but if he was, he held it in. Before the moment became unbearable, he turned the engine on and headed toward the river.

The public bathing areas were closed this time of the year. La Florida wouldn't open its beaches until November, but Diego parked in an empty lot that overlooked the water.

"Here," he said.

The river's soft waves caressed the outline of Rosario, and the bridge to Victoria glittered on the horizon. Round, low, dark clouds embraced the full moon like a cloak.

We got out of the car, and Diego took the paper bag from the back seat, then his backpack from the trunk. He handed me the bakery bag and put a package wrapped in shiny blue-and-yellow paper under his arm.

"What's that?" I asked, trying not to put too much weight on my foot. It throbbed.

He'd taken off his hat, and a curl fell in his eyes. When he brushed it away, I saw an impish sparkle. "You'll see."

He held my hand and slowly led me down to the riverbank. My feet slipped in the sandals, so I stopped to take them off. The coarse sand was cold and pleasant. Diego led me to the middle of the little beach. It was deserted, as if we'd walked through a tear into a magical place where it was just the two of us, no strings to reality—past or future—attached.

Diego took a blanket out of his backpack and spread it on the ground; then he set a green Stanley thermos on top and took out a plastic container of yerba and another of sugar.

"You're prepared." I sat on the blanket. My left leg immediately seized up in a cramp so intense that I groaned.

Diego knelt in front of me and held my foot. "Point and flex. Point and flex." I wanted to shake him off. I was sweaty and stinky, and his hands on my naked skin made it harder to concentrate on relaxing my muscles. But then the pain eased, and soon the cramp was gone. He rotated my ankle a few more times and finally placed my foot gently on the ground. "Now," he said, "when that happens to me, Massimo massages my thigh to loosen the muscle. He makes me drink at least a liter of mineral water, too."

"Massimo?"

"The team's physiotherapist." He rummaged in his bag and grabbed a glass water bottle. "Drink."

"Fancy," I said, studying my reflection in the bottle before I drank. The water was slightly salty, but I was too thirsty to let it bother me.

Diego shrugged. "I get sick now when I drink from the tap. So mineral water it is for me."

"It's all the sugar you're eating, nene."

He smiled sheepishly, and I could see the tip of his tongue between his teeth. He prepared the *mate* and took a sip. The first sip is always the strongest; it leaves a bitter green aftertaste. He didn't even flinch. All the leftover tension that knotted my muscles drained away as I watched him do this ordinary thing.

"You bought all this for just the two of us?" I asked, looking at the assortment of facturas in the bag. Tortitas negras, vigilantes, cream and marmalade. He'd brought two of each at least. I took out a croissant. It melted on my tongue.

"They had an after six p.m. half-off sale. Happy hour." He shrugged. "I couldn't resist."

We ate and drank *mate* and water from the same bottle and the same straw. He pulled out his phone, and at first I thought he was checking his texts, but before I could complain, music started playing softly. A man's voice sang in Italian. Diego sang along softly, slightly off-key. He put the phone back on the blanket.

"How did you know I'd be at the little pitch?" I asked.

Diego changed la yerba and shook his head. Here by the river, his hair had taken on a life of its own; it curled luxuriously in ringlets. He took an elastic from his wrist and tied it into a bun on top of his head. I'd seen him in designer suits on a red carpet and in fancy rock star clothes driving his BMW, but dressed like this, like a regular boy who had never posed for photographers, he was irresistible.

"I didn't know."

"Then how did you find me?"

"I already told you, Mama."

"But it's hard to believe. The evidence"—I gestured to the picnic he'd come with—"shows that you were stalking me."

"And why would I do that?" He raised an eyebrow.

Just like that, the words evaporated from my lips. The scent of the night, humid and kind of fishy, erased my thoughts. I wasn't going to make this easy for him.

"One piece of advice Paulo gave me as soon as I arrived in Turín was never to forget my roots."

"Paulo as in *Paulo Dybala*?" Paulo "la Joya" Dybala was Diego's *friend*. I'd known this, of course, but Diego had never flaunted his connections before. Not that he was doing it now. It was just . . . *Dybala*.

Diego's whole face lit up, dispelling the awkwardness that tried to creep between us. "I know, right? I wouldn't say we're *friends* friends, but I've been over to play FIFA or have dinner with his family."

"Going over for FIFA and dinner makes you friends."

Diego bit his lip. "I guess . . . and we play together. Like, on the *same team*. Camila, I have his old number!"

"Twenty-one!" we said in unison.

Diego went on. "First time I saw him, I couldn't speak. I was like this." He put his straight arms against this body and made a stunned face. I smiled, imagining the whole thing. "But he pretended not to notice and passed me a *mate* and an alfajor cordobés."

"Your favorite."

"He's totally down-to-earth, and yes." He laughed. "He's my favorite."

I realized Diego had been bursting to share this. Had no one given him the chance? Maybe the boys were afraid that he'd changed now that he couldn't even drink our water. Maybe they were jealous that he had everything they wanted. Everything *we* wanted.

"Dybala told you not to forget your roots, and so you went to that pitch?"

"When I was eight and lived with Father Hugo, I used to play on that field. That's where the Central scout found me."

Pablo had started in the academy at twelve, and by the time Diego moved in with Ana, he and Pablo had been teammates and best friends for a while.

"He found you in Newell's territory?"

Diego bit his lip and ducked his head. "I might have been one of the Old Boys in another life."

"Impossible."

"I didn't know any better. But I've been one hundred percent Scoundrel ever since." He hesitated for a second, and then he added, "My mom and I lived in that barrio before . . . before she left. I kept going back, hoping I'd see her or someone who knew where she was."

"You haven't heard anything even now?"

Diego looked toward the bridge that tied Rosario to Victoria. He shook his head. "No. I keep thinking now that I'm—" he hesitated.

"Famous?" I offered, and he smiled timidly.

"Yes, I keep thinking she'll contact me. Even just for money. But she hasn't, and I hope that she's safe wherever she is. It's my last night in Rosario. I had to go to my lucky field."

I stretched out my hand to press his. "Lucky field?"

"Lucky field." His gaze was so intense I had to look down. "You were magic out there. You have that joy . . ." He rolled the edge of the blanket between his fingers. "You're like a female Messi, a Dybala. You could defend pretty well when you played with Pablo and me. But I had no idea you were this good. Why didn't you tell me?"

Diego's compliments mixed with the chill of the breeze and made me shiver. I wrapped my arms around myself. "I'm not like Messi or Dybala, or even you. I'm like Alex Morgan. Like Marta. My team doesn't compare to yours, but one day I'm going to play in the Unites States with those women."

He stared at me.

"Do you even know who Marta is?"

"Five-time Ballon d'Or," Diego said, and now it was my turn to be impressed. "Of course I know Marta, nena. I met her in Monaco a couple of months ago."

A cargo ship crossed the river, and a few seconds later, tiny cold waves lapped the shore and licked my naked feet. I hadn't been swimming in the river in years.

He'd met Marta. In Monaco.

"Is that why you want to play in the States?" he asked. "Because Marta's there now?"

"Marta's one reason," I said, surprised he even knew where she played. Pablo had no idea. "In an interview, she said she was switching from Sweden to the North American league because the best players in the world played there. Besides, English's easier to learn than Swedish, you know?" He smiled on cue and motioned for me to continue. "I've always wanted to play." I looked up to see if he was about to laugh at me, but his face was still and serious, so I kept going. "Their league is professional. But imagine . . ." I didn't know how to explain myself, but he waited for me to find the words. "I know it's far-fetched, but if I do well in the Sudamericano, maybe I can get called up for a professional team. Even the U.S. women's league . . ." My heart pounded in my ears as I poured out my dreams at Diego's feet. "It's not Juventus, I know."

Diego grabbed my hand and pressed it. "One day it could be, Camila."

"It sounds stupid, but I want to play."

"And you will, Cami." He unknotted the red ribbon, his good luck bracelet, from his wrist and tied it around mine. "You have to keep fighting, even if you're hurt now," he said. "Come back stronger. You're doing it on your own. Here I was, thinking I was coming back to rescue you, and you're becoming your own savior."

I held his hand. "Is that why you came back? To rescue me, Titán?" I'd meant to sound playful, flirty, bantering, like always. Instead, my voice was deep and hoarse. I couldn't stop looking at Diego's lips.

He leaned closer, and just like that, we were shoulder to shoulder. I traced a finger over his barrio tattoo, and he lowered his forehead to mine. Tentatively, I put my hand on the nape of his neck. His skin was hot under his curls.

The music played on in the background. I took a deep breath, about to jump into one of Paraná's whirlpools. I wouldn't resurface the same.

I leaned in first. My mouth was soft and hot on Diego's.

He kissed me back. A shuddering breath escaped us both, and he pulled away. Although clouds covered the night sky, I could see the Southern Cross and the whole Milky Way reflected in his eyes. I took hold of his worn-out sweatshirt and pulled him back to me. He closed his eyes, but I was afraid that if I closed mine, I'd miss something. Soon I couldn't fight the urge anymore. I let the whirlpool take me. I didn't even know how to swim. My eyelids dropped.

Diego wrapped an arm around my waist. Before I knew it, we were kneeling on the sand, facing each other, the blanket bunched up around our legs, the *mate* knocked over and forgotten. La Furia met her equal in el Titán. The latent goddess inside me pulled at her bindings until she snapped them. Together, we held on to this boy who'd come to wreck my world.

My mouth moved down to his neck; skin recognized skin. His hands burned against my back, climbing up, up, up.

In a lucid second before I took off my jersey, I remembered we were out in public.

Nothing would happen to Diego, but if someone saw us like this, the consequences for me would be dire. I'd break my mom's heart. I'd become a hated tool in my father's hands. Roxana would think I'd given up on everything I'd worked for.

"Te quiero," Diego said in my ear, trying to catch his breath.

With my hands on his chest, I gently pushed him away. "Don't lie to me."

"If anyone's a liar, it's you, Furia. Who taught you to kiss like this?"

Like I would ever tell him he'd been my only one. I laughed. "Who taught you?" I teased him back.

In reply, he kissed me again and again and again.

"My knees are killing me," he said when we broke apart to breathe. He fell back on the sand but didn't let me go. He pulled me up onto his lap, his arms wrapped around me. His heart beat hard against my back.

"In La Juve, the mister always says life is a bianconero business. Love is black and white; there's no in-between. Camila, I've loved you all my life. I can't pretend I don't. Not anymore."

He turned me around and kissed me again, softly this time, like we had all the time in the world, like he wasn't leaving the next day.

But he was.

"What are we going to do?" I asked, my soft voice an echo of Furia's desperate cries.

"I have a plan," Diego said. With every sentence that left his mouth, I said yes with a kiss. He pulled me down on the sand while raindrops baptized us as they fell from the pregnant clouds.

18

EVENTUALLY, THE RAIN CHASED US AWAY. DIEGO HELPED me get back to the car. The moment by the river was already gone.

We carried our shoes, the *mate* things, sand, and something else, a link that made me hurt every second I wasn't touching him.

Thunder shook the car. Diego looked at me, his curls plastered to his forehead, goose bumps covering his strong arms. His sweatshirt must have come off at some point.

I looked at the clock on his dashboard. "My parents are going to kill me."

"I'll come up and tell them the truth. I mean, it's not like they won't have guessed. I *told* them I came back for you." Diego kissed my forehead.

Vestiges of the old Camila climbed out of the smoldering pile of senselessness that couldn't quite bury her.

Somehow, I wiggled out of his arms. "Wait," I said. "We're not telling anyone."

"But why?"

Diego knew my parents, but would he understand if I told him about the fight with my dad the night we'd gone out? Or my mom's warnings the morning after?

"Diego, I . . ."

Say it, say it, la Furia chanted, echoed by my drumming heart.

But I couldn't say I loved him. If I did, I'd be defenseless, and I was afraid that I'd do something we'd both regret forever. The girl Diego said he loved was the strong one, the winning Camila, the one with a future she was forging for herself. The one who was still fighting. If he rescued me, if I quit for him, I wouldn't be the girl he loved. I wouldn't be *myself*.

He let me sort out my thoughts and pushed a button on the console. Soon, heat warmed my seat.

"You don't have to tell anyone if you don't want to," he said. "How do you live carrying so many secrets?"

Diego had a face like a book. I wasn't that fluent in the language of love, but anyone could have seen it painted all over him. In my family, love had always been a weapon to be used against the weakest at their most vulnerable. I wouldn't let my parents use it against Diego.

"Listen," he said. "I can't ask you to wait for me. You're not the kind of person who'll just knit a scarf or sit on a pier like the girl of San Blas."

Why was it always the girl waiting and losing her mind?

"But *I'll* wait for *you*, Camila. Until you're ready to give me a chance."

"You say that now . . ."

Lightning flashed, and I counted to three before thunder rumbled. He wanted a chance. He wanted to wait for me. Until I was ready.

My fantasies with Diego usually reached embarrassingly romantic points, but I'd never even dreamed of something like this.

He took the package from the back seat and handed it to me. The paper was stained with water and muddy sand. "I've been wanting to give you this since I arrived."

I carefully placed my finger under the Scotch tape, but he said, "Rip it for good luck."

Feeling guilty because this paper must have cost a fortune, I tore it off and opened the flat, white cardboard box. What I was certain must be the scent of Europe, clean and sharp like the expensive stores at the shopping center, filled the car. My fingers brushed the silky fabric of a jersey.

"What's this?"

"Take it out and see for yourself."

Carefully, I lifted the jersey. It cooled my fingers like water. It was an original, Juventus and Adidas, with all the official stamps, and on the back, above the number twenty-one, was my name: CAMILA.

"Had I known," Diego said softly, "I would've had them print Furia. You know, they have a women's team. Maybe one day . . ." In the space of the ellipsis, I saw our future like in a movie.

"Maybe," I said. I wanted him to take me somewhere else right now, while we had the chance. I wanted him so much, I could've done it right there in the back seat of his car.

He leaned in to kiss me, the same raw hunger in his eyes. Before our lips touched, his phone buzzed. My first impulse was to tell him to ignore it. We couldn't stop now. But Diego glanced down at the screen, and his eyes widened in alarm. "It's Pablo," he said. "He's asking if I know where you are."

As if midnight had struck and turned the car back into a pumpkin, the illusion vanished. Pablo and the rest of my family might as well have been sitting in the back seat, watching my every move.

I looked at myself in the small, fogged mirror on the visor. I looked just like someone who had played a brutal fútbol game and then spent the last couple of hours rolling in the sand by the river. How was I going to hide all this?

Rain drummed on the car roof, amplifying my nerves. Diego said, "He's worried. What should we say?"

"Nothing!"

He looked at me like I wasn't making any sense. "I'll come up and tell him and the whole family—"

"No!" I exclaimed a little louder than I intended. I saw it all so clearly now. "Pablo just gave us the best excuse for being together tonight."

"He's going to tell. He's not stupid. He has to know about us."

I took Diego's face in my hands and kissed him. "Here's what we're going to say."

Diego trusted me so implicitly, he texted what I dictated to him without once questioning me. He sat up and typed staccato lies to his best friend.

Never had I felt this much power over anyone else, or even my own life, and the taste was intoxicating.

———

Diego sped home, but still the storm beat us to 7 de Septiembre. By the time we crossed Circunvalación, the rain and wind were wreaking havoc on the west side of Rosario. Water ran through the streets. Torn tree limbs had brought down power lines, dooming the residents to darkness and warming refrigerators. An empty 146 bus moved aside to let us pass. The beams of its headlights brightened the dark road. The BMW wasn't built for the fury of Santa Rosa. She was drowning us.

"I'll see you tomorrow," he said.

"How?"

"I'll find a way."

When I got out of the car, the pelting raindrops couldn't wash away Diego's last feverish kiss or the memory of his hands all over my skin. I felt him watching me as I limped slowly up the stairs. My leg didn't hurt so much anymore. Diego had said the hamstring was probably only strained but that I should be careful. Luciano had played after a tweak in his knee, and by the time the doctors realized his meniscus was shot, it was too late. None of the stories my mom told to scare me into behaving had ever terrified me the way Luciano in his blue La Valeria uniform had.

Once I was on my floor, I waved at Diego, and finally, he drove away.

I wished he'd taken me with him. But there was no avoiding my family.

Nico barked from inside the apartment, giving me away, and my dream of coming in unnoticed vanished.

To my surprise, we still had power. The only person home was Pablo, sitting in front of the TV, drinking straight from the orange juice bottle. Once Nico had licked my hand to his satisfaction, he made his way back to my brother.

The clock on the TV read just after eleven. There was no sign of my parents. Where could they be at this time?

Relief flashed in Pablo's eyes before he had time to

camouflage it with frustration. "Where the hell were you?" He sounded so much like our father that I recoiled.

Pablo must have heard *him* in his voice, too, because he put the bottle down and said softly, "You scared me."

Encouraged by his effort to calm down, I made my way to him and kissed him on the cheek. He smelled like Diego's new cologne.

"At work, Pali. I thought I'd wait out the storm, but it just got worse."

Pablo shook his head. "You were with Diego the whole time."

It was easy for Pablo to imagine the truth. He'd had plenty of similar experiences with Marisol and the other girls he'd hopped between since he'd discovered his good looks and blazing smile.

Thunder rumbled outside, making Nico whimper. The temperature had dropped at least ten degrees, and my skin prickled. I put the kettle on and made myself a ham and cheese sandwich. "Do you want one?" I asked, looking over my shoulder. He was flipping through the channels.

"Sure," he said.

It was almost like traveling back in time to when Mamá worked at her atelier downtown and it was just the two of us most days. I never had Pablo to myself anymore.

When I brought the sandwiches and *mate* to the table, Pablo was laughing at a *Simpsons* rerun like it was the first time he'd seen it. The episode was almost over. He took a bite of the sandwich and smiled. "Thank you. I was so hungry."

"You could've made something, you know? Your balls aren't gonna shrivel up and fall off if you feed yourself."

He laughed. "But you made the sandwich for me. My tactic worked."

I stuck my tongue out at him. "Next time, I'll let you starve."

The *Simpsons* episode ended, and the transmission jumped to coverage about Central having all its players, even the reserves and youth teams, attend workshops about domestic violence. Pablo rolled his eyes and turned the TV off.

"Why did you do that?" I asked.

"I have nothing against the workshops, negra. Some of the guys are violent because they don't know any better, and they can learn. But, I mean, a lifetime of hard work can go down the drain because of one moment of anger, and like Papá says, some women like the rough, bad boys . . ."

It was one thing for my father to say that and quite another to hear it from Pablo. I tried to remind myself that I wanted to keep my brother on my side, that I needed a lifesaving favor from him. Arguing wouldn't change his mind, so why should I hurt myself trying? But I spoke up anyway. "So many girls are getting hurt because of that mentality. Look at me tonight. I was scared to come home on my own. I can't even walk to the bus stop without being afraid someone will attack me. And you were scared, too."

Pablo clicked his tongue. "Now, don't exaggerate. Of course it's not okay, but that's the world we live in, nena. Maybe you shouldn't be working at all. When you aren't home, we worry you'll be on the next poster. If you aren't careful, it'll be your fault if you are."

"I'm not going to be a missing girl," I said.

None of the girls and women whose faces plastered the walls of our city had ever intended to become statistics, either, but they were blamed for the crimes committed against them.

"Did you and Diego really go out again?" Pablo asked. "When I texted him, he said he was driving you home. Why didn't he come up with you?"

I had all my answers ready at the tip of my deceiving tongue. "We didn't go out. It was a coincidence he found me," I said. "When I couldn't venture out into the storm, one of the nuns said Diego was coming over to bring some donations, so I just waited for him." Pablo nodded, accepting the lie Diego and I had created. "Then everyone wanted to see him and get pictures with him, and before I knew it, it was late. He promised Ana he'd be home tonight, since he's leaving tomorrow."

Pablo yawned. "I don't know why he's driving that car in this weather. I guess when you have enough money to throw butter at the ceiling . . ."

The jealousy in his voice shone neon green. This was my cue to head back to my room and install the new doorknob. I didn't want to see this side of Pablo. I picked up my backpack and ruffled his hair before walking away. "Good night, Stallion. Don't forget to come pick me up when you have your own BMW."

He scoffed. "My red Camaro, you mean?"

"On these streets? You'll fall into a pothole and resurface in China."

Pablo threw his head back in laughter. "At least the Chinese like Argentine fútbol players."

Now was the time. He wouldn't deny me.

"Pali . . ." I willed him to read my request on my face.

My brother knew some things were too important to put into words.

He pressed his lips into a hard line, but his eyes were still velvety soft like the old Pali, the one nobody saw anymore. Finally, he nodded and said, "I won't tell them you came home so late. But don't do it again."

"I won't."

I walked away, and just when I thought I was in the clear, Pablo called me out. "What happened to your leg? You're limping, and your pants are all muddy."

"I got hurt in a scrimmage," I said.

Pablo laughed. "Stop trying to be funny. Really, what happened?"

I shrugged. "Walking to Diego's car, I fell in a pothole, turned up in a fairyland. But I had no choice but to come back to real life." The joke revealed too much, but he still smiled.

"Just be careful, okay?" he said. "Everyone knows fairylands are full of wolves."

DID SOMETHING COUNT AS A MIRACLE IF IT WAS POSSIBLE only because of a lie? I didn't really want to find out, so I put Deolinda's estampita in my nightstand drawer.

In the shower, sand fell from my tangled hair and gathered like crumbs at my feet. After, wrapped in my towel, I curled up in bed, hugging the Juventus jersey, which still smelled like Diego. The nightstand was covered in dry petals.

In between pangs of pain in my leg, my body thrilled at the memory of tonight. I repeated Diego's words and promises so I wouldn't ever forget them, so they could make me stronger.

He had power over me, but I had power over him, too.

I fantasized about what it would be like if I were flying out with him tomorrow. Heading to the glamorous new life he had in Italy. I wasn't the first or the last girl dating a fútbol player to do this.

My body was on fire. I hovered at the edge of dreamland, feeling Diego's gentle fingers on my skin, his soft mouth on mine.

I hadn't pushed the dresser in front of the door to protect me. Nico had stayed with Pablo.

I heard someone come into my room.

"Camila, what's wrong?" my mom exclaimed, shaking my shoulder. I bolted upright. "Hija, are you okay?"

My heart hammered painfully all over my skin, as if that's all I was, a heart. My mom held my face in her cold, cold hands and pressed her lips to my forehead. For a moment, I was afraid that she'd sense Diego in me, and all the things I'd been hiding from her.

Then I remembered. Today was Diego's last day.

"I didn't hear the alarm," I said, gasping as if I'd run sprints. My voice was raspy.

"Mi amor, I think you're sick," she said, looking around the room as if searching for someone or something to blame. She stared at the flowers and then at me. "Is it because Diego leaves in the afternoon?"

Rationally, I knew he had to go back to Italy. I didn't want him to stay in Rosario. I would have hated it if he turned his back on the dream of his life just to be with me. Last night, like the two lovesick kids we were, we'd promised we'd wait for each other; we'd make the long-distance relationship work. It wouldn't be like the last time he left.

I clenched my body to control the shaking, and all I got was another cramp in my calf. Diego wasn't there to help me flex my foot, and I didn't have a physiotherapist to make me drink fancy water.

Mamá looked worried. "Pablo told me you fell in the street yesterday. Are you okay? Maybe you should stay home today."

I hadn't missed a day of school since the bus strike in third grade. School and the fútbol field were my sacred safe spaces.

"I can't miss," I said. "I have a history quiz and a math test."

Mamá walked around my room, inspecting it. If I didn't distract her, she'd find the Juventus jersey hidden under the pillow. My name on the back could complicate things more than if Diego had given me a diamond ring.

"Where were you last night?" I asked.

She smiled, her eyes shining. "I had to turn in a dress, and since it was raining, Papi offered to drive me." She bit her lip and clasped her hands like a little girl bursting with gossip. But Mamá had practice at hiding things, too. She started picking up my laundry and said, "Later, he drove me to get some fabric for a special dress I'm planning, and then he took me out to eat. Isn't that wonderful?"

She tripped, and when she picked up the new door-knob I'd left on the floor, a cloud passed over her face.

"What's wrong, Ma?"

She looked at me as if she was peeling layers of time off me to see the little girl I'd once been.

"You look terrible. I think you're ojeada." She shook her finger at me. "I told you, be careful with the promises you make to random saints. You were looking pretty just the other day."

Her cruelty left me speechless.

"I wish you were still little." She sighed and put a hand over her heart. "I wish someone had the recipe to keep kids small and safe."

I hated it when she said things like this. Like it was my fault I couldn't stay ten years old forever. It wasn't like I'd had any say in how fast my breasts grew or when I got my period. Why was she making me feel guilty for being alive?

She got up to leave, taking the doorknob with her. "I'll go ahead and install this. I should've done it already. Now, get going. You're going to be late."

My limbs were lead, my muscles bruised, but I didn't waste any time getting dressed.

"Have you talked to your parents?" Roxana asked when the lunch bell rang, and I had no choice but to follow her to the school courtyard. "Mine were sad I had to choose between the graduation and the tournament, but priorities, you know? My mom ordered my dress already and everything. But now she's spearheading the fundraising for the team."

I'd been so distracted by everything with Diego that I hadn't thought about the conflict between the tournament and graduation, or the paperwork my parents had to sign for my FIFA registration, or all the money I had to save. Fundraising would only take us so far.

The gravity of my secrets and all the lies I'd spun to cover them pressed down on me.

I put my head in my hands.

Roxana wrapped an arm around my shoulders. When the warmth of her body grounded me, I realized I'd been shaking again. Georgina and Laura eyed us suspiciously from the hallway. The year before, two girls in the class below us had been caught kissing in the bathroom, and ever since, there had been "a hunt for the gays," as Roxana called it. Our country had legalized same-sex marriage way before the U.S., but prejudice didn't read or obey laws. It was a hard weed to pull from people's hearts.

Roxana didn't let go of me but inched closer. "Let them think what they want."

My laughter made me shake even more, and Roxana made a worried face.

"We got caught in the rain last night, and I think I'm sick."

"Wait . . ." she said. I could practically see her mind trying to make a timeline. "How long were you and Diego together?"

"Not long," I said, feeling myself turning as red as her can of Coca-Cola. "He's going back today, anyway."

She tugged at the red ribbon tied around my wrist.

The bell for last period, math, rang. It saved me from having to explain or lie.

What had happened with Diego the night before had been inevitable yet unexpected. Roxana loved me, but our lives were so different. She'd never understand. Lying to my best friend was probably the worst sin I'd committed so far, but it was too late to back down now.

I blundered through my math test. I probably wouldn't scrape even a six, which would put a dent in my GPA.

At the end of the school day, Roxana walked out to Alberdi Avenue with me.

"Well, well, well," she said. "I didn't expect he'd actually give up so easily. I really thought he'd pull a *Tres Metros Sobre el Cielo* and come pick you up on his motorcycle."

"He doesn't have a motorcycle," I replied. Although I knew I'd see him later, my eyes still scanned the street for his car.

"BMW—same thing," Roxana replied.

I kissed her cheek and walked away before she pulled the thread of my lies and unspooled the truth.

On the bus, my eyes searched for Diego. Every black car I saw made my heart race. Sweat beaded on my forehead in spite of the return of winter weather. But every time I caught a glimpse of the drivers, my hopes were shattered.

In the end, Diego's car was not the one that gave me a jolt.

It was my father's. I got off the bus a block too late and saw his red Peugeot in the carport of a house just around the corner from El Buen Pastor.

At first, I thought my mind was playing tricks on me. But the Rosario Central banner that hung from the rearview mirror along with the blue-and-yellow rosary beads confirmed that it was my father's car.

The rain pelted my legs, and the wind pulled at me, trying to snatch my umbrella.

What was he doing here?

The door of the house opened, and in the least stealthy move ever, I shielded my face with the umbrella. I couldn't stand in the middle of the sidewalk like this, so I darted to the kiosco across the street. From the display case, I grabbed a Capitán del Espacio alfajor. I hadn't seen this brand of chocolate cookie for years. I checked the expiration date just in case. It was good.

While I waited to pay, I peeked over my shoulder. The front door of the house was still open, and a young woman, not much older than me, walked out. She had dyed blond hair and looked unnaturally skinny in her jeans and leather jacket. Her black boots had heels so high that she walked like a stick bug. Then my father followed her out of the house, opened the car door for her, and got in the driver's seat. His whole face glowed with happiness.

I stared at him while the car backed out and finally merged into the boulevard's traffic.

"Nena, are you going to pay for that?" the kiosco guy asked me. An unlit cigarette hung from his lips. When I didn't respond, he took the cig out of his mouth and put it out on the counter. Then he continued, "Only the alfajor? The things I had to do to find those cookies . . ."

I handed him some money and looked back at the car. My father lifted his gaze to the rearview mirror, locked eyes with me, and then drove away.

20

THE FIRST PERSON I SAW AT EL BUEN PASTOR WAS KAREN reading by the window. The Alma Maritano book covered her face. The sight of her awakened a smile I didn't know I had in me.

Father Hugo had been right. It was all worth it just for the one.

Karen and I were on different paths headed in the same destination: freedom, a place as mythical as heaven. She looked like a younger version of me, poring over Alma's book, making sense of the secret code the author had woven into the pages for furious girls like us. If part of our souls stayed in the books we read and loved, I hoped Karen was getting some courage from the little Camila I'd once been.

Karen felt my eyes on her and looked up at me. She

didn't smile but held her finger up, asking for a second as she glanced back down at the book.

How many times had that same gesture ended in a fight with my mother? Too many to count.

Keep going, Karen. Keep going.

She turned the last page of the book and closed it softly, her little fingers caressing the worn covers. A satisfied sigh escaped her chapped lips. Her Mona Lisa smile made my eyes burn.

"Did you like it?" I asked.

Karen hugged the book against her chest. "Tell me there's more." I nodded, and she exclaimed, "Do you have the next one? I need more Nicanor and Gora."

I took *El Visitante* out of my backpack and placed it on the table carefully. "It's about Nicanor and Gora, but wait until you meet Robbie."

Karen leapt from the chair, raising her arms in the air like I did when I scored a goal. "Yes!"

The boys arrived in a whirlwind of shouts and smells. Apparently, a pipe had burst in el barrio, and now the street was flooded. Water had blocked the boulevard, and sooner or later, it would reach the sanctuary's entrance. I thought of our ruined practice field a couple of blocks away in Park Yrigoyen. How long would it take for the mud to dry before we could use it again?

"No mass tonight!" Javier said, high-fiving the air in front of Miguel, who hadn't reacted fast enough.

Karen sent them a scathing look before diving back into *El Visitante*. Lautaro and Javier eyed her suspiciously, but they left her alone.

Miguel grabbed me by the hand. "Come, Seño Camila." He pulled me toward the door. "You have to see this." His little face sparkled.

I wasn't remotely interested in seeing sewer water carrying toilet contents into the street, but I had no choice. I followed him. So did the rest of my class.

Diego stood under the balcony that overlooked the internal courtyard. Three giant plastic bags filled to bursting rested at his feet.

"Hey, Mama," he said. I'd have run into his arms to *fare l'amore con lui* in front of the Good Shepherd himself, but it was Karen's presence that forced me to mind my manners. What example would I be setting if I behaved like an airhead botinera?

"Hola, Diegui," I said.

If only there were a way to stay in this moment forever. If only the rest of the world didn't matter.

When I reached him, Diego kissed me on the corner of my mouth. He, too, seemed hyperaware of the kids watching us.

"I told you I'd find a way to say goodbye. Also, I brought some gifts," he said, and the kids shrieked with excitement.

"Order, order," Diego called. "Make a line next to Seño Camila." Then, in the most ridiculously seductive voice, he said to me, "Seño Camila, help me out with my balls."

The kids exploded into laughter, and I swatted his arm. From the corner of my eye, I saw Karen was trying not to smile.

Sister Cruz watched benevolently from the kitchen, where she was kneading bread. With this humidity, the dough would take forever to rise, but she was a woman of faith.

The kids lined up as if it were Christmas, and Diego gave away the contents of the bags. Footballs, sneakers, T-shirts, notebooks, pens, pencils. There was a package with stuffed Juve giraffes and other toys. He put that aside. "For Sister Cruz and her babies," he said.

Karen hovered at the end of line, *El Visitante* clutched against her body. When it was her turn, Diego asked, "A football for the little ones?" and she nodded. From the bottom of the duffel bag, he took out two backpacks, a black one and a pink one.

"Here's a backpack just for you, Señorita Karen."

Miracle of miracles, Karen's eyes shone like stars. "Can I . . . I choo . . . choose?"

"Of course. Whichever you want."

Without hesitation, she took the pink backpack and filled it with school supplies.

When Karen was done, she patted Diego on the arm. He met her eyes, and when she said, "Gracias," his whole face turned red.

She didn't hug him like the boys had, and Diego didn't pressure her to. She quietly walked to the classroom, but even though her backpack was bulging with stuff, her shoulders weren't slumped.

Diego asked the older kids to help Sister Cruz give out the toys for the babies.

And then, as if by magic, we were suddenly alone. I looked at my watch. If he was going to make his flight, he had to leave now.

Diego took me in his arms and held me tight until the world stopped spinning.

"I thought you had left already."

"How could I leave without saying goodbye? I had to see you," he whispered in my ear. "I want to take you with me right now. I want . . . so many things."

The kitchen door closed softly, and I sent a silent thank-you to Sister Cruz for the kindness. I raised my head and kissed him. I wanted to stop time with that kiss and believe we were breaking a curse. I wanted to reinvent our history, but then his phone rang, forcing us back to reality.

"I have to go," he said. "La Serie A doesn't stop in December. Why don't you come after graduation? Or as soon as your exams are over. You don't need to be at the ceremony."

"That weekend is the tournament."

His eyes narrowed almost imperceptibly. He was trying to remember what tournament I was talking about. Frustration roiled inside me, but Diego was leaving. I couldn't ruin this last moment with him.

"I'll come here, even if it's just for a couple of days," he continued, speaking fast, like he too could feel the time rushing past us. "There's a FIFA date in January, and I'll try to . . ."

In January there would be team signings. If I got what I wanted most of all, who knew where I'd be then?

Before I could put another wedge between us, I kissed him. How many times had my father promised my mother he wouldn't cheat on her? How many times had Pablo lied to girls for a moment of pleasure and then forget his promises as soon as he zipped up his pants?

If Diego could promise me anything, it was to be ruthless on the field. To never let his dreams go, because if he could make it, maybe I could, too.

He broke away first. "I brought you something, too."

I opened the black backpack he handed me. I must have looked like Karen as I rummaged through the T-shirts, shorts, socks, training jacket, and best of all, a pair of brand-new Adidas cleats in classic black and white.

"These won't give you blisters. And those shirts repel sweat, so they won't stink like your old ones. Camila, if we bottle that scent, we could sell it to the government as a weapon of mass destruction."

I didn't know how to thank him. He wouldn't have brought me all this stuff if he didn't believe in me, right?

"Gracias," I whispered, holding the boots against my pounding heart. "I can't play the scrimmage on Saturday, but—"

"You have to recover. Train harder every time. Don't give up," he said, and like that, I forgave him for forgetting my tournament.

He took out a slick cardboard box the size of a chalkboard eraser. "There's also this." When he opened it, the glass screen mirrored the shock on my face. It was a phone. The kind of phone not even Pablo could afford. The kind of phone boys in the streets literally killed for.

"Why?" I asked, while in my mind I was doing cartwheels. Now I could be part of all the team chats.

Diego's mouth curved into a smile.

"You need a phone, right? We'll be in touch. We'll talk every day. See? There are apps for music, and you can keep track of your trainings, and . . . we can talk all day long if we want to." He sounded like he'd been practicing that speech all week long.

"But the Wi-Fi . . ."

"I prepaid for service. There's an international plan with enough data that we can chat on WhatsApp all day." He misunderstood my stunned expression. "We *can* make this work, Cami. If you want."

"I do," I said. I wrapped my arms around his neck, careful not to drop the phone that was worth more than all my other possessions combined.

In my ears, the ghosts of my abuelas whispered like a Greek chorus that their dreams ended with those exact words—*I do*—but I pushed their advice to the bottom of my mind.

21

FROM DOWNSTAIRS, I WATCHED A MAN WALK OUT OF MY apartment. A black beret and a dark scarf covered his head and his face.

My mom was home alone. What was he doing?

Adrenaline jump-started me. Ignoring my hurt leg, I climbed the stairs two at a time. Just when I was about to reach him, my fists ready, he lifted his face. It was César. The fight left me in a rush. He pushed his thinning hair behind his ear.

"Princesa." His silver tooth glinted in the corner of his mouth when he smiled.

"César? What are you doing here?" My mind was trying to connect the dots, but no image formed.

Rain dripped from the metal railings, and from the corner of my eye, I saw movement in the downstairs neighbor's window. Franco waved at me from behind his grandma, who was peeking through the curtains.

"Hola, Doña Kitty," I said, waving, and she darted back.

César lifted his eyebrows. "These neighbors are better than the secret service, right? I think she's been keeping track of how long I was alone with your mom. Vieja de mierda."

I couldn't help it—I giggled. César was one of those people whose insults made me laugh instead of flinch.

"What were you doing?" I asked.

César shrugged and opened his denim jacket to show me a Juventus T-shirt. "For one thing, I hadn't seen Diego. He texted me that he'd be here, and I said I'd come over to say hi." César's eyes were sparkling. Now that he didn't have to pretend not to care about Diego in front of my dad, he was starstruck. "Then your mom and I kept talking. You know how it is." He always looked down when he talked about my mom, and I wondered why he tried to hide their friendship. But then, my suspicions, Doña Kitty's spying from behind the curtains—it was all proof that a friendship like theirs would always be an anomaly.

"You're not going to the game with my dad and Héctor?"

When he looked back up, sadness veiled his eyes. He said only "No," but the word hung in the air, as if waiting for me to guess what he couldn't say. He took a breath. Were my father's secrets fighting to stay put in the bottom of César's heart?

César had to know about that girl in the short dress. Had he been talking with my mom about my dad? But then he exhaled in a puff, ruffled my hair, and said, "You're going to get sick in this weather. Go in. Your mother is just starting el *mate*."

I nodded, realizing how my cold had vanished at the sight of Diego.

"You look just like she did at your age, you know? Be nice to her." He kissed me on the cheek and continued down the stairs, his hands pushed into the pockets of his jacket.

The melancholy of his words stuck to me like honey. When I walked into the apartment, Mamá looked up. When she saw it was me, the surprise on her face turned into annoyance, as if the mere sight of me had ruined her day. She reached for her phone, and the music playing died.

"You missed Diego."

All the intentions I had of being gentle with her disintegrated. Why was she so mean to me? Why did she take her anger out on me?

Then I noticed she was also wearing a Juventus T-shirt. The letters stretched across her breasts were a little distorted. The black and white showed off her curves. For a second, I got a glimpse of that young girl César had known. That girl whose dreams had died when she'd chosen to follow someone else's was buried under layers of expectations, responsibilities, and lies, just like I kept la Furia hidden. That girl had suffocated under all the rubble.

My anger collapsed in on itself. Twenty years from now, would that be me? Would I be resigned to my fate, pushing my daughter toward the light so she could be free? Or pulling her down so I wouldn't be alone in the dark?

I took my shoes off and left them next to the space heater.

"I know. César told me Diego came over."

My mom busied herself trying to thread a needle so thin it almost looked like she had nothing pinched between her fingers. "Ah, you saw him?"

I hobbled to the kitchen. "Yes. I didn't know he came over when Papá wasn't here." My voice sounded way more accusing than I had intended.

My mom looked up and shrugged. "Cesc and I grew up together. Almost like you and Diego."

What did she mean? That their relationship was like Diego's and mine because of how long they'd known each other? Or that there was something else? Did she have any idea what pictures her words brought to my mind?

"Diego stopped by El Buen Pastor, too," I said. "He . . .

he gave everyone presents. The kids were so glad. He brought this for me."

I showed her the backpack, because there was no point in hiding it. But I didn't mention the phone weighing down my jacket pocket.

She looked inside the backpack, her forehead wrinkled. "You could get quite a bit of money if you sell this. It's all name-brand clothes. With the tags, even."

"I'm not selling anything, Mami." I felt like Paola when she'd shown me the autographed picture.

"Suit yourself, but why would you need cleats?" my mom asked.

Since I couldn't heal my ankle without help, and getting back into shape was imperative, and keeping secrets was so exhausting, I decided to come clean.

"Look." I pulled down my pants and showed her the bruise that spread over my thigh and knee. It was like a green-and-purple map of misery.

My mom covered her mouth with her hand. I'd expected surprise, but not the flames of anger rising behind the fear. "Who did this to you?" She stretched out her hand, but before her fingers grazed my skin, I pulled the pants back up and rolled up one leg to show her my ankle.

"Camila, por Dios!" she exclaimed at the sight of my swollen foot. "How did this happen? Pablo said you fell in the street last night, but I had no idea . . . Did Papá . . ." She left the sentence hanging.

With a sigh, I lowered my foot and sat down next to her. "I have to tell you something."

Tears sprang to her eyes, but before she got carried away, I said, "I've been playing fútbol for about a year."

My mom sucked in air through her teeth. "You what?"

After a deep breath, I told her the rest of the story. "A while ago, I started playing in a night league with Roxana. She's a goalie. Her team needed a striker. I hadn't played since I was twelve, but I don't know . . . it all came back. Then this woman, Coach Alicia, saw us playing and invited us to join her team."

The more I spoke, the more my mom's face hardened. The paper napkin I'd been shredding made a little mountain on the tablecloth. "We played in a league championship game last Sunday. We won." I wondered if it was too pretentious to say we'd won because of me.

"We qualified for the Sudamericano tournament—a real FIFA tournament—it's in December, here in Rosario, and we—"

"We're going to Córdoba in December," she said. "Papi promised that after Pablo's last game and your graduation, we'd go to Carlos Paz for the holidays. Our first real family vacation."

"I'm not going anywhere." I shook my head. "Least of all with *him*. My team needs me."

Her mouth fell open.

"This coach from the U.S. saw me in a scrimmage

yesterday." My throat burned, but I talked through the pain. "She says I have something special."

My mom shook her head, her hand wiping nonexistent crumbs from the table.

"I know it's a long shot —"

"It's impossible. It's insanity. It's a waste of time!" She didn't have to raise her voice to topple my house of cards. "What about medical school, Camila? Have all your studies been for nothing? I have been sewing my fingers off so you could concentrate on school next year. I've been designing your dress for graduation. Since you didn't have a quinces party, I wanted to go all out for this."

My mother threw her sacrifices at me like knives.

"I haven't been studying for med school, Mami."

She cried out as if I'd stabbed her. I saw her dreams for me crumbling.

"You lied about med school? I've been telling everyone how proud I am of you. What will people say now, hija?"

But these were my dreams, not hers. Even if the path I chose led to more heartbreak, the decision would be mine.

"I'm sorry," I said.

I took the tournament forms from my backpack and placed them on the table. They were the same forms Pablo had filled out when he officially signed with Central. The humidity had curled the corners of the paper.

She glanced down at them. "Eva María?" she asked with a sneer. "What kind of team name is that?"

If I'd had any tears, I would've cried then. I was ready for my father's ridicule, for Pablo's, even, but not hers. Pushing my pride aside, I said, "I know it's not Central, Mami, but it's a good team. Coach Alicia is a good person. You'd like her."

She bristled at the mention of Coach. To her, any other woman was an enemy.

"And she does this out of the goodness of her heart? What's in it for her if, like you say, you do have something special and a team signs you?"

Usually, I knew what she wanted to hear. Now I was lost, so I stayed silent.

"I'm not signing anything until I meet this woman, Camila."

"My team has a scrimmage on Saturday. We can talk to her then."

"I can't go. Your brother has a game in Buenos Aires."

"But you don't even go to his games, Mami! You can listen on the radio or watch it later on TV."

Her eyes softened, but she shook her head. "Your father's gone tonight. He's traveling with the team. He needs to look this over and make sure you're not signing your life away to this woman."

She stood up and started clearing the table. My blood rushed in my ears, and I saw myself telling her everything: that my father had lied to her. He wasn't with the team. He was with that woman with the blond hair and high heels. I wasn't going to let him sign my papers and control my life like he controlled Pablo's.

Just when I was about to lose control of my tongue, she put a hand on my arm and said, "You need to get that leg seen. It looks horrible. How can you even walk?"

Who knew what kind of war was raging inside her while I fought my own?

"I just want to play, Mami." I tugged at my hair, trying to pull some of the pressure from my head. "Why is it so easy for Pablo, but for me it's a disgrace?"

She paled, and I was afraid I'd gone too far. If she had to choose between my brother and me, I didn't stand a chance. But then she shook her head and, surprisingly, brushed her hand across mine. "Remember that Christmas when you asked for a size five ball and you got a doll?" Her voice was soft. It always was when she traveled back in time to the days when Pablo and I were little and she was the queen of our hearts. She smiled. "You were what, eight or nine?"

"Nine," I said. I was in fourth grade. That was the year Roxana had moved to our school.

"I found you and Nico playing with the doll's head in the laundry, remember? You kicked, and he guarded the goal. I got mad at you and left you in the corner. After that, I went to my room and cried."

The mere thought of my mom crying had more power over me than any shout, threat, or sneer. It tore at my heart.

230

"Why did you cry, Mama?"

"Because you reminded me of myself when I was that age. My dad, bless his soul, never let me play. He didn't want me to become a lesbian. Can you believe it?" She dabbed at the corner of her eye with the inside of the Juventus jersey.

Seconds passed. I had nothing else to say. If she wasn't going to sign my papers, I needed another plan. Just as I was about to head to my room, she said, "Leave the papers. I promise I'll take a look. That way, I can prepare your father so he won't say no before you can explain."

Hope flared inside me like a torch. I had to give her something in return now. "I can still be a doctor if you want, Mami. I can do both, you know?"

My mom smiled through her tears. "Mamita, you can't have it all. You'll see."

Although I wanted to yell that this was the greatest lie told to girls like us for centuries, seeing the defeat in her eyes, I couldn't find my voice.

22

WHEN I WAS ABOUT TO FALL ASLEEP, DIEGO CALLED ME.
He'd set the ringtone for his number to the Central
anthem.

Un amor como el guerrero . . .

"Hola!" Even with everything going on, his name on
my screen had the power to make me smile. "You made it?"

"Hola, Mamita. I just got to Buenos Aires," he said.
"I'll be home in eighteen more hours, give or take . . .
hang on."

In the background, I heard muffled conversation.
Someone had recognized him, and he agreed to a picture. During the half hour we tried to talk, this happened
five more times. Everyone wanted a piece of this boy, and

things would only get worse—or better, depending on your perspective.

Between interruptions, I told him about my conversation with my mom and how my leg still didn't feel any better.

"I'll send you the contact information for a doctor at the polyclinic on Martínez de Estrada, across from the sports center in el barrio. Doctor Facundo Gaudio treated me back when I hurt my ACL, remember? He's also seen Pablo. Your mom will know about him. The polyclinic is free—"

A robotic voice announced the next flight to Rome.

"That's me." He couldn't quite hide the excitement in his voice. Like he'd said, he was going home.

"You're going to Rome first?"

The familiar envy snaked inside me again. I wanted to go to Rome. If I were another type of girl, I'd be there with him instead of staring at the humidity stain on my ceiling. But one day, maybe, it would be me getting on an airplane to join my own team.

"It's only a layover. Next time you'll be with me, right? The flight is too long to endure on my own." He was so cheesy that I started laughing.

"Listen, I'm sure there are plenty of girls who'd be more than willing—"

"I only want you, Furia. I've only ever wanted you."

I held my breath until the world stopped spinning, until I could stop myself from saying he was all I'd ever wanted, too. For a long time, that had been true. But it wasn't anymore. I wanted so much more than Diego's love or money could give me.

"Welcome, Mr. Ferrari," a young woman's voice said. "Have a safe flight, and thanks for flying with Aerolíneas Argentinas."

The interruption saved me from needing to respond.

"Have a safe flight, Mr. Ferrari," I said, imitating the woman's sultry voice. "I'll see you on TV next time."

He laughed. "I'll see you in my dreams and on FaceTime. Every day and every hour, know I'm thinking of you, and your lips, and those killer legs. And remember, next time, I won't come back to Italy without you. That's a promise. Te quiero, Furia. Get better soon. You owe me some shots."

He hung up before I could say anything, and I stared at the ceiling, half wanting to squeeze myself inside the phone and half relieved he was now far away.

There was a teacher's strike on Friday, which gave me a chance to stay off my hurt leg. My mom and I didn't talk about either Diego or my team, but I could think of nothing else.

The next day, I was restless.

Saturday mornings were chore mornings, but Mamá must have decided to sleep in, because the familiar sounds of the washing machine and her radio competing with the neighbor's music were absent.

Raindrops echoed in our apartment, which seemed empty without my brother and father. I stretched in my bed, careful not to overextend my leg. It still throbbed. The only other sound was Nico's breathing in the hallway between my room and my parents'.

Pablo was with the team. Central's game against Colón de Santa Fe was at three in the afternoon, and the bus wouldn't be back until late. My father was . . . who knew where?

Coach Alicia's words rang in my mind: *no days off.* Yesterday, I'd done some push-ups and sit-ups in my room. But today, my work for the team had more to do with the administrative aspect of the game than the physical one.

I had to convince my mom to sign the forms before my father came back.

By the time she got up, I'd already folded the laundry she'd left drying on the Tender by the space heater. I'd prepared her *mates* and gotten her favorite facturas from the bakery on the corner. I'd put away last night's dishes and swept and washed the floor. The kitchen smelled of strawberry Fabuloso. If only I knew how to make the tiny stitches for the hem of the dress she'd left on her worktable.

When she walked into the kitchen and saw her chores completed, her eyebrows rose with delight.

"You went down to the bakery on that leg?" she asked.

"I paid Franco with two dulce de leche facturas, and he went for me." I pulled a chair out for her like I'd seen waiters do in movies. She smiled as she sat and picked up a tortita negra, her favorite kind of biscuit. She grinned, black sugar dusting her smile. "I forgot how good these are." She patted the table and in a conciliatory voice said, "Come, sit with me."

We drank *mate* in silence, and then she said, "I've been thinking . . ."

I put my factura down on a napkin as she continued, "I felt like Pablo had no choice but to become a fútbol player. Once he started walking, he was always chasing after a ball." She swallowed as if the words were too bitter. "Abuelo Ahmed once told me you had a good foot, that he'd seen you playing with Diego and Pablo, and panic seized me." She clutched her shirt like she was trying to grab the fear still wriggling inside her. "When he saw how upset I was, he said you'd save us all."

My father's words about Pablo blared in my ears.

He'll save us all.

And Héctor's declaration: *He'll make us rich.*

I shook my head. I was just a girl with a strong will. A girl who told too many lies. How was I going to save us?

"I don't want you to save us, at least not in the way everyone else does. I want you to break the cycle, Camila. That's why I want you to go to school. Why I don't ever want a boy around you, even if that boy has a good heart and a good future and money. Fame and money eat good hearts like rust eats metal. Even the strongest perish, mi amor."

Before I could reply that Diego wasn't like that, she placed the forms on the table, her clear signature at the bottom.

"What's he going to say?"

We both knew who *he* was.

She placed a finger on my lips. I tasted the sugar from the pastry. "The hunger for money and power eat away like rust, too, hija. I love your father, but . . ."

She didn't finish her sentence, and I desperately wanted to know what she was going to say. But she loved me more? But she didn't trust him?

"No matter what, you can't play with that leg, hija."

"Diego said that Doctor Gaudio at the polyclinic could help?"

She wrinkled her nose. "He's kind of a jerk, but we'll go Monday. He's not in on the weekends. In the meantime, I know someone else who can help."

I trusted her. For the first time, I felt like she was my friend.

While my mom got dressed to go out, Roxana called the house to tell me the scrimmage was cancelled because of the rain, but the meeting was still on.

"It's better this way," she said. "You'll have time to rest your leg, and we can find a replacement for Sofía."

"Sofía left? Ay, our defense is destroyed."

"We'll find someone."

"We need more than some*one*. We'll need subs."

"Let's talk more at the meeting," she said. "Don't be late. Write down the address . . ."

My mom made a sign for me to hurry. I hadn't imagined she'd be ready so soon. I lowered my voice so she wouldn't hear me. "Send me a text. I got a new phone. Here's the number."

Roxana's surprise traveled through the line. "What? How?"

"Pablo." Roxana didn't press me for more information, and I left it at that.

"The taxi is waiting," my mom called. I hung up and joined her outside. The rain had stopped, but the fog was thick. I was basically inhaling water.

"A taxi? How far are we going, Mami?"

She pressed her lips together and winked at me. "You'll see."

In the taxi, she turned to the window with wonder, as if she had forgotten how powerful a Santa Rosa storm could be and how the city looked with its face washed. How long was it since she'd been out beyond Circunvalación?

We arrived at a nondescript house in Arroyito just as Central's game was starting. The streets were deserted, but I felt the energy and anticipation radiating from every house on the block as fans gathered around TVs, radios, computers, and phones.

An older lady opened the door. She smelled like cigarettes and roses. Seeing my mom, she clapped a hand over her mouth.

"Hola, Miriam," my mom said, a smile in her voice.

"Isabelita, nena! It's been too long! Since . . ."

My mom and the woman shared a charged look. Words seemed insufficient to describe the last time they'd seen each other. Then the woman turned her attention to me. Her eyes roved over me.

I averted my gaze as she scrutinized me, but her features were already imprinted in my mind. The deep wrinkles crisscrossing her face and the bright red lipstick contrasting with her white skin were not the marks of a witch, but there was something about her that screamed the word. Hair too golden to be natural framed her face in stiff curls.

"Nice to see the woman you've become, Camila." She had a deep smoker's voice. She moved out of the way so we could follow her into her house. "Last time your mom brought you here, you were seven months old and had pata de cabra." Her fingers gently touched my shoulder, urging me inside. Electricity zipped along my spine, stopping at the base of my back. I didn't remember this woman, but something inside me did. The door clicked closed behind us.

I tried to catch my mom's eye, but she didn't notice.

A set of rattan chairs and a sofa were the only furniture in the living room. A white cat peeked at me from the kitchen, but when I smiled at it, it hid behind a vase of lush devil's ivy.

"Carmelita likes you, but she's shy," the woman said. "She likes bright, pretty things."

My mom cleared her throat. "Thanks for seeing us so soon. This is urgent."

Miriam scanned me up and down. Her yellowish teeth flashed briefly in a sad smile. "You got it bad, don't you?"

I felt myself burning up. The image of Diego kissing me on the beach flashed in my mind, and Miriam laughed, clapping her hands.

"No, it's not that." My mom spoke too loudly to sound natural. "She has a sprained ankle. The doctor won't be in until Monday, and by then, you might cure her already?"

After a nod, Miriam motioned for us to take a seat. "You know better than that, Isabelita. I don't cure. It all depends on your faith and the will of the Lord. I'm just an instrument in the saints' hands."

"Which saints?" I asked, looking around to see if there was an altar, but she didn't even have a cross on the wall.

Miriam shook her head. "The saints that guard you. I can see their protection all around you, bonita. The prayers of so many are layered upon your head." She hovered her

240

hand over my hair. I felt a current of energy, of warmth, flow from her palm to my head. I shivered.

"It's the left leg?" she asked, her eyes looking beyond me. "A strained muscle, swollen tendons in your ankle."

I nodded, and she grabbed a handful of rice from a porcelain bowl that sat on the table. I looked at my mom for an explanation, and she smiled nervously.

Miriam dropped the rice into a cup of water. Immediately, most of it sank to the bottom, but five grains rose to the surface, making a circle that spun and spun.

The hairs on my arms prickled. Once again, I looked at my mom for an explanation. In reply, she placed a calming hand over mine. Miriam muttered under her breath, and a scent like a summer breeze enveloped us, bringing the smell of the Pampas's wildflowers and hierbabuena.

For a second, my whole body tingled. When the rice stopped spinning, Miriam took my hand firmly and closed her eyes. She muttered a prayer. Her nails dug into my flesh. I couldn't catch the words, but I felt they were good. Light came in through the window, falling on the three of us like a blessing.

When she was finished, Miriam smiled. She looked tired, the wrinkles under her murky green eyes more pronounced. "I'll pray again tomorrow and Monday," she said. "You don't have to be here for it, but try to rest the leg as much as you can."

"Will this work?"

Just like the boy who had sold me the estampita, Miriam shrugged. "It depends on your faith."

My mom opened her purse and took out a roll of bills, which she placed on the table.

Miriam's eyes dropped. "You don't have to, Isabel."

"I want to," my mom said. "You have cured my babies of empachos, pata de cabra, evil eye, and more. And me? You saved me last time. You helped me with my marriage, and I've never given you enough. Now that I can, this is the least I can do."

The corners of Miriam's mouth turned down. "Isabelita, that atadura . . . I regret doing it for you. It tied your husband down, but it tied you down more. I see it in your face."

My mom's eyes flickered in my direction, as if I were a child to be shielded from the truth. But I'd been a witness to her struggles with my father all my life.

My mom led me to the door, holding my hand tightly, and before I walked out, Miriam whispered in my ear, "Lies have short legs, guapa. Don't forget, or you won't run."

23

THE STREET THAT LED TO THE HEART OF BARRIO RUCCI WAS so crowded, the taxi driver had to let us out a block away from the community center. This wasn't an ideal meeting place, but it was free.

When we got out of the car, my mom looked across the street to the Natividad del Señor parish and crossed herself. Then she followed me. I tried to walk slowly, hyperaware of my injured leg, but I was too excited to hold myself back. The two most important women in my life, my mother and Coach Alicia, were about to meet for the first time. To my surprise, my leg didn't even hurt that much. Maybe it was my imagination, or maybe Miriam's prayers and rice were already working.

My mom and I followed the smell of fried bolitas de fraile and hot chocolate and the sounds of girlish chatter to the main room of the community center.

Surrounded by players and parents, Coach Alicia looked like she hadn't slept in days. When she saw me, relief flashed across her face. Her shoulders relaxed. She put her phone down on a table and came up to me, her arms outstretched. "Furia," she exclaimed. "You're here! You're here!" She hugged me tightly and kissed my cheek.

The self-assurance my mother had shown that morning was gone. She eyed Coach Alicia timidly.

"This is my mom," I said, standing between them. "Mami, this is Coach Alicia."

The two shook hands, and then Mamá smiled a little more confidently and leaned in to kiss Coach on the cheek.

Coach beamed at her and then said, "Thank you for letting Camila play. Five of my players have dropped from the team."

"Five?" I asked, dismayed. "Who?"

Roxana walked to my side and draped her arm over my shoulder. "You know about Sofía and Marisa. The others are Abril, Gisela, and Evelin."

"What are we going to do?"

Coach pursed her lips and pointed to the other side of the room with her chin. "Rufina, the girl from the Royals, brought a few of her teammates along. Carolina, Julia, Silvana . . . I forgot the other names."

Roxana added, "Milagros and Agustina."

My mom craned her neck to take a better look at Milagros and Agustina, who were holding hands, and when she turned back to Coach, she asked, "Are those girls . . . a couple?"

Coach Alicia put a hand up and said, "Señora, my players' personal lives are private and not subject to scrutiny. I think more than one person here is happy to have a full roster, right, Hassan?"

I flinched. "I didn't complain at all, Coach."

"I was just asking," my mom said, shrugging one shoulder.

I elbowed Roxana, who quickly changed the subject. "Carolina is a goalie, though. Another goalie? Aren't you happy with me?"

"I'm delighted with you." Coach laughed and ruffled Roxana's hair. "We need a plan B just in case, Chinita. But don't worry, you and Furia are irreplaceable."

My mom cleared her voice. "Furia?" Her eyes shone when she looked at me.

Roxana said, "Look at this, Señora Hassan." She placed her phone in front of my mom, showing her a video. The reporter, Luisana, spoke in the foreground, and images of my last goal of the championship game played behind her.

"They showed it on TV?" Mamá asked.

"They put it up online," Coach Alicia said. "It didn't go viral, but it's created some buzz for the team. Rufina recruited some Royals who know our style of play, but some players came from as far as Pergamino."

Yael joined our group. She watched the video play on a loop on Roxana's phone and said, "With la Furia and Coach Alicia, we have a good chance."

My mom looked at me as if I'd turned into a butterfly.

Suddenly, whispers rippled through all the Central fans in the room. The newcomers all seemed to be Lepers. No one screamed in victory, but the look of glee on their faces was obvious.

My mom checked her phone. "Ay, no," she whispered. "Colón just scored. Central's down by two now."

I locked eyes with Rufina. She smirked, and I felt heat rise to my cheeks. Coach Alicia saw everything and in her megaphonic voice said, "No, no, no. Señoritas, we're not doing this. When we're together, we're all Eva María. There won't be any Newell's or Central here."

"What about Boca and River? Or Independiente and Vélez?" said a dark girl who towered over everyone else in the room, including Coach.

"The goalie, Carolina," Roxana whispered in my ear.

Coach sent Carolina a look that made the girl shrivel. That'd teach her not to be cheeky with Alicia Aimar.

"Like I said, when we're together, we're all Eva María, and if anyone has a problem with that, she can walk out the door right now. We need players, but I assure you, if I send out a public call, I'll have enough candidates to make three teams. Don't try me." Her gaze swept across the room, and no one moved, not even the parents or Rufina's boyfriend or Luciano Durant.

There was another chime, and my mom looked down at her phone. She closed her eyes briefly but didn't say anything. Her reaction could only mean that Colón had scored again. Three to zero. Poor Pablo.

Coach Alicia continued, "Like I said, today is the last day to turn in the forms and the first payment. We'll play hard, play to win, and have fun. Claro?"

"Like water," the original Eva María players intoned. The newcomers joined in a beat too late, but now they knew for next time.

Parents, including my mom, swarmed around Coach with questions. Someone started playing cumbia through a speaker, and before long, the gathering resembled a party. Two of the newcomers—I assumed Milagros and Agustina—danced in perfect synchronicity.

The memory of Diego and me dancing by the river made me blush.

Roxana and Yael stood next to me, the three of us surveying the bubbling excitement rippling through the players, old and new.

"This team is stacked," I said, rubbing my hands.

"If everyone is one hundred percent by December, I think we have a chance," Yael said. "How's your leg, Furia?"

"My mom took me to a curandera. I should be better

by Monday." I laughed, but she lifted her eyebrows in plain disapproval.

Luciano walked up to us and added, "You still need to go to Doctor Gaudio. He can make sure you're totally okay." If anyone knew about being cautious with an injury like mine, it was Luciano. "In any case," he continued. "I told your mom I'm here to help you or anyone with anything you might need."

"Why, Mago?" I asked, unable to stop myself. "What's in it for you?"

He shrugged. "I want to coach. Why not coach women's fútbol? Once you explode, everyone will want a piece of the phenomenon."

Roxana stared at him.

My mom stepped into the group and, holding my arm and Luciano's, said, "Camila, since Yael lives in our barrio, Luciano agreed to be your ride to and from practices to make sure you're safe."

"On your motorcycle?" I asked, imagining the three of us squeezed on his Yamaha.

"I can give her a ride." Roxana said, an edge to her voice that my mom didn't seem to notice. "I've been doing it for a year."

"I can just take the bus," I offered.

But my mom wouldn't listen. "Thank you, Roxana, but I don't want you to drive all the way into el barrio and then out again. It's settled. One hand washes the other, and both wash the face. I told Luciano I'd pay for the gas for his new car."

"New car?"

Luciano shrugged, his freckled face mottled with embarrassment. "Just a Fiat 147. It's not a BMW." Like there had been an invocation, Diego's presence suddenly loomed gigantic among us. I avoided everyone's eyes. Luciano continued, "But it does the job. I'll be driving Yael anyway, so really, Furia, it won't be a problem."

"In that case, I guess I'm in." My mom smiled at this small victory.

Roxana glared at me. "I'll go tell my mom not to worry, then. She was already making plans for nothing."

My mom, seeing Mrs. Fong for the first time, exclaimed, "María!" and ran after them.

Luciano stared at Roxana's back.

He *liked* her.

Poor boy. He didn't have a chance.

———

I hadn't felt this close to my mom since elementary school. In the taxi back to the barrio and then at home, she didn't stop talking.

"I have to say, I'm impressed with Coach Alicia. She has a good system. And the respect you girls have for her is palpable! Of course, the respect is mutual, because she stood by those two girls holding hands in front of everyone.

Times are changing." She sounded like she'd been asleep for decades and was just waking up to a new world.

For a moment, I considered sitting down next to her, putting my head in her lap, and telling her about Diego and me, and then, if I was brave enough, asking her what Miriam had meant about an atadura, a binding. But after we ate, she turned the TV on. The commentators were shredding Central.

"What's wrong with the Stallion?" Luisana asked.

"What does she know about fútbol, anyway?" my mom hissed from her worktable. But Luisana had been the one to compliment my skills.

Another commentator added, "Pablo had a great opener, but this game was laughable. Lately, Hassan hasn't been the player we saw last season in Rosario. He looks tired; he can't run. Look at that!" The TV showed a clip of Pablo missing a high pass. "He lost every ball he touched."

My mom closed her eyes in agony, and then she switched the TV off. She left the dress unfinished in the kitchen. Quietly, she locked herself in her room, and when I got the message that she wouldn't return, I went to my own.

Nico followed me. I wanted to comfort my mother, tell her that those commentators had never stepped on a pitch and didn't know what it took to perform at the top every game. But no matter what I said, it wouldn't be enough.

In my room, I looked at my phone for the first time

all day. Roxana would believe that Pablo had bought it for me, but my mom would know who it was really from.

I turned it on. The screen glowed in the semidarkness of my room as notification after notification popped up and made the phone vibrate. Nico's ears perked in alarm.

"Shhh," I warned him, a finger to my lips. "Don't give me away. It's that silly boy sending me stupid love notes." I covered my mouth with a fist to stop the giggles from escaping.

Part of me felt guilty that I was euphoric even though my brother had played an awful game, but how could I help it? My mom knew about my team and supported me, and Diego loved me, even if he was far away.

Miriam's warning echoed in my mind, but I pushed it down, down, down to fester along with my worry for my brother and dread over what my father would say if he ever found out my mom was my agent and manager.

I unlocked the phone and scrolled to Diego's first message. It was a picture of him, his hair rumpled, his eyes tired but still shining. The ocean inside me rippled with pleasure.

> Just arrived. The mister wants me to
> report to practice tomorrow. I can't wait but
> I think I have a cold. Wish me good luck.
> When's your next game? Score a goal for
> me and I'll score for you! Te quiero.

After that, he'd sent a link to an article about famous couples who were both successful in their careers. The first picture was of Shakira, no introduction needed, and Gerard Piqué, the Barcelona defender. She was *by far* the more famous of the two. To compare Shak and Geri to us was totally apples and oranges.

And that's what I texted him: emojis of apples and oranges and a meme that said KEEP TRYING.

Instantly, he replied with a laughing emoji.

It was midnight in Turín, four hours ahead of Rosario. He should be in bed, especially if he was sick.

What about the other couples? he asked.

I scrolled down.

Mia Hamm and Nomar Garciaparra had been divorced for years. When I told Diego, he sent me a picture of his laughing and dismayed face. I brushed my hand over the screen, longing to touch him.

The next couple was Alex Morgan and her husband Servando Carrasco.

How did those two make it work while playing on teams on opposite coasts? Would Diego and I ever be able to pull that off?

I replied with a picture of me wearing just the Juventus jersey and a caption that said, **I like this couple much better. She's a world champion, and hardly anyone knows who he is.**

The three dots at the bottom of the screen made me nervous. Maybe I'd offended him. It had been a joke, but not really. Was it really so outlandish to suggest that maybe one day I'd be more famous than he was?

Finally, his answer came, **I won't be able to go to sleep now knowing you're wearing my jersey in your dark room. You're cruel, Furia.**

I sent him a laughing emoji, and he replied with, **Soooo jet-lagged. So tired. Dream of me.**

He hadn't really said anything about my comment.

I missed his lips on mine. His strong arms around me. The smell of his hair.

Dream with the angels, I texted him and put the phone away.

MY FATHER'S VOICE THUNDERED FROM THE KITCHEN AND
woke me with a start. I pulled the phone from underneath
my pillow: it was three a.m.

Witching hour, when demons come out to wreak
havoc, babies' fevers spike, and Death calls to collect her
souls.

"What I don't understand is what she went there for,"
my father yelled.

"Andrés, please," my mom begged. "Let's talk tomorrow, mi amor."

"You, shut up!" My dad's voice reverberated through
the house.

I held my breath so he wouldn't know I was awake.
Would the new doorknob and chain protect me?

"Leave her out of this." Pablo sounded exhausted. When had he gotten home? "Mami, go to bed."

I listened to my mother's footsteps rush through the hallway, but I didn't hear her go into her room. She must have been waiting, ready to jump back into the kitchen. I should have gone to comfort her, but I stayed in my bed like a coward. We'd been so happy with him gone.

"Just explain to me why she went to Santa Fe. Don't you turn your back on me!"

I clung to my covers. Pablo was a man, but since he still lived at home, he had to take this. I strained to hear my brother's answer.

"She just went to the game. Is it so hard to imagine than she wanted to see me play?"

"But why, Pablo? You already spend all the time you're not playing with her. Do what you want with her! I don't blame you if you're constantly fu—"

"Stop talking about Marisol like that!" my brother snapped, but my father just laughed at him.

"So it's true. You were just with her."

Pablo didn't answer. I imagined his anguished face, his tight fists, all the words stuck in his throat, choking him.

My dad continued, "She'll leave you if you aren't on the first team, if you don't make enough money. You know that, right? Save your little *meetings* for after the games, or you won't last another season. Do you want to end up working in the factory with me, like Luciano Durant?" If

I listened carefully, I could find a hint of concern in my dad's voice. "When she runs to Diego because you're a nobody, don't come crying to me."

"¡Basta!" Pablo yelled.

I threw my covers off and stood next to my closed door.

Stop, Pablo. Go to bed. Go to Marisol's.

But Pablo remained in the kitchen.

"The news is all about him. Diego this, Diego that, and he wasn't even playing!"

Pablo was crying now. The sound pierced me, and I unlocked the door, my breath ragged and painful.

Finally, my brother managed to say, "He's the pride and joy of the city, me included."

His voice was like ground glass in my ears.

"He's a nobody! No family, no past. I've always been beside you, Pablo. Always!" My dad changed tactic and said softly, "Don't throw this talent away, son. Think of your poor mother." As if *he* ever thought of my *poor* mother. "You will break her heart. Control that girl. Put fútbol first. Don't be the idiot I was, letting a woman ruin your life."

"She's pregnant," Pablo said. "It's done. Marisol's pregnant."

I hoped against all reason that my mom wasn't listening to this.

"She finally got what she wanted!" my father yelled, making me shudder. "She's only after you for the money. You're an idiot, Pablo, just like I was an idiot when your mother ruined my life, tying me down with a baby. Why, why did God curse me with such useless children!" He huffed like a bull. "Mark my words, Pablo—Marisol won't see a cent from your contract. Not one coin!"

Without thinking, I stormed into the hall. The despair on my mom's pale face turned into horror when she saw me. "No, Camila. Go back to your room."

She tried to pull me back, but I shrugged off her hands. *No more, Mami. No more.*

"Pablo," I said, my voice stronger than I felt. "Go. Go now. You don't have to take this anymore."

My dad laughed, but I was ready for him.

"And you? You talk about my brother being an idiot when you . . ." I couldn't catch my breath. I was drowning. "How could you? How *dare* you?"

The ridicule died on his lips. He knew what I was talking about. He'd seen me at the kiosco, hiding behind my umbrella. He knew what he'd done. And he also must have known I wasn't the weak girl he could manipulate and abuse anymore. I had things to tell. With a sneer, he walked past me as if I were a thing too insignificant for him to care about.

Instead, he towered over Pablo and in a dismissive voice said, "Go to your room, Pablo. We'll speak more tomorrow. I can't deal with your sister's hysterics." But my father was the one who headed to his room, slamming the door behind him, the lock turning ominously.

Pablo turned to me, outrage on his face, and said, "I had everything under control!" He shook like a wet duckling. This terrified boy was going to be a father. And everything he knew about being a father was based on the man who had just stormed away.

Behind me, my mom stood like a salt statue. Nico stayed next to her, and he whined before curling up at her feet.

We were all safe, but my brother and my mom didn't thank me for stepping in. Instead, they both looked at me like I was deranged.

Without another word, I went back to my room. I lay on my bed in silence, regretting the burst of courage that hadn't really accomplished anything.

At five in the morning, my period started after not coming for two full months. I peeked out my door to make sure it was safe to go to the bathroom and put a pad on. I rolled up my stained underwear and put it inside a plastic bag, which I placed on top of the bathroom window. I'd have time to wash it in the morning.

I stayed awake, watching the shadows on the wall fade as dawn approached. I tried to pray for my brother, for my mom, even for my dad, but the words died on my lips.

I didn't have enough faith. Getting away from this, far from my dad's reach, was the only way I could survive. I wouldn't be like Pablo.

———

My brother left before dawn. I'd hoped for a chance to talk to him, to make sure he was okay. But he surprised me.

I imagined him packing his brand-name clothes and his *Dragon Ball Z* figurines before he vanished like a ghost at the sight of the sun. I was happy for my brother and proud of him, but part of me seethed. Now that he was about to have his own family to take care of, he'd left me behind.

My underwear was gone from the bathroom window. I hoped it hadn't fallen, because then Nico would've for sure found it. Slowly, I ventured out to the kitchen. Although my leg felt better than it had yesterday, my whole body was sore from bracing for my father's explosion.

The expectation had been worse than the actual fight.

My mom sat on her throne, Nico at her feet. She and I looked at each other. It felt like we were both washed-up shipwreck survivors. She wasn't sewing today. She just sat by the window, nursing the *mate* in her hands. Usually after one of her fights with my dad, she looked wounded, teary, but now she just looked defeated.

A cramp stabbed me, and I pressed my hand against my belly.

My mom smiled, and her eyes turned velvety, soft, grateful. "Gracias a Dios your period came. I was praying you wouldn't be pregnant, too, mi amor . . . I don't want you to go through what Marisol will suffer. Stupid girl!"

My face went hot. If I were a cartoon, steam would have been coming out of my ears. "Why would you be afraid I was pregnant?" My voice cracked. "My period's always irregular."

She shrugged one shoulder and waved my embarrassment away with a hand. "Camila, I was seventeen once and in love with a boy everyone wanted. The difference was that I gave in to the love, and I fell."

"I'm not stupid," I said. She hunched her shoulders, and immediately I wanted to take the words back. But it was too late.

My mom passed me a *mate*, a gesture to show me my comment hadn't offended her. "No. You're not like me," she said, tapping at her phone. "You're smart enough to go to the university. And because you were born under a star, you also have the chance to play fútbol. Fútbol, of all things. You have many opportunities . . . don't waste this chance."

Maybe if someone else had said those words, I would've accepted the advice. But coming out of her mouth, it sounded like an accusation.

She rose from the chair and headed to the bathroom. Her phone was unlocked, resting by the thermos. I looked at it, and blood rushed to my head, making me dizzy.

On the screen was a picture of Diego and me at the beach a few days ago. We were on our knees, my head was thrown back, and his mouth was on my neck.

A picture was supposed to be worth a thousand words, but this one didn't contain the beauty of finally being with him, the thrill of feeling him tremble when I touched him, or the glimpse I had into a limitless future in which we could dominate the world together.

Instead, it showed a girl selling herself for a chance with . . . what had my mom said? A boy everyone wanted.

All the other girls, las botineras whom I'd always looked down on—what were their stories, their feelings and intentions? What got erased by scandalous pictures?

I clicked on the screen and saw the picture had been posted on one of those wives and girlfriends gossip blogs that twisted every relationship a footballer might have for clicks and likes.

I ran to my room and grabbed my phone. There were hundreds, if not thousands, of accounts dedicated to footballers' romantic lives. I found whole profiles devoted to Diego's every move, and the picture of us by the river was on all of them.

Working-class boy, one of the accounts described him. *Workhorse who doesn't party like the rest of the players his age. Who's el Titán hiding? Who's that girl?*

I felt sick.

Before I could make myself stop looking, I got a text from Roxana.

> **Really, Camila? You weren't going to tell me at all? What game are you playing, huh?**

I called her four times, but she never answered.

25

BY THE TIME I MADE IT TO DOCTOR GAUDIO, THE MASTER healer of torn muscles and other athletic afflictions, a week after my injury, my leg was almost back to normal. I didn't really want to go, but Coach Alicia wouldn't even let me practice again without a doctor's note. My mom was too busy pining after Pablo, who refused to come to the house even if my father wasn't there, to come with me. So I skipped school and went to the polyclinic by myself.

I sat in the hard plastic chair, trying to ignore the nurses and receptionists as they drank *mate* and chatted. They didn't seem to notice the line of people who had gotten up before the sun to see a doctor.

Diego texted, encouraging me and trying to distract me. This clinic couldn't possibly compete with the photos he sent of his medical checkups at the Juventus headquarters. The brightness of the futuristic facilities dazzled me through the screen. And I didn't want his pity. He'd sat in this waiting room plenty of times before, but time and distance softened the sharpest edges of even the worst situations. When he said he actually missed the polyclinic, I told him I'd text him later.

I caught the eye of a mom sitting across from me, holding her crying baby on her lap. I couldn't tell how old the little boy was, but he had big brown eyes and even darker hair. He cried in a monotone, yellow snot running from his nose to his chin. His chubby cheeks were chapped from the cold. I wondered what Pablo's baby would look like, and I imagined Marisol here with him. Or her.

My mom thinking I'd ever want to become a doctor was proof of how little she knew me. I wasn't made for this calling.

It was almost noon by the time the receptionist called my name. A nurse weighed me, measured me, and then led me to an examination room. Like the reception area, the walls were covered in peeling eggshell paint. It smelled like creolin, antiseptic, and humidity.

"Come in, Hassan," said Doctor Gaudio, a white man who looked to be in his late forties. His salt-and-pepper hair was long for a guy his age. His smile was tired, and his fingers and teeth had the characteristic yellow tinge of nicotine.

"Good to meet you, Doctor."

He got straight to the point. "What's going on?" After visiting Miriam, I could see why my mother found him abrasive. He leaned against an examination table covered in a gray sheet that should've been retired long ago. He motioned for me to sit on the table and took a seat next to an ancient computer.

"I . . . got injured playing fútbol, and my coach won't let me play without a doctor's note."

His eyes brightened. "You play fútbol? Following in your brother's footsteps?"

"I wouldn't say that . . ." I realized that if I were following in anyone's footsteps, it was my father's. Both Pablo and I had devoted our lives to our father's sport. I didn't know what that said about us.

After a few seconds of uncomfortable silence, Doctor Gaudio said, "Show me the injury. I didn't notice you limping or favoring one foot when you walked in, but I've been surprised before."

I didn't know how to do what he was asking, so I just stared at him. After a minute, he understood, and his face softened. "Just a second." He walked toward the door, opened it, and hollered, "Sonia! Come here for a minute."

Sonia came straight away. She'd been one of the nurses drinking *mate* and laughing behind the counter, but now she seemed attentive. "What do you need, Facundo?"

"Please stay here while I examine her."

Sonia nodded, and after a quick glance in my direction, she stepped into the room.

I pulled down my warm-up pants and sat on the examination table. Although the leg didn't hurt anymore, the bruise still looked like a rotten steak. I caught the look that passed between the doctor and Sonia and felt the need to explain. "I got cleated during my championship game," I said too quickly. "This girl was a steam engine . . . and then I stepped in a hole . . ." I stopped talking before I sounded more ridiculous than I already did.

He pressed his lips into a hard line, but his eyes remained soft. "May I?"

Sonia observed from the corner of the room with a somber expression on her face.

I nodded, and he inspected my thigh. I hadn't noticed him putting gloves on. The doctor pressed softly on the bruise and asked, "Does this hurt?"

"No," I said, suddenly terrified that the reason it didn't hurt anymore was because it was injured beyond repair. The doctor checked my ankle next, turning my foot, but that didn't hurt either.

He exhaled and smiled tightly. "I think it's a good idea to do some X-rays to rule out any fractures, especially in your ankle, but I'm pretty sure that it looks a lot worse than it actually is. I guess a truly gifted curandera did her job right."

I knew better than to admit I'd gone to a curandera in front of the doctor. Still, I felt like I owed him an explanation. "My brother and Diego Ferrari and even Luciano Durant, remember him? They told me to come here. Luciano is my coach's assistant . . . and . . ."

"And Diego Ferrari is your 'friend'?" Sonia asked. The way she said *friend* made me want to curl up like a potato bug.

"Sonia will take you to the radiology room," the doctor said, and I could tell he was trying not to smile.

I pulled my pants back up, but before I left the room, he coughed softly. I turned to look at him.

"Camila . . . if there's something other than fútbol going on, know that you have options."

"I got cleated and then I fell," I said, dismayed that after everything I'd said, he still hadn't believed me.

The doctor turned his palms up in a conciliatory gesture. "In the case that these injuries are the result of a particularly vicious opponent and mere distraction, I advise that you warm up and cool down properly. Eat plenty of protein. Sleep well. Drink water. But then, Pablo, Diego, and Luciano will have already told you all this. But in case there's something else a curandera can't cure with a handful of rice or a measure of ribbon, then know that there is help out there. Regardless of the way the news makes it seem, there is help for girls and women like you . . ." He paused, swallowed. And then he added, "There is help for you and your mother."

A whirlwind of anguish opened up under my feet. I hadn't ever seen my father hit my mother, but what did I know?

"Thank you," I said, and followed Sonia to the X-ray room.

26

ON SATURDAY, I HEADED TO THE SCRIMMAGE WITH
Luciano and Yael. They made a perfect team. Yael served
as lookout. Luciano drove like a Formula 1 racer, dodg-
ing a horse-pulled garbage cart first and then a brand-new
black Jeep Cherokee. All around me, there were reminders
of Diego.

The cousins chattered like parrots and never forced me
to chime in.

Pablo and I had once been like that. Now he didn't
respond to my texts. Neither did Roxana.

I texted Diego to see if he'd heard anything from my
brother, but he didn't reply, either. He must have been
training. It was the day before his first home game of the
season, after all.

By the time we arrived at the indoor field, I was feeling carsick.

Mr. Fong waved at me from his parked car. I waved back and headed to my first official scrimmage since my injury.

Coach Alicia had let me sit out practices, but now that I had the doctor's green light, it was time to gear up for the Sudamericano.

I was used to having Roxana next to me as we warmed up, but now the team was divided into two camps: Roxana's and Rufina's. I was in neither. I stretched by myself between the two groups, the target of vicious looks from Rufina's girls and of Roxana's cold indifference. Yael and Cintia looked at me and smiled awkwardly.

Coach Alicia grabbed my doctor's note. She studied it as if trying to see if it was a fake. Typical Alicia, but there was something wrong with her, too. Like repelling magnets, the more I tried to approach her, the more she pulled away from me.

She nodded and pointed me to the center mid, my least-favorite position. Without protesting, I ran in. We were facing a team of boys a little younger than us, but they looked like baby giants. Gangly, pimply-faced giants.

The whistle blew, and the game started. I couldn't find my feet on the turf pitch. I tried to summon Furia, but the spark wouldn't ignite.

Half the team yelled directions at me, and the rest gloated over my downfall.

Finally, Mía passed me a good ball, but my first touch was off, and I lost it to the other team. A blond, soft-cheeked boy grabbed it, dribbled through our defense, and scored. I felt like the industrial ceiling of the warehouse was falling on me.

"Sub!" The cry came, as I knew it would. I didn't look to the bench, because I didn't want to see Coach Alicia's disappointed eyes.

Mabel went in for me, but she didn't even slap my hand as I went out. Instead, she shoulder-checked me so hard I staggered.

"What's wrong with you?" I yelled.

She flipped me off.

Speechless, I finally looked at the bench. Luciano pretended he was studying one of his charts. None of the girls looked at me, their attention focused on the game, but Coach Alicia's laser eyes made me shrink.

"What?" I asked, and I regretted it instantly. As the team captain, disrespecting the coach was a capital offense.

Coach Alicia only scoffed and turned to watch our team. Roxana saved a killer shot. "Good job, Roxana!" she shouted, and in a softer voice, she told Luciano, "She's the only one improving consistently."

Luciano sent me an accusing look, like it was my fault the whole team was floundering. Couldn't *I* have one bad day? It was just a practice.

Coach never put me back in, and we ended up tying, thanks to Roxana at the goal, and Yesica, who scored at the last second.

The girls looked to be in better spirits than the boys, who didn't take the tie gracefully, mumbling loudly enough for everyone to hear that they went easy on us.

A tall, dark-skinned striker who reminded me of Pablo at that age told Luciano, "It was a lose-lose situation for us. We can't celebrate a win against a girls' team, and if we lost, imagine the shame. It's against a *girls'* team."

Luciano grimaced. "Loco, it's just a scrimmage. Get it together, man. Your balls aren't going to shrivel up and fall off."

He was spending so much time around us.

The boy smirked but didn't say anything else and walked off.

I told Luciano to head out without me. "Sure," he said without pressing me for details, and followed Yael.

My team left one girl at a time, but I knew to wait for Coach to apologize, at the very least.

Roxana left without glancing my way. Even though I was watching her like an alma en pena.

I needed her there next to me, telling me I had the right to one bad day.

Finally, Coach Alicia turned toward me, took a long breath, and said, "What's all this talk about Diego Ferrari taking you to live with him when he comes home for Christmas? Is all your work, *my* work, going down the drain, Camila? Is this team a distraction until he comes back to whisk you away?"

When she put it like that, it sounded ridiculous.

"He's not coming home for Christmas."

Coach didn't look impressed. "Camila, when the river sounds, it's because it brings water. I know you and Diego have something. My sister is moving heaven and earth to publicize the tournament with the NWSL scouts for you. Are you going to throw it away? Diego's a good boy, but I'm . . . disappointed."

I didn't care if the rest of the world was disappointed in me, but I couldn't take this from Coach.

"It was one bad scrimmage in months, after an injury, and all of a sudden I'm throwing my team and all my opportunities away? I'm one hundred percent in."

Coach Alicia wasn't one for sentimentalities, but she patted my shoulder and said, "In your world, Furia, one mistake can be fatal. Keep your goal in sight. Keep your priorities straight, and it will all be worth it. I promise."

Father Hugo and the kids didn't expect me at El Buen Pastor on Saturdays, but Coach Alicia's words felt like too heavy a burden to carry on my own. Roxana had always helped me process the messes at home and at school. Without her, I had no one to talk to.

Diego and I could text all day long, but when he asked me why Roxana was angry, I didn't want to unload my drama on him. He didn't need to worry about my problems, and deep down, I didn't want him to. What could he do from the other side of the world?

I didn't want to go back home. Mamá would be there, quietly working in the corner, a Penelope who refused to accept her Ulysses was a monster. She constantly moped over how much she missed Pablo and blamed me for him leaving. El Buen Pastor, once a prison for incorrigible daughters, was now the only place where I felt welcome.

A group of kids played fútbol in the dappled sunshine of the inner courtyard. Sister Cristina was the goalie for one of the teams, and when she blocked a shot, all the kids ran to her in celebration. She saw me and waved happily before turning back to the game. Lautaro was already kicking off again.

My eyes prickled. I had forgotten how beautiful fútbol was. Without referees, lines on the ground, trophies, tournaments, or life-changing contracts, the ball was a portal to happiness.

A little hand tugged at my sleeve.

"Seño, do you want to play goalie for my team?" Bautista asked. His brown eyes were huge, his little face flushed from the exercise. His invitation was tempting, but I could hear voices coming from my classroom.

"I'm having fun watching, but thank you," I replied.

"You come in if you get tired of standing here like a palm tree, okay?" He ran back to his team, his too-big Juventus jersey flapping around him.

In my classroom, Karen sat at the head of the table, my usual spot. She didn't stutter as she read from *Un Globo de Luz Anda Suelto*. It was as if a new Karen had emerged.

Five other girls encircled her, hanging on her every word. They were all about the same age, that awkward stage right at the beginning of puberty. Baby faces, budding breasts, bashful eyes. Dark-haired golden goddesses with the latent power to change the world if given one chance.

Their enraptured faces turned to Karen as if she were the sun, the light in her voice germinating the seeds Alma's words planted. I tried not to make a sound. I didn't want to break the spell.

Eventually, one of them looked up, and, puckering her lips, pointed in my direction. Karen felt her friends' restlessness and followed their gazes. When she saw me, she smiled, her nose crinkling adorably.

"Seño," she said, "The girls kept asking about the books, and I told them it was b-b-best if I read to them."

Bautista, followed by a younger boy with Down syndrome, burst into the room and bellowed, "Time for the semifinal!"

The girls turned toward Karen, and she rolled her eyes but nodded. One by one, they left in respectful order, then broke into a run once out the door.

"What was that all about?" I asked, sitting next to Karen, who'd placed a bookmark on her page, put the book away, and taken another from the pink backpack Diego had given her. It was *Locas Mujeres*, by Gabriela Mistral. I hadn't read it, but the title alone made me laugh.

"Karen," I said, "where did you get that one?"

"The library," she said, chin lifted high. "There's a version with the English translation, but I don't like it as much, so I'm doing my own translation."

"And why weren't you reading this to the girls?"

She scoffed. "Apostle Paul says that first, you must feed the babies with milk, and then, when they're ready, you give them meat."

I shivered. I wasn't worthy to stand in her presence. "You're amazing."

She blushed. "So are you, Maestra Camila." Then she hesitated. At first, I thought it was her stutter, but then I realized she was trying not to offend me. "Are you going to leave us, too? Are you going to go live with Diego in It–Italy?"

Now I was the one having a hard time finding the right words. "Diego and I . . . we've loved each other since we were little kids, you know?"

"Like Nicanor and Gora?" she asked.

"Like Nicanor and Gora," I said. "But I have my own dreams, too. I play on my own fútbol team. I want to play professionally one day."

Her eyes widened at the revelation. "But you're so smart! You speak English. You go to school; you have choices."

"I like to play, and I happen to be very good at it. I have choices, and fútbol is my choice. I won't ever give up when I have a chance to make it."

"Not even for Diego?"

"Not even for him."

"Does he know yet?"

"I'm following my own path, chiquita."

"But he's your true love." Karen sounded like any little girl hoping for a happily ever after. When she saw me, she saw her teacher, a role model to follow. I didn't want her to think that to be free and happy, a woman had to turn her back on love, but I didn't know how to do both.

Outside the window, the frogs and crickets sang to the setting sun. "He said he'd wait for me."

Karen nodded slowly.

She was only ten. She wanted to believe that love was possible for crazy, incorrigible girls like us.

27

AT THE END OF A SCRIMMAGE ON A MUGGY NOVEMBER morning, Coach Alicia gathered the team. The months of preparation had blurred by, and the tournament was almost here. I gave Luciano an envelope containing my second payment, and he distributed copies of the final schedule for the games. For the next thirty minutes, Coach went over our rivals: Praia Grande, Tacna Femenil, and Itapé de Paraguay. Praia were the defending champions, but Tacna and Itapé were new to the tournament, like us. Two teams from our group would move on to the next phase. After semis, one would claim the trophy in the final. Somewhere in Brazil, Perú, and Paraguay, similar groups of dreaming, hopeful girls must have been wondering what kind of team Eva María was. They would see soon enough.

Rufina and I had a competition going to see who could score the most, and I was still soaring off a hat trick that had put me ahead. The outcome of the games didn't matter—we played to get minutes—but it felt good to be in the lead.

"Nice goal," Rufina said when the scrimmage ended, the corner of her mouth twitching. From her, this was basically a full-on friendly smile.

"Start from zero on game one?"

"You're on!" We shook hands to seal the deal.

The team's mood was bubbling, and Coach Alicia looked like she had gained an extra five years of life. A winning mindset was the road to victory, she always said.

In front of me, I saw Roxana's eyes sparkle, but when I tried to get her attention, she turned around and left. I watched her walk away with Cintia and Yesica. They'd been riding to practices and scrimmages together for weeks. The jealousy didn't torture me anymore, but I still missed her.

The team scattered, everyone studying their packets, as if reading and rereading the schedule would give them a glimpse into the future.

As I was leaving, Coach Alicia called me aside and said, "Now, Furia, if you play the tournament the way you've been playing in the scrimmages, we'll be set."

"I'll do that," I said, and laughed to hide how much her words of encouragement affected me.

"Are you and Roxana still not talking?" she asked, her voice uncharacteristically soft.

The question took me aback, but I was glad she'd asked.

"We're not," I said.

"Not even at school?"

I crossed my arms tightly. "Not anywhere. She didn't let me explain about Diego when I tried. She'll never forgive me for keeping it secret, but she doesn't understand."

Coach gathered up the gear and slung it over her shoulder like Papá Noel.

"You're right about that. She doesn't understand, but at the same time, remember that your life is yours, Furia. At the end of the day, are you playing for yourself or to prove others wrong? Love is the same."

"So now you're telling me that this thing with Diego isn't the worst idea?"

We headed toward her car, and I helped her load equipment into the trunk.

Finally, she said, "I don't know about that. What I mean to say is, fútbol is life, but so is love, and so is family. My intent in coaching the team was never to create fútbol-playing machines. I know how much all of you sacrifice to play. I just wish you weren't so hard on yourself."

"But maybe it's better this way, Coach. The rest of my life is a mess, but at least on the pitch I get to do what I love."

Coach placed a hand on my shoulder. "And you've been amazing."

I glowed with satisfaction, but it dimmed when she added, "It's just that there's something missing."

I'd tried to do everything right. I'd been sleeping well, eating better, cutting out distractions. Without Roxana, I hardly ever talked to anyone other than the kids at El Buen Pastor and Diego. Even when he traveled for Champions League games, we always spoke before he went to sleep.

Last night, he'd said, "If your voice is the last sound I hear and your beautiful face is the one I see before falling asleep, then I dream of you. That way we're always together."

Butterflies danced in my stomach at the memory of his words.

"What am I missing? I've tried so hard," I asked Coach.

Her eyes softened as she brushed my cheek with her fingers. "Joy. Fun. Abandon. You're playing with too many voices in your head. Remember, you get in your head . . ."

". . . you're dead," I finished.

Coach continued, "There are too many people whose opinions control how you perform. Let them go. Be yourself. You're la Furia, but remember, the game is beautiful."

Then she tapped her finger on my chin and waited for me to look up at her before continuing, "How are things at home? I haven't seen your mom in a while."

My mom had spiraled since Pablo had moved out. Marisol had dropped out of school two months before graduation. Every time she posted on her Instagram about decorating their apartment downtown or what she was planning for the nursery, my mom sank deeper. I wanted to help, but I didn't want to fall in with her.

I couldn't tell Coach that, but part of me hoped she could read my mind. Finally, I said, "She's fine. I thought she'd come to the tournament, but Central's home that weekend, so she might have to watch Pablo."

My mom wasn't doing fine. She had never planned on making it to my games. Central was playing in town then, but that small truth didn't make my words less of a lie—the first I'd ever told Coach. My cheeks burned with shame.

"You go find that joy in playing again, okay?"

"Are you telling me to smile?" I asked, faking outrage.

Coach laughed, throwing her head back. "No, Hassan. I'm demanding that you make everyone who watches you smile."

———

After the talk with Coach, I stayed at El Buen Pastor until Sister Cristina kicked me out. It was First Communion season, and she had to prepare the church for the first of many celebrations. I wanted to help, but she pointed at my short shorts and my muddy legs and sent me home. She wouldn't budge even when I changed into my warmups.

On the bus, my phone chimed. I peeked at the screen and saw that Juventus had won, thanks to two goals by Diego. I itched to watch the replays, but the bus was full, and I didn't have earbuds with me. Besides, I wasn't going to flash a phone this fancy in public. The phone was my connection to my team, to Diego, to the rest of the world. I couldn't afford to lose it.

When I arrived home, the TV was on at top volume, my father, Héctor, and César eating a picada of cheeses, salami, and bread while my mom cooked in the kitchen.

"Hola, Camila," said César, ungluing himself from the TV long enough to smile and nod at me.

"Hola to all," I said so I wouldn't have to kiss anyone. But nobody really paid me any attention.

When I walked over to see what was so mesmerizing, I realized they were watching the Juventus game. I almost choked when Diego appeared on the screen.

"There he is," César said, stating the obvious.

Héctor glanced at my dad nervously.

My mom left the dishes in the sink and stood next to me, crossing her arms.

Instead of showing the team's warm-up, the camera panned over the Allianz Stadium. It was filled to capacity. The sky was already dark. The game had started at six in the evening in Turín, but in mid-November, it was almost winter there.

My breath seized when I saw Diego jogging to the sideline to talk to one of the coaches. He zipped up his warm-up jacket. Someone from the crowd said something to him, and his eyes crinkled deliciously as he smiled.

He was the same Diego as always, but on TV he looked like an alien on another world impossibly far away.

Jay, Juve's giraffe mascot, ran behind him, urging the crowd to cheer, but there was no need for that. A solid roar rose when Diego waved, and I got goose bumps. Central's fans were passionate, but this was something more. There were so many people in the Juve stadium. They all cheered for el Titán.

"Diego!" my mom whispered. It was a prayer that my brother would one day be where Diego was.

After warm-ups, the team headed back to the locker room, and a reporter sprinted over to Diego.

"Titán, unas palabras!" he begged in an unmistakable Buenos Aires accent.

Diego stopped, but glanced at his teammates.

"Juventus loves you, Titán," the reporter said. "Do you still think you'd like to return to Rosario later on in your career, or do you want to remain a bianconero forever?"

"Ooh!" my father exclaimed. "Now he's done for."

It was such an unfair question. If he said nothing compared to playing in Italy (and how could it?), the Central Scoundrels would never forgive him, but he couldn't snub his adoring tifosi.

"I have a contract for three more years. I'm grateful for it, and I'm trying not to think beyond that. But I'll never forget I'm from Rosario. I'm a Scoundrel until the day I die and beyond. I'm a Juventino until the day I die and beyond. Central gave me the chance to be here in this cathedral of fútbol. How can you make me choose?"

My dad's stone face softened. The reporter must have felt chastised, too, because he changed the subject. "Who's watching you back home?"

Diego looked straight into the camera like he was looking directly at me. When he licked his lips, my hands prickled.

"My mamana, my friends from 7 de Septiembre. The kids from El Buen Pastor."

Like it was just the two of them exchanging confidences at home and not on TV for the world to see, the reporter said, "You know what I mean." He laughed, but Diego looked at him, uncomprehending. "Okay. I'll ask on behalf of all the girls who wish they were here with you—is there a special friend out there cheering you on?"

Diego's gaze strayed from the camera. He actually blushed and tried not to smile, biting his lip. "Yes, there is someone. My first goal today is for her."

"Someone," Héctor said, turning to look at me.

I pretended not to notice.

"Give us a name," the reporter insisted.

But Diego looked over his shoulder. Someone was calling for him. He shrugged and ran off.

I was fire turned into woman. If I moved, I'd combust into flames.

My first goal today is for her.

My mom announced that dinner was ready: milanesas, mashed potatoes, and fried eggs.

"I'm happy for him," César said.

I went to the kitchen to make myself a plate.

"My first goal!" My dad threw his hands up. "He's an arrogant prick."

"Fast-forward," Héctor added. "Let's watch the goals."

I carried my plate back to the table. I wanted to watch the whole thing. Fútbol was more than goals, but it was best to stay quiet and avoid my father's attention. I sat in silence as my dad fast-forwarded to Diego's first goal and celebration. The stadium exploded in cheers, but Diego was the best part. He kissed a bracelet made of white tape and lifted his tight fist to the sky.

I felt the hotness of his lips on my skin, searing through me.

"He's still the same old Diego," César said, a smile on his face. "Look at him. That spark . . . you can't manufacture that. He plays like he's still in the vacant lot."

"And not like he has a stick up his ass, like Pablo," my dad said.

The three of them started arguing about the pros and cons of playing in Europe, the pressure of having a family, the pressure of being paid millions. My mom had disappeared into her room, and quietly, I went to mine to text my boyfriend and thank him for the gift.

28

THREE DAYS BEFORE THE TOURNAMENT, ROXANA TEXTED the team's group thread.

> Eda, Marisa's sister, is missing. At seven, the family and neighbors are marching to the police station to demand the police look for her. Who's with me?

I sat down hard on my bed.

One by one, the girls of the team replied, echoing each other's shock and support:

> Ay, Dios mío. Eda? Not her!
> I'll be there.

On my way.

Count me in, Coach texted.

Everyone knew a girl who had gone missing. Most times, they turned up dead.

I'll be there, I typed with shaking hands.

Heavy-hearted, I turned the TV on. A grainy picture of Eda as the flag bearer at the math Olympics took up half the screen. She was twelve years old and hadn't come home from school. Her seventh-grade graduation was the next day. There was no reason for her to run away.

Not wanting to go to the march by myself, I knocked on my mom's door. She'd been locked in for days, coming out only to make dinner for my father.

She didn't reply, so gingerly, I turned her doorknob and walked in.

"Mami," I called.

She didn't answer.

Bright sunshine filtered through the cracks in her shutters, but it only made the rest of the room seem darker. The heat and stale air felt like a wall.

I sat by her side on the bed and shook her gently. Slowly, she opened her eyes, and when she realized it was me, she bolted upright with a gasp of terror. "What happened? Is Pablo okay?"

My first impulse was to reply that who cared about Pablo? He was obviously okay, loving playing house. But that would only have made my mom feel worse. Instead, I tried to summon the voice Sister Cruz used when Lautaro was having one of his tantrums.

"Everything's okay," I whispered, thinking of Marisa's little sister. My mind replaced her face with Karen's, Paola's, the faces of the other girls from El Buen Pastor. Even Roxana's or my own. My mom's.

Mamá's eyes softened and fluttered shut like butterfly wings; she was fast asleep again before I could tell her the truth. Everything was wrong. I wanted to lie next to her like when I was little and feel the warm safety of her arms. But she looked so fragile in the bed, I also wanted to protect her. On the bed, there was a gigantic set of mahogany rosary beads, but nothing else in the room showed that this was her private space. Careful not to disturb her, I fixed the covers and left. I wrote a note that I put on the table so she wouldn't worry about me if she woke up alone.

Right before I walked out the door, I texted Pablo.

> **Mamá isn't doing well. Come over. She won't get up. You know how she is.**

The message showed as delivered, but he didn't reply.

Nico watched me. I thought about texting Diego and asking him to help me convince Pablo to come over, but it was ten at night in Turín, and Diego and I had already said our good nights. In any case, I needed to get to the march.

On the way to Marisa's house, I counted seven boys and one girl wearing Diego's Juventus jersey. In el barrio, it used to be only Central and Newell's jerseys with the occasional Barcelona one because of Leo Messi, but now everyone wore Juventus twenty-one. I wondered if someday I'd see kids wearing my colors, my number, my name. It seemed like a fantasy that would never actually happen. But I'd fantasized about kissing Diego and him telling me he loved me on TV . . .

After the game, Diego had shown me that under the top layer of tape, there was another layer with my name on it.

You're why I do everything I do, Camila. Without you, all this effort would have no meaning.

Part of me had melted like sugar over fire, and the other part had wondered what he expected in return for all the love.

The bus approached Arroyito, and I got off and joined the crowds of people heading toward Avenida Génova. Although most of the team had promised they'd be there, when I arrived, I only saw Roxana. She must have felt my gaze on her, because she looked up, and her face crumpled when she saw me.

The months of silence vanished like they'd never happened. I rushed toward her and hugged her tight, tight, tight while she cried.

"They found her body."

The crying around me turned to hushed tones as the news of what had happened to Eda spread.

"She didn't tell anyone she was meeting this guy," Roxana said between hiccups. "Her phone was unlocked— they found it at the bus stop—and the police went through her messages. It's horrible. She was just a little girl."

The door of the house opened, and a woman walked out with a young girl hitched on her hip. It took me a second to recognize Marisa. The rest of the team started trickling in, including Coach Alicia, whose eyeliner was smeared. Even she had been crying.

I don't remember who gave me a candle, but Roxana, the rest of the team, and I joined the neighborhood in a silent march, demanding justice for Eda.

Mothers clutched their daughters' hands. Fathers carried posters with Eda's picture. In one of them, she celebrated with Marisa, who was dressed in her Eva María uniform.

People opened their doors, left their houses, and swelled the ranks of heartbroken and furious friends and families. A few of them carried signs with the same picture of a smiling Eda that had flashed on the news. Miriam Soto waved at me from her stoop, and I waved back.

Roxana cried silently, her shoulders shaking. Inside me, a fury grew and spread until I couldn't hold the words in anymore.

"Queremos justicia!" I shouted.

Justice.

We wanted justice, but what would that mean for Eda and all the girls and women like her? In a perfect world, it would mean that every person involved in their suffering would pay. An eye for an eye. A tooth for a tooth. And then every girl would be safe.

But even though I didn't want to let the cynical voice in my mind win, it was hard to imagine that Eda would be the last one.

Who would be next, and who would get to grow old?

"Ni una menos," I sang out. "Vivas nos queremos."

The chant spread like wildfire. Every voice, every heart demanded that the world let us live.

After the march, the team gathered in Roxana's elegant living room. In the kitchen, Mrs. Fong spread out boxes of pizza, but no one seemed hungry.

I looked around at the faces of my teammates scattered on the sofa, the silk-upholstered chairs, the marble floor. None of the new girls had known Marisa or her sister, but everyone looked affected. Milagros and Carolina still had tears in their eyes, while Rufina's jaw was set. She caught my eye and quickly looked away. I loved my team, but I realized I didn't know much about their lives off the pitch, especially the new girls. What personal horrors were they revisiting as we reeled over Eda's murder?

Roxana held my hand tightly. I was her anchor to reality, and she was mine. I'd missed her so much.

Finally, Coach stood up, and her gaze swept over the room. She looked like one of those ancient prophets, and we were the parched girls at the edge of a daunting desert.

"Chicas," she said, "Marisa just texted me. She asked me to thank you all for being there with her today. She also wished you good luck in the tournament."

"But Coach," Roxana called out, surprising everyone, "we can't play. We can't go out there and have fun when girls are dying every day."

Coach Alicia took a big breath and said, "Daring to play in this tournament is a rebellion, chicas. Not too long ago, playing fútbol was forbidden to women *by law*. But we've always found a way around it. Those who came before us played in circuses, in summer fairs, dressed as men. How many of you had to quit when you were around twelve, the same age as Eda, just because you dared to grow up?"

I raised my hand, and so did most of the other girls.

"Here we are. Incorrigible, all of us," Coach said, her eyes glinting. "Many people may think it's just a game. But look at the family we've made."

Roxana leaned in and hugged me, and I hugged her back.

"Things are changing, and you ladies will have opportunities women of my generation never dreamed of. Vivas nos queremos, and fútbol is how we Argentines play the game of life. Let's honor Eda and all the other girls we've lost by doing what we love and doing it well."

Her words reignited the fire in me. I imagined the same thing was happening inside each of the girls, and even in Mrs. Fong, whose eyes blazed.

"Chicas," Mrs. Fong called. "There's pizza. Come and eat."

Without being told twice, we all joined her in the kitchen. With three *mates* going around, we grieved together like sisters, but I also felt the prickle of the challenge Coach had set for us.

One day, when a girl was born in Rosario, the earth would shake with anticipation for her future and not dread.

29

YAEL DROVE ME HOME IN HER FATHER'S LITTLE CAR. WE were quiet most of the way, but when we reached el barrio, she blurted out the question that must have been burning on her tongue since Roxana's house. "How old do you think Coach is?"

My mind raced with speculations. I'd never even thought about it. She was certainly older than my mom. "Fifty?"

"So old? I think she's just wrinkly. My mom's forty-five, and she can't run a block without coughing up a lung, and Coach? She can outrun me."

"Let's look it up."

The car made an ominous sound, and Yael cringed and hurriedly switched gears. "Ay, I got used to Luciano's automatic."

"Fancy!" I teased her.

She gave me a side-eye. "Not as fancy as what you-know-who drives."

"Voldemort?"

Now she laughed. "You're such a great deflector. No, Diego, boluda."

I forced myself not to blush or smile and said, "You're the one changing the subject."

Yael pulled into my monoblock's driveway. The engine of her car grumbled, impossible to ignore. Doña Kitty and Franco seemed to be coming back from Ariel's market, plastic bags in hand. They both looked curiously at us. I waved. Franco waved back, but his grandmother pretended not to see us.

"Nosy neighbors, huh?" Yael asked.

"You have no idea." I leaned in to hug her.

"*You* have no idea what the neighbors say about Luciano and me. They're disgusting."

Just thinking about it, I shuddered. "But no one is asking if you need help, right?"

We shook our heads in unison, and I said goodbye. Dashing past Doña Kitty, I ruffled Franco's hair and climbed the stairs two at a time.

Although the Southern Cross already shone in the sky, I was determined to get my mom out of bed. She hadn't helped me become a futbolera when I was younger, but she'd helped me get to the tournament. I wouldn't be here without her, and she needed me.

"Hola, nena." Pablo said when I opened the door. He sat in front of the TV, the volume muted for a commercial. Nico sat next to Pablo, his head on my brother's lap.

"Pali!" I said, running to him. I hugged him tightly, blinking quickly so I wouldn't cry. "You came back!" He laughed and kissed my forehead, and I looked into his dark eyes. "I missed you, tarado."

He just smiled. That was Pablo. He hadn't missed me, and he wouldn't lie. I let go of him and asked, "Is Mamá still in bed?"

The TV sound came on. It was a *Ben 10* episode, and Pablo reached over to lower the volume again. "She's in the shower," he said. "We talked for a while, and then she said she wanted to get changed." I could hear her singing.

"How long have you been here?" I asked.

"I came as soon as I got your message. I was in the area anyway. You never see me, but I'm always around."

He might have meant well, but his words sounded too much like something my father would say.

"Where were you?" he asked.

"I went to a march for the girl that died today."

"Another one?"

I crossed my arms tightly to stop my shivers. "Her name was Eda. She was twelve."

Pablo's jaw clenched.

"Marisol's having a girl. I mean, we're having a girl."

A girl.

My brother was going to be the father of a girl. I was going to be an aunt.

I hugged him again. "Congratulations, Pali. I'm so happy for you."

It wasn't a lie, but there were so many things unsaid that my words sounded false anyway. How were we going to protect her? How did he feel watching the world destroy us?

"Let's celebrate with some *mates*." I headed to the stove. From the corner of my eye, I saw a suspicious puddle in the middle of the floor. "Nico," I sighed, and my dog, knowing exactly what I meant, whined pitifully.

Pablo just laughed as I cleaned up the mess.

After the initial burst of emotion, an awkwardness fell over us. I hated the feeling, like a wet fog that pressed me down, but I didn't know how to talk through it. The only words that came to my tongue were accusatory or mocking. Why had he left Mamá? Why hadn't she been invited to the ultrasound? Was that why she'd been so depressed? How could he not tell me about the baby when he first found out? And why did he have to wear the same cologne as Diego's? But nothing good would come if I started interrogating him.

Pablo might not have been an active liar, but he knew to stay quiet when he didn't have the advantage. Lying by omission was lying, too.

Since talking about either of our lives felt off-limits, I turned to the one subject that always united us: our father.

"And where is *he*?" I asked.

"I don't know where he is now, but we had a meeting with the boss at the club. Papá's trying to change the contract for the loan." Pablo's tone of voice suggested he'd more than made peace with our father.

"Loan?"

Pablo rolled his eyes at me, and the urge to smack him was so strong I clutched my hands together. "I have an opportunity to go to Mexico next year. On loan, but still."

All my diplomatic good intentions vanished. "Why didn't you tell me?"

His lips parted a couple of times, but no words came out. He finally crossed his arms and said, "Look who's talking." The venom in his voice found its mark.

My pulse quickened. "What do you mean?" I asked, walking over to where he sat. I wasn't afraid of him.

He shoved his phone in my face. It took my eyes a second to adjust and read the words. It was a headline in *La Capital*.

LEAGUE CHAMPIONS EVA MARÍA COMPETING IN FIRST SUDAMERICANO TOURNAMENT TO TAKE PLACE IN ROSARIO.

I scanned the article. It was mostly about Coach Alicia "la Fiera" Aimar. How she had been part of a team of women's soccer pioneers who'd played in the U.S. in the early nineties. It also mentioned me, but not by name, only as Pablo Hassan's sister and Diego Ferrari's latest love interest.

"I can't believe they named only you and Diego in an article about a team of girls. The patriarchy! It burns," I said, laughing to dispel the toxic cloud around us.

But when I looked up, I saw that Pablo was livid.

"You think you're so much better than me, playing for the love of the game and all that? What do you know about playing fútbol? Love can only take you so far. All my life, I've busted my balls with one purpose only: saving our family, Camila." Somewhere in the back of my mind, a part of me registered that Mamá had stopped singing.

"I didn't ask you to save me."

My words only made him angrier. "I gave my whole life for this family."

"Playing fútbol, Pablo," I reminded him. "It's not like you're enslaved."

"I never had a choice. Why couldn't you just leave with Diego when you had the chance? You could've managed his career. No matter how much you try, you'll never make it. You'll never make the kind of money we need—"

"You think this is all about the money? You think I'm going to be like your little Marisol? What does she know about anything? What does she say about Mexico, *Stallion*?" I taunted him. "I thought she wanted to go to Italy . . ."

His lip curled in a vicious sneer. "She'll go where I go; she's expecting my child."

"She's not even eighteen years old! What does she know?"

"And what do you know? It's easy to claim girlfriend status from far away. If you cared about Diego, shouldn't you be with him? But maybe he's just playing with you, like I said he would."

He hadn't yelled at me since we were little kids, but when he did now, his voice thundered like our father's. I recoiled from him.

But I wasn't backing down. We were both our father's children. We carried the curse of hot tempers and quick, lashing tongues. "You have no right to say anything about Diego and me."

He laughed, and the cruelty in his voice slashed at me. "Negrita, you really think he's in love with you? ¡Vamos, por favor! He scored in Barcelona today. Why would he come back to you when he could have anyone?"

I slapped him. The sound reverberated around the kitchen, mixing with Nico's frantic barking.

Pablo inhaled sharply. His face drained of blood.

The palm of my hand stung.

I'd never hit Pablo before. And in spite of what we'd both grown up with, he'd never lifted a finger against me.

An apology was blooming on my lips. Pablo's face was already softening, forgiving me before I spoke.

"What's happening here?" Mamá asked, stepping into the kitchen, a towel wrapped around her head.

Before either of us could answer, the front door slammed open.

My father walked into the apartment like he was bringing in a Sudestada storm on his shoulders.

Pablo's face transformed, and something in me withered seeing my brother, the father-to-be, cower.

"Camila," my father asked. "Where were you just now?"

My mom's eyes found mine. In hers, there was a silent plea for me to find a good excuse.

But I was tired of running. We were all buried underneath mountains of blame, shame, guilt, and lies.

I wouldn't hide anymore. I'd let him deal with the surprise or disappointment. I was done carrying this load.

"Where were you?" he asked again, his face close to mine, spittle flying from his angry mouth.

He was so much taller than me, but I wouldn't shrink.

"I was at a march for the missing girl."

"Why do you waste your time protesting instead of doing something productive? I better not find out you're part of that green-handkerchief group of abortionists."

"Abortionists?" My mom looked at me like I'd killed a baby on national TV. "Camila, we've raised you better than that. Why are you involved with those people at all?"

"Listen," I said. "First of all, the march wasn't about abortion or anything related to it. We carried the Ni Una Menos signs, and yes, some people wore green handkerchiefs, but it was about the girl, Eda. She was my friend's sister."

"There have always been rapes and killings." My father wouldn't stop. "The media makes everything seem worse than it is. If she hadn't been running around with the wrong crowd—"

"Wrong crowd? She was walking to school."

"Her sister had a baby in second year, though," my mom added. "Isn't it Marisa's sister we're talking about?"

I wanted to cry and scream and pull my hair, but they would never understand.

Instead, I took my chance. I threw up my hands in exasperation and tried to head to my room. My father grabbed me by the arm, pressing it so hard that I cried out in pain. I wasn't going to be tossed around like a rag doll. I twisted out of his grasp. He reached for me again but lost his balance and fell, knocking me down with him.

My mom and Pablo were screaming in the background, but I couldn't understand what anyone was saying. Nico ran around us in a panic.

The old ghosts came back, wailing that this was all my fault.

But the guardian angels Miriam had seen around me came, too. They screamed at me to rise up.

I scrambled back to my feet. My dad was older, but he was still an athlete. He grabbed me by my ponytail and slammed me back down. I couldn't breathe.

"Don't touch me!" I yelled.

Pablo was crying, and my mom stood helpless, saying, "Don't hit her, Andrés. The neighbors are outside."

"What do I care about the neighbors?" He took off his belt, stretching it with a slapping sound.

"You're not going to hit me," I said, putting my hand up, still on the floor.

He moved so fast. I tasted blood. My ears were ringing. Pablo and my dad were suddenly wrestling.

"You won't touch her anymore," Pablo yelled, but his voice was small and hoarse.

My father ignored him. He reached down to grab my phone. It must have fallen out of my pocket.

My nose was runny, and I wiped it with the sleeve of my Adidas jacket. The blood seeped quickly into the blue fibers.

Now the one laughing was my father. "'Back to Turín after beating Barça in the Champions, Furia! Next time, we'll be here together.'" He looked at me. Then he looked at my mom. "See? You're sewing your fingers to stumps, and the little lady here has this expensive phone, an Adidas jacket, the promise of travel . . . What else is he paying you to play the little whore?"

Of course he didn't want an answer. He drew his hand back and smashed the phone against the floor.

"Stop it!" my mom said, finding her voice perhaps for the first time. "Andrés, stop now."

"So now I'm the bad guy? Years and years of sacrificing for this family. And for what? You're mixing with the wrong crowd, Camila. That girls' school and all that reading have fried your brain. And playing fútbol has turned you into a marimacho. What? Did you think I'd never find out about your little hobby? My eye is always on you. I know everything."

I didn't want to be afraid, but my blood chilled anyway. Then he turned to my brother. "And you? You are a failure. I give you six months in Mexico before they find out you have less talent than your sister. Your mother is dead weight. If it weren't for all of you, my life would have been so much better."

"So leave already, Andrés," my mom said. She helped me up, and when she looked at my swollen face, her eyes welled with tears. "Leave."

He stepped back.

It was now or never. I wasn't going to let him off easy. Not after holding us hostage and blaming us for his failures. Not after destroying Pablo's confidence, staining my mom's love.

"You can hit us, and yell, and try to run from the consequences, but your time to pay is here, Papá," I said, shaking.

For the first time, he seemed at a loss for words. And then he smiled.

"If you think you're going to blackmail me . . ." He rubbed his hands as if they hurt. "Your mom knows about her, and the others before. Your mother and I have a little agreement, don't we, Isabel?"

Mamá started crying, but she didn't crumple like he wanted her to.

I heard voices outside, but I couldn't stop now.

"Mami," I said, afraid that the moment was gone, her courage spent. But she surprised me.

"Go," she yelled at him. "You won't hurt us anymore."

He lunged at her, but Pablo and I both stepped in front of her.

In a corner of my mind, I thought, *This is how people die.* All the news in the papers about domestic violence, crimes of passion—they all must have started like this.

But whatever the consequences, my mom, Pablo, and I were breaking the cycle today.

Somehow, my father had three scratches on his face. He was pale and didn't seem so big anymore. "You really want this, Isabel? If I leave now, I will never come back. You'll be all alone when your children leave you, too."

Someone knocked on the door. "Police," a woman's voice rang out.

My father looked around like a cockroach trying to scurry back into the darkness when the lights come on.

"It's open," Pablo bellowed.

My father didn't have the chance to attempt an escape or to take us down with him.

The police came in.

Pablo, my mom, and I raised our hands in surrender. But the officers went straight for my dad. A dark-skinned woman in a blue uniform came to my side. "You're safe now, corazón," she said in a soft voice. "He can't hurt you anymore."

Neighbors gathered by our door. One or two talked with the police.

Leaning on my mom's shoulder, I finally cried.

WHAT DOESN'T KILL YOU MAKES YOU STRONGER: WHAT A lie. I didn't feel stronger repeating the fight over and over for the police. Hours later, I felt sick and drained.

Any strength I could spare, I summoned for going to El Buen Pastor the next day. Karen gasped when she saw my swollen cheek, but she didn't ask how I'd been hurt. Instead, she handed me one of her poetry books.

"Maestra, since you like kids' books, I found this book of Mistral's poems for children. Maybe you'll like it, too."

She left before I could thank her. That night, I read the poems aloud, and the sound of my own voice lulled me to sleep.

I didn't feel strong the following morning, when I opened the door to see Coach Alicia and Roxana. "We heard the news this morning, and then you weren't at practice, so we had to come," Roxana said, and hugged me. Now that I had finally cried, I couldn't stop. But she held me up.

"I failed my daughter," my mom said.

Roxana looked at me, her eyes full of tears. "We all failed her."

Coach Alicia put her hands on mine and my mom's and declared, "You did not, Isabel. And neither did you, Roxana."

"I failed myself," I said.

Coach pressed my hand. "You didn't fail anyone. If anything, it takes a strong person to fight back, Camila."

I nodded and said all the things she expected me to say, and when Coach asked for a few minutes alone with my mom, Roxana and I went to my room. She hadn't been here in years.

She looked at the picture of Diego, Pablo, and me easting nísperos in a tree. Pablo had brought it over yesterday before joining the team at the hotel for Central's next game. It was my brother's way of saying he was sorry, but I'd already forgiven him.

The cycle was breaking with me.

"I'm sorry for not telling you about Diego," I said, sitting on my bed.

Roxana sat next to me and held my hand. "I'm sorry for acting like a jerk every time you talked about him."

I elbowed her softly. "Why don't you like him?"

"It's not that I don't like him," Roxana said. "I was scared that he was like every other footballer, your brother included. No offense."

I turned to look at her. "And now you don't think that?"

She shrugged. "I don't know. Seems like his fame and money haven't changed him . . . that much. He's actually kind of adorable when he talks about you."

"What about you and Luciano?" I asked, and now she was the one blushing. "I've seen how he looks at you . . ."

"He's not bad," she said. "But for now, we're partners. He's team manager, and I'm one of the captains. We'll see what happens later."

Nico trotted into the room and flopped on the bed, sprawling out and ignoring both of us. We laughed. Laughing felt like a miracle.

"Ready for the tournament?" Roxana asked.

"Not really," I said.

Roxana seemed to guess what was troubling me and asked, "Does Diego know about everything that happened?"

My heart fluttered as I wondered how he'd react to what had happened with my father. "Pablo said he told him last night. My phone's destroyed."

She rummaged in her purse and offered me her phone. "Here. Take your time. I'll be in the kitchen with your mom and Alicia."

"Gracias, Ro."

"That's what friends are for," she said, and closed the door softly behind her.

I didn't trust that I wouldn't cry, but I needed to hear Diego's voice. I called him, and the phone rang and rang, but he never answered. After the third try, I typed a long message, telling him what had happened at home, including how my phone was broken, the reason my father was in jail, and my fears that when he got out, he'd come for my mom and me.

Standing naked in front of Diego wouldn't have been more revealing than writing that message. For a few seconds, my finger hovered over the delete button.

He didn't need any distractions. He'd worked hard to get where he was. But I knew he loved me. He cared about me.

I hit send and waited for a reply, but the seconds turned into minutes, and the only answer was silence.

━━━━━

Coach left with strict instructions for me to rest. But when Mamá said she was going to the store, I said, "I'll come with you." I couldn't let her face the neighbors' curiosity on her own. "I need to change, but I'll be ready in a second."

"Don't," she said, grabbing the shopping bag before she headed to the door. "I won't be long. Besides, Belem, la brasilera from building thirty-two, might bring the first payment for her wedding dress. Give her this receipt and leave the money in my room."

She left before I could insist on coming.

On a whim, I turned the TV to *The Bachelor*, indulging in a mindless game of love, yelling at girls making stupid decisions.

Someone knocked, and I grabbed the receipt for Belem. But before I reached the door, a dark fear sneaked into my mind. Maybe it was my father, out of jail, or that woman he'd been sneaking around with, coming to teach me a lesson. I was paralyzed until I saw Nico's ears perking up, his whole lower body shimmying with excitement.

I peeked through the peephole, but I couldn't see who was on the other side.

Finally, I armed myself with courage. I was la Furia, after all.

I opened the door.

Diego stood with his hands in his pockets.

"Hola, Furia," he said.

My body went cold, as if I'd seen an apparition, but I blinked and fell into his arms.

He closed the door behind us, and when he hugged me, he picked me up and held me tightly.

"Shhh, I'm here. Don't cry," he whispered.

My tears stung my skin.

He kissed my bruised face softly, but his eyes flashed. "I'm going to kill him"

I never wanted to hear words of hatred from his lips, so I kissed him over and over until the anger left. Somehow, we ended up on the sofa.

"You taste like sugar," I said before passion overtook us. My mom could arrive any second.

"I ate an alfajor at the airport. I was starving."

Diego's eyes seemed to drink me up, and I basked in the feeling of being loved.

"I was afraid you wouldn't want anything to do with me after you heard what's been going on," I said, lowering my gaze. I was ready for everything except Diego's pity.

He pushed my chin up with a finger. "How could you say that?"

I didn't have an answer, and I snuggled against his chest. He wrapped his strong arms around me.

"After Pablo called me, I took the first flight here. By the time I got your text, Roxana was already home. The distance has never hurt so much."

Diego should've been in Turín. The team didn't have a break until the next FIFA date in a few weeks.

"Don't you have practice? How did you get permission to travel? What's Giusti going to say?"

"I'm skipping practice. I don't care what Giusti says." Even though the heat in the apartment was unbearable,

I shivered when he added, "He'll understand once we're safely back at home."

I sat up. "What do you mean?"

Diego bit his lip. It was easy to speak through a phone screen, but now the words wouldn't come.

An alarm bell rang inside me that I couldn't ignore.

"Diego . . ."

"I came to take you with me, Camila."

The blood rushed in my ears.

"He'll never touch you again."

"But I can't leave," I said. "What about my team's plans?"

Diego looked confused. "Your team's plans? What about your dad? What if he comes back? Coach Alicia and your mom will understand. But also, who cares what they think? You need to leave. This is the perfect time . . ." His words faded.

"I have my tournament this weekend, Diego."

"But you might not win, mi amor."

"I can't win if I don't even play."

"What are you going to do if things don't go well?"

"There's going to be a new national women's team convocation. There's a World Cup in two years, and I . . . I want to try."

The blood drained from Diego's face.

"I bought your plane ticket already," he said.

Nico felt the tension and whined.

"I can't just leave with you," I said. "And you shouldn't have left the team without permission."

"You don't mean that." He held my hands, and his eyes shone with the glamour of his fantasies. "It's now or never. Imagine the two of us in Europe! I'll show you everything. Everywhere. We'll go to Barcelona and visit La Sagrada Familia. We'll go to Paris for Valentine's Day. You'll love the apartment, but if you'd prefer a house, we'll find one in the old city, like the one Luís Felipe and Flávia just moved into."

I closed my eyes for a second. I could almost smell the fancy streets; I could almost feel the magic of playing house with him.

"What about *my* dreams?" I didn't want to yell, but why wasn't he listening to me? "What about *my* career, Diego?"

Diego put his head in his hands and breathed deeply. "I thought your dream was to be with me."

"It's one of them, Diego."

"*My* greatest dream is being with you. What's in the way? You could play in Turín. I'll see if you can get a try-out for the women's team, but you don't need to worry about anything ever again. I'm getting you out of here before your father hurts you, Camila. Why aren't you happy about this?" Diego never lost his temper, but his voice was rising, matching mine.

Why was he making me choose?

"I'm not going to run away."

Diego stared at me. But this time, I didn't lower my gaze.

"I'm sorry you bought a ticket. I'm sorry you left the team to come rescue me. But Diego," I said softly, caressing his hand, "you should've at least talked to me before you did that. I have opportunities here. Even if I have a bad tournament and we lose el Sudamericano, there are other tryouts, and I'll get them on my own. I'll keep trying."

"And I don't mean anything to you?" He stood up.

I stood up, too. "Of course you do. Te quiero." I said it. I finally said it. "Nothing will change that, but I won't abandon everything I've worked for. If I do, then *he* wins. Can't you see? We can keep doing long distance . . ."

"I can't keep doing long distance."

Diego was the type of person who either committed wholeheartedly or walked away. How had I not seen it before? He'd gotten offers from smaller European teams, but he had only agreed to move when Juventus gave him a contract. He'd play for the best or no one. He'd only pursued me when he was sure my feelings for him hadn't changed. He'd only come back because he believed I'd follow him.

Now he looked unmoored.

"It's all or nothing for you, Diego—that's why you're el Titán. For you, it's only black or white. But in my life, things aren't so simple. I have to compromise. I can't separate the parts that make me who I am: a daughter, a sister, a captain, your girlfriend. La Furia. You can't ask me to choose between you and my dreams. Don't. Please don't."

Diego's eyes brimmed with tears. "I left everything for you."

I hugged him. I could feel his heart racing. "I didn't want you to. We can still fix this, mi amor. We can make it work." I stood on my tiptoes to kiss him.

He didn't kiss me.

I stepped back, and he said, "This can never work."

"Diegui." My voice wavered as my world came crashing down on me. "Don't ask me to leave everything for you, please."

He shook his head. "You never had to ask. I never hesitated. I'm sorry that what we had didn't mean the same to you."

And before I could fight back, make him understand, the love of my life walked out the door.

31

BY THE TIME MY MOM CAME BACK FROM THE STORE, I WAS in bed, willing myself to sleep so I wouldn't have to think about Diego and the life he'd offered me, the life I'd turned down. But all night long, I heard his broken voice, saw the tears in his eyes. Every time I woke up, I wondered if it had all been a nightmare. But I still smelled his cologne on my skin, tasted the sugar of his lips, and sadness roiled deep in my belly.

I had lost so much, and I had hurt him *so much*. Coach Alicia had told me to get rest before the tournament, but when the sun came up and the benteveos started singing, I was exhausted.

My life was in shambles. All I could do was get my uniform ready for the day. Tidying up my room, I breathed deeply, reminding myself that I was still la Furia. That I wasn't the first girl with a broken heart, and I wouldn't be the last. I'd sacrificed so much for this tournament. The least I could do was give my all to make it count.

Outside, the air smelled of jasmine. Spring had painted Rosario purple and red with blooming jacarandas and ceibos.

El Sudamericano would take place over the next three days. Two games on Saturday, one on Sunday. The semifinal was on Sunday afternoon, and the final was on Monday. Five games that could change our lives forever. A win counted for three tournament points. A tie was one, a loss zero. For a moment, I imagined what it would be like to sweep the whole thing.

The bus left me just a block away from the pitch, and when I arrived, Rufina and Milagros were already stretching on the sidelines.

There was no way they didn't know about my dad, so I saved us all the awkward conversation by staying on the other edge of the pitch. When Coach arrived, she acknowledged me with a simple nod and studied her clipboard while we got ready with Luciano.

The girls from Praia Grande FC were giants compared to us. Coach reminded us to keep our eyes to ourselves, but it was difficult. The Brazilian girls had won the Sudamericano multiple times. They walked and behaved like professionals, going through their warm-up like rehearsed choreography, smiling for the cameras, ignoring the curious looks from the sidelines.

"Are you okay?" Roxana asked, her face already gleaming with sweat. "I heard that Diego came to see you."

"Did you talk to him?" I looked around, hoping to see him on the sidelines. Maybe if he saw me play, *really* play, he'd understand.

Roxana shook her head. "He already left."

My throat tightened, and I clenched my jaw.

It was a testament to her unconditional love that she let me be.

When the ref called the captains, Roxana and I trotted onto the field. Maybe because I oozed bad vibes, we lost the coin toss. We'd have to play facing east, and the sun would be in Roxana's face for the crucial first half.

The field was full of recently filled holes and bald spots, but the lines were freshly painted, bright white. Before the ref called the teams in, a little girl ran along our lineup, handing out black mourning bands. "For Eda." They gave us the incentive we needed to vanquish our fears.

Praia Grande was famous for playing an expansive game full of long aerial passes we had no chance of stopping. If we wanted to control the game, we needed to shrink the field and force them to play on the ground.

Coach Alicia said, "Play smart. Play hard. But above all, have fun."

We all ran to our places.

The ref whistled, and the game started. I tried to summon la Furia, but she didn't answer the call.

My jaw, still bruised where my dad had hit me, throbbed when I clenched my teeth. My mind flashed to Diego's wounded eyes before he walked away.

"Loosen up," Coach Alicia yelled, and even without looking, I knew her words were directed at me.

I unclenched my jaw and stopped fighting the memories.

—

I ran like the warrior princess in Diego's stories. I'd turned my back on him, but our history was part of me. He was imprinted in every memory, every dream.

The sad, the difficult, the beautiful.

La Furia took charge of my legs and my mind. I muted my heart for now.

The game was locked at 0–0. I let it consume me, blocking every distraction. Here and there I heard a cheer, but when the ref whistled for halftime, I felt like I was coming out of a trance.

All I wanted was water. I couldn't drink enough.

"Are you okay to keep going?" Luciano asked me.

I nodded, and he made a note in his book.

Then Coach Alicia said, "We're going to defend and counterattack."

Nobody contradicted her. Now that I had the chance to look, I noticed a solitary TV camera with a skinny, tall boy at the helm and Luisana, the reporter, standing under the shade of a paradise tree.

From us players to the coaches to the families and reporters, we were all part of something that went beyond the white lines of the pitch. We were all making history.

"You're going to play wingback, Furia. Ready?" Luciano asked before I headed back out for the second half.

For the rest of the game, my job was to protect the goal and Roxana. I was much shorter than the Praia Grande strikers, but I was strong and fast, and no one crossed over my line.

Time slipped by, the sun glaring into my eyes, but the game remained scoreless. My blue-and-silver jersey stuck to my skin. A little tightness in the back of my thigh warned me to play smart.

When the ref marked the end of the game, the Brazilian girls looked at us with a little more respect, and my team walked off the field a little taller. Tying against the favorites was a feat, but I remained hungry for more.

"Why the long faces? We tied!" Luciano said. "A tie is one point. And it's especially impressive against this team."

He passed out water and Gatorade, and I gulped mine down so fast I didn't even know which I had drunk. Now that the adrenaline had stopped pumping through my body, I smelled my sweat and the smoke of choripán cooking on a makeshift grill. The cicadas screamed, and nearby, graduating students chanted and celebrated.

On the way to meet Coach Alicia under the shade of a mora tree, I caught conversations in Spanish, Portuguese, and English. I recognized the official-looking men and women with clipboards, but there was no sign of Coach's sister, Gabi Tapia.

"This isn't the ideal result," Coach Alicia said, "But like Luciano said, we got a point. This is historic. Not only is Praia the defending champion, they have a direct pipeline to several professional teams, and you, chicas, held them back."

The parents who had crowded around to hear Coach's speech applauded proudly. I looked back, just in case, but my mom wasn't there.

So much hung on the results of our games. But like Coach had told me months ago, no one had any expectations of me. Not even Diego had really believed I could make this a career. We didn't have to win. We didn't have to score. We just had to show that we were *something*.

"Now," Coach continued, "drink plenty of water and eat a good lunch. Rest. Don't go too far. We warm up in four hours. Meet me beside field number seven."

Without being told twice, my teammates and I followed the scent of food. Choripán in hand, most of us watched other teams, marveling at the beauty of their style in some cases and laughing at their blunders in others. Some of these girls had never been trained, and it showed. But they still played with heart and grit, which was nothing to underestimate.

Finally, after one last shared lemon popsicle, Roxana and I headed back to meet Coach. Field number seven was right next to the bathrooms. The temperature had climbed into the low thirties, and sweat ran down my back just from doing basic stretches. I felt a pull in the back of my leg. "Not now," I muttered.

"What's wrong?" Roxana asked next to me.

I grimaced. "The leg . . . it's tight."

"Let me help you." She walked over and helped me stretch my leg. "I hate to say this, but if it gets worse, you know you have to tell Coach."

I knew. At the same time, if I told Coach my leg was tender, she'd bench me. I couldn't let that happen.

Our next game started. Tacna wasn't as disciplined a team as Praia, but they had a tougher style that disrupted our rhythm. Every few seconds, one of our players was sprawled on the ground, but soon the ref stopped calling fouls in our favor. Tacna took control of the game, and we ran in every direction, our lines in disarray. For the first fifteen minutes, we couldn't seem to find our legs. Then, taking advantage of a blunder in their defense, I passed wide and far to Rufina. She kicked, and the ball crossed the line in a perfect arc.

For a second, we were all too stunned to celebrate, but someone on the sidelines broke the silence, and we all ran to Rufina and jumped on her. She clasped my hands in hers. "I'm winning, Furia." She winked, and I laughed.

The competition between us felt silly and small now. We all won, or we all went home.

The minutes went by in a rush. Mabel scored a free kick, and Rufina passed me a beautiful heel. All I had to do was softly push the ball with the tip of my foot. The ball kissed the goal line, and I pointed my fingers toward heaven, thanking the angel on call.

I had scored at an international tournament. Scoring a goal is almost like kissing. The more you do it, the more you want. I wanted to keep scoring until it hurt.

Rufina hugged me.

After that, we knocked and knocked on Tacna's goal, but the keeper was like a spider, blocking every single shot. With seconds to go, Julia made a run from the back. She shot a cannonball that no human could stop, but it bounced off the crossbar.

The ref blew the whistle. Roxana remained undefeated on the goal. Our team danced and sang in celebration. We had four points. Day one had been a success.

32

THAT NIGHT AT ROXANA'S HOUSE, IN THE GIANT BED HER mom had prepared for me with crisp sheets and fluffy pillows, I couldn't sleep any better than I did in my tiny twin with Nico fighting me for room. My fingers itched to take Roxana's phone and text Diego. Not even the victory was enough to fill the void he'd left in me. Although we'd been apart for months, we'd talked every day. I missed him in the core of my heart—his jokes, his silly memes, the glimpses into his day-to-day life. But now we were worse than strangers.

"He must hate me," I said.

"He could never hate you," Roxana said, hugging me tightly after she found me crying. "But he's impulsive and proud. One day, he's going to realize what he was really asking you to do, and he's going to regret it."

The next morning, Roxana and Mrs. Fong drank *mate* in the kitchen, poring over the report of the games. Unlike yesterday, when all the teams had started with a clean slate, the standings were all over the place today.

"Where do we stand?" I asked, helping myself to a croissant.

"Itapé won both their games yesterday," Roxana explained. "Three to zero and one to zero. They have six points. We have four. Praia has one, and Tacna has zero."

"Two teams go on to the semifinal with the other bracket?" Mrs. Fong asked, and Roxana nodded.

"So we have to win or tie."

"And if we lose, then Tacna has to beat Praia, but we need to have a better goal differential."

All the way to the field, we speculated on possible results, which was the most useless way to pass the time. If I'd been a nail biter, I would've been chewing my elbows. Instead, I pulled on the red ribbon tied to my wrist, trying to coax some magic out of it.

The atmosphere at Parque Balbin was completely different from the day before. There were several food stands with coal already smoking, vendors selling T-shirts and flags, manteros displaying everything from watches to purses to little made-in-China Monumento a la Bandera replicas. Players arrived by the busload and camped out in any shade they could find. I envied the little kids heading to the pool in their flip-flops and swimsuits, but my feet prickled with the desire to play. TV cameras were stationed under a white tent and on the sides of every field. I spotted Luisana with the same skinny camera guy in tow. She waved at me and then answered her phone.

I followed Roxana to the meeting spot by field number seven. A cooler of bottled water and Gatorade served as the team beacon and meant that Coach was already here. Roxana's mom placed a bag of energy bars next to it, and Rufina stepped in front of the cooler, protecting it until we really needed a drink.

We high-fived each other as girls trickled in. Finally, Coach arrived with her sister and a Black woman whose shirt had the NWSL logo. Everyone fell silent. "Good morning, team," Mrs. Tapia said. "This is Coach Jill Ryan. She's a National Women's discovery scout. Coach, these are the Eva María girls."

Coach Ryan smiled at us. "Hello, Eva María." She had a slight accent I couldn't place but spoke perfect Spanish. "I'm already impressed with what I've seen, and I'm eager to find some gems today and tomorrow. No matter what happens next, I expect to see excellent soccer." We stood there in stunned silence.

Mrs. Tapia winked at me, and a fire ignited inside my

stomach. Roxana elbowed me excitedly, but Coach Alicia was speaking, and I didn't want to miss a thing she said.

"I hope you have all seen the game plan by now. Those who don't have phones, I hope you've been updated so we can move on."

I, along with a couple of other phoneless girls, nodded, and she continued, "We need to win. Itapé is the toughest team in our group. They are great all over the field. Their back is solid, and they have a number nine who is fast as hell and strong as steel. You all know what to do."

We jumped to our feet and began to warm up. From the corner of my eye, I saw Luciano heading off to watch the game between Praia and Tacna. My belly squirmed with anticipation, but I had to push any distraction away.

Coach approached me to hand me the captain band for the game. "We need you to be unstoppable. I know you can do it. More than that, though, I need you to be a leader. The girls are nervous, but if they see you're collected, they'll catch on to that. Claro?"

"Like water," I said, but I was anything but collected. Luckily, she couldn't see me quivering inside. The Itapé girls in white and red looked like they could eat us for appetizers before moving on to the main course in the semifinals.

The ref called the teams, and I won the coin toss. This time, the sun wouldn't glare in Roxana's eyes. I brushed my thumb along the red ribbon bracelet Diego had given me. I needed its power more than ever. Hopefully, it would work even if we weren't together. Rufina's boyfriend in the eternally horrible red-and-black jersey cheered for her. I remembered the championship game when she'd cried and he'd held her. I envied her so much.

And then I heard her. My mom. "¡Vamos, Camila!" Her voice jolted my whole body like an electrical current.

I looked at the crowd, and as if my very soul knew where to find her, I saw my mom waving a blue-and-silver flag. My eyes became cloudy. She was here.

"¡Vamos, Furia!" she yelled again.

The game started, and soon, number nine from Itapé, Natalia, made a shot that Roxana blocked. The first warning. Natalia wouldn't make the same mistake twice.

In a counterattack, Rufina and I formed a wall together with Agustina that reached all the way to the Paraguayan doorstep. But Rufina took too long to pass, and the defender stole the ball from her.

With my mom's cheering in my ears, I pushed to recover the ball. For several minutes, it was back and forth across the field, ours and theirs, both sets of midfielders struggling to create a strong wall. After a few minutes, Itapé's number five sent a long shot to their number eleven, who was thankfully offsides.

Itapé was testing the waters, but I felt my team stretching to cover each square centimeter of the field.

Natalia broke away and kicked the ball with a killer curve, and this time, Roxana couldn't deflect the shot. The goal was like a stab wound. We started hemorrhaging confidence and imagination.

Now that Itapé had found the crack in our system, their pressure was so strong, my team couldn't resist much longer. They scored twice more with almost identical plays, free kicks expertly sent at an angle not even Elastigirl could have caught.

The whistle blew, and we plodded to Coach's side, eyes downcast in humiliation. Down by three goals, our shot at winning the tournament was over.

Coach Alicia looked lovingly at us. "We're playing hard," she said. "Winning is not the objective anymore, but what about having fun, huh? What about going out there and playing with joy? Do you think you can do that?"

Back on the field, I muted everything else. The sounds, the white glare of the sun, the ache of this lost chance. What if this was Furia's last moment to shine?

I ran as if I were back in the clover fields with Diego. I played the kind of fantasy moves that made opponents go mad with frustration, that made boys mad, megging one defender, sending a rainbow over another. But when I kicked toward the goal, the shot was too high.

Then Rufina got the ball and dragged half the defense after her, leaving me all alone with the goalie. This time,

I didn't miss. With a soft touch to the lower right, the ball crossed the line.

Pandemonium exploded all around me. I screamed so loud it left my throat sore. When the other team kicked off, I was still flushed with ecstasy.

Itapé was out to liquidate us, but Julia stole the ball, and in a tiki-taka worthy of Guardiola's Barcelona, I chested it down and passed to Rufina. She shot, and the keeper blocked it with her open hands. I was ready for the rebound and sent the ball in with my shin.

We didn't waste time celebrating. Not yet. We were close to tying, and time was running out.

For the next few minutes, we attacked and attacked, but an invisible force seemed to block the goal until finally, Rufina and I were once again in the box.

Instinctively, I knew she'd run around the defenders to shake off her mark. But a voice in my head whispered that if I scored, I'd have a hat trick. My mom, Mrs. Tapia, Coach Ryan, the reporters, and an enormous crowd of people were watching.

But then I saw Rufina all alone.

If I took the shot and missed, she wouldn't reach the ball in time for a rebound.

The seconds were rushing away.

I made my choice.

Channeling my inner Alex Morgan, I crossed the ball through the wall of defenders. Rufina received it like it was a kiss and shot it with such force the keeper didn't even see it coming.

Now we celebrated.

Rufina ran to a corner and kneeled down, screaming, "GOAAAAAAL!"

Tied 3–3 with only two minutes to go, this was the moment of truth.

While Itapé got ready to kick off, I looked around the crowd. I caught a glimpse of green from the Praia players, some of whom were hugging each other and watching the game while others prayed on their knees. They were praying for us to lose. Luciano yelled, "Get back in the game!"

Itapé pulled back to defend, happy with a tie. Rufina, Cintia, Mabel, and I sent shot after shot at them, but nothing cracked their armor. Until Natalia, number nine, made a run all the way to Roxana. I ran to defend, pumping my arms hard, my eyes always on her back. Yesica reached her first with a tackle that earned her a red card and gifted Itapé with a penalty kick.

Roxana stood in the goal, her outstretched arms trying to shrink the space.

My breath came in gasps.

The Itapé player stepped back several feet and then ran up to get momentum. I closed my eyes and held my breath.

And as the crowd moaned and cheered all at the same time, reflecting all the emotions of the human soul, I felt peace. I'd done all I could. I felt joy for being alive, playing a sport that a generation ago could have landed me in prison.

A hand fell on my shoulder. I looked up at Rufina; her face was red from exertion and sunburn. Tears ran down her cheeks. The ref whistled to signal the end of the game, and the capitana in me took over, collecting my girls. I picked them up one by one as Praia Grande celebrated around us. I led Eva María to congratulate every Itapé player.

"You have pasta of campeona, number seven," Natalia told me when we shook hands. "I know we'll play again."

———

Coach Alicia wouldn't let us wallow. "Give yourself time to rest and heal, but remember, no days off," she said.

All around me, brokenhearted teammates lamented our lost chance. I kept my cool until I saw my mom, and then everything around me disappeared as I ran into her arms and sobbed on her shoulder, my tears mixing with her sweat.

"You are incredible," she said, crying too. "I'm la yeta. I made you lose."

I pulled away to look at her eyes and said, "Mamita, without you, I wouldn't even have played."

A little farther away, César waved timidly at me.

Soon, strangers and family alike showered us with con-gratulations. Coach Alicia's praise echoed around us.

"That was an amazing game. You almost had it," said a man with a thin mustache.

By the time Mrs. Tapia found me drinking a Gatorade, I'd run out of tears, but the disappointment lingered. Coach Ryan was talking to a group of Praia Grande girls, and I tried not to look jealous.

I must not have done a good job, because she ruffled my hair and said, "What you did in the last goal was heroic. To sacrifice personal glory for the team is something to be proud of. Not a lot of players would do that, but you did."

"Thank you," I said.

She wasn't done. "There are rumors that the federation is putting together a seleccionado for Copa América and the World Cup in France in a couple of years. Keep play-ing hard, and I'll do what I can so you have more chances. This won't be the last time we talk, Furia. I promise you that."

THE NEXT MORNING, INSTEAD OF GOING TO PARQUE
Balbin to network with coaches and watch other girls live my dreams, I stayed home with my mom.

While she worked on yet another dress, I watched cartoons with Nico. Coach had said no days off, but after a short run to the soy fields and back, I allowed myself the luxury of laziness.

Soon, I fell into a routine. The days stretched into a week, and one afternoon, when my mom went out to meet with Marisol and her mother to plan the baby shower, I realized the commentators on TV were talking about Diego.

They sounded like kids on Christmas.

"AFA has just released the list of World Cup qualifiers,"

the man said. "The one newcomer is Diego Ferrari, Juventus's wonder boy."

His female companion added, "Diego had previously played well, but after missing that game against Roma, he came back and had a hat trick and two assists out of a FIFA video game. The boy is on fire! We can't wait to see what he does next to Dybala, Messi, and company."

I turned the TV off.

Weeks later, my mom gave me a laptop as an early Christmas present, and I used it to pore over tryout schedules for women's teams. Urquiza and Boca Juniors in Buenos Aires had put calls out for players. Roxana and I would head there in January.

Rufina was still deciding if she'd accept an offer from Praia Grande, who had defended their title and won another Sudamericano. They were going pro, and they wanted her.

An incoming message chimed, and I opened the email. It was the file I'd asked Luisana to send me. For the next ten minutes, I watched the video version of Furia she'd edited together. It was mesmerizing. I saw the joy, the sparkle in the championship game, the bits and pieces of practices, and the Sudamericano tournament.

Luisana had made me look like a player any team would want, and before I chickened out, I sent the video to Mrs. Tapia.

What could I lose?

Christmas came and went. Pablo and Marisol spent the holiday with her family, so my mom and I headed over to her sister's, my tía Graciela, whom I hadn't seen in years. Now that she was free of my father, Mamá had plans to open an atelier downtown. Her sister was helping her find a locale.

My eighteenth birthday was on Three Kings Day, January sixth. Of course, I wasn't expecting presents. But just as I was coming back from my run with Yael, the home phone rang.

"Camila? Is that you?" Gabi Tapia asked.

At the sound of her voice, I had to sit down.

When I recovered enough to speak, I said, "Yes, Gabi—I mean, Mrs. Tapia."

"I got your video."

"You did?" I probably should have been speaking English, but I was so nervous I could hardly remember my own name.

"First of all, you're eighteen today, right?"

"Yes."

"Happy birthday. Do you have a passport?"

My father had made all of us get passports when Pablo signed with Central, in the event the call came to move across the world. "Yes," I said.

Mrs. Tapia sighed in relief. "The national league is expanding. I've been offered the position of assistant coach on a new team, the Utah Royals. I want you as a discovery player. I hope you haven't already signed with another team?"

I shook my head, and then, realizing she couldn't see me, I said, "I was going to try out for Urquiza and Boca next week . . ."

"What do you think about giving *us* a chance? I know you have to talk to your parents, look at the details. It's not an offer for a contract yet, but the lead coach wants to see you in person. Can you be here next week?"

"Yes," I said.

With the money I'd saved from El Buen Pastor and my mom's help, I could afford a ticket, even if it was the kind that stopped in every time zone.

"I know you will have many questions. I can talk to your parents."

"My mom," I said. "She's my agent."

"Good," Mrs. Tapia said, "I'll talk to her in more detail about where you'll stay and the paperwork you'll need. But for now, do you have any questions?"

The first thing that came to mind was, "What are their colors?"

Mrs. Tapia laughed and laughed. "Navy blue and yellow, just like Central."

———

While I was packing, I found the estampita of La Difunta Correa in my nightstand drawer. Roxana and I made it to the shrine on the highway to Córdoba the evening before my flight. I placed a bottle of water next to the others that covered the altar, along with a brand-new number five ball.

I'd asked Deolinda for a miracle, and this was my life now. My best friend by my side, my mother finally free, the chance to play on a team in the States. But a part of me still longed for more. I put that old yellow lollipop next to the ball.

Roxana and I walked back to the house, savoring the heat and humidity. Around me, my city glowed green with life.

At El Buen Pastor, I placed my stack of old, loved books in Karen's hands.

"They're all for me?" she asked.

"All for you, Karen."

The pure words of Laura, Alma, María Elena, and Elsa, the fantasy kingdoms of Liliana's books, the poetry of Alfonsina, and even the romances of Florencia's colonial heroines had shaped my world. They had shown me that I could do impossible things.

The sense of wonder and possibility—*that* I owed to the Argentine women who had fought for freedom before the universe conspired and the stars aligned to make me. Pieces of little Camila's soul were in those books. I hoped they would guide Karen toward her own impossible dreams.

I couldn't figure out how to capture the smell of ripe green grapes growing in the vacant lot. Or the sight of the barrio kids pretending a donkey was a noble steed. Or the sound the next morning when the whole monoblock gathered along the staircase to see me off with cheers and applause, as if I were going to the moon. The neighbor played Gustavo Cerati's *Adiós*.

I wanted to gather the stars so when I was in my apartment, I could paste the Southern Cross on the ceiling. That way I'd never be lost. Still, I tried to pack everything in my heart.

The small Fisherton airport was almost empty. Posters of missing girls plastered the wall next to the bathrooms. Young, innocent, small faces. I saw them. I read every one of their names.

My mom, Roxana, Karen, Mrs. Fong, and Coach Alicia kissed me on the cheek, and it felt like a blessing. My mom took a picture of me and posted it online with the caption, Furia la Futbolera.

"Call me every night," she said, and swallowed. "Te quiero."

"Te quiero, Ma."

I grabbed my luggage and headed to the gate. Everyone waved as I went up the escalator.

On the airplane from Buenos Aires to Miami, there was a Mormon missionary boy going back home to Utah. When he heard I was from Rosario, he showed me his

Central jersey and said, "I got it signed by Pablo Hassan *and* Diego Ferrari! They were playing in a field like two little kids. Have you ever met them?"

I shook my head because I couldn't speak. At immigration, the officer hesitated for a second when he saw my Arabic last name. In the end, the visa and the letter from the club were enough, and he let me through.

At the end of another escalator down to baggage claim, Mrs. Tapia waited for me. "Welcome, Furia."

Epilogue

Seven months later

Sometimes I wake up, my throat parched, my arms tangled in a Juventus jersey after dreaming of a boy with swift feet and soft lips, and I wonder why the air is so dry, why the morning is so quiet. And then I remember, and all these months rush back to me in a tsunami of impossibility.

I left Rosario, but Rosario hasn't left me.

Diego was right. It is possible to love two places with the same intensity. I love the majestic mountains covered with snow, but I miss the endless plains and the expansive river.

My team practices on a beautiful turf field. The girls here complain about it all the time, and I get why they do—my legs have the scars to prove how brutal turf can be. But when I remember the state of Parque Yrigoyen, I can't help but feel I'm in paradise.

During the American national anthem, I catch a glimpse of Mrs. Tapia on the jumbo screen. When she squints her eyes, she looks so much like Coach Alicia it takes my breath away.

I'm about to play against the Orlando Pride. I'm going up against Marta. My team warms up, but I can't stop looking at her. When the announcer says my name, the stadium erupts in cheers. "The public loves you, Furia," Mrs. Tapia yells. Little girls and boys wear my jersey. Men and women celebrate my goals.

Life is a wheel, I hear my mom say in my mind.

The sun shines brightly behind the Wasatch mountains as I jog to the center of the field to join my teammates.

In Rosario, Central is playing their opening game. On both Juventus and the national team, Diego's still breaking records. The press has run out of adjectives to describe him. Now that he's cut his hair short, he looks more like an avenging angel than a titan.

With a deep breath, I summon the spirits of my loved ones. Abuela Elena, the Andalusian with all the regrets and the broken heart. My Russian great-grandmother Isabel and her pillows embroidered with sayings. Matilde and her stubbornness. My mom and her newborn freedom. She's opened her atelier and is living with Tía Graciela in an apartment downtown. My niece, Leyla, and her pure eyes.

Roxana and our eternal friendship, even though we're on different teams now. Eda and all the other missing and murdered girls, resting in love. Karen, growing in power. All the unnamed women in my family tree, even the ones forced into it against their will, those who didn't ask to be my ancestors. I have their warrior fire inside me. I summon their speed, their resourcefulness, their hunger for life.

The ref starts the game, and I unleash everything in me. After months of professional training and nutrition, I am faster than ever before. My stride has grown as if my legs have gotten longer. Or maybe it's that I've stopped lying. No one can stop me but myself, and I'm never going to stop.

I fight for every ball, and although I don't always win, no one can say I hold back. I leave my soul on the pitch. I relish what my body can do, appreciate its unorthodox beauty. The eyes of the crowd are on me, and I feel like a goddess.

With my assist, one of my teammates scores. We win the game. I laugh at the way the girls say Furia, over-rolling the *r*, but they try their best.

I try to memorize every moment so I can tell Roxana about it all during our nightly call.

When I finally leave the field and head to my car (my car!), two Latina girls run to me.

They must be around nine years old, dressed in pink versions of my team's jersey, their hair braided and beribboned. There's room in this beautiful game for girliness. That's something I've learned here, and I'm grateful for this gift. I'll never take it for granted.

"Can we get your autograph?" one of the girls asks.

"Of course, chiquita!" I sign their jerseys. "Always be proud to play like a girl," I say, and they run off.

They join the man waiting for them. He high-fives them.

Their dad.

He waves at me, grateful, before taking their hands and walking away. They are so lucky.

"Bye, Camila!" Mrs. Tapia calls from her red convertible. "Good game."

Just as I get in my car, my phone goes off. It's the ringtone that takes me back home.

Un amor como el guerrero, no debe morir jamás . . .

I let the phone's song die down, but it rings again insistently.

In a far corner of the parking lot, Nuria, my roommate from Spain, is talking to a girl who comes to see her play every game.

Finally, I rummage in my purse.

Diego smiles in his profile picture, but I don't pick up. Two hours ago, when my head was fully in the upcoming game, he sent me a message, and I want to read it first. I take a deep breath and jump into the whirlpool.

Hola, Camila. I don't know if you'll see this, but weeks ago, I had a dream we were drinking *mate* and eating alfajores at El Buen Pastor. We were talking about fútbol—what else?— and at the end, you gave me a hug. It seemed so real. Mamana says sometimes our souls find our friends when we sleep. Above all, you and I were always friends first, and I've missed you.

Last night before I went to sleep, hoping to dream of you again, I saw your goal from last week in the highlights. You were glorious.

You made the right choice, and I'll always regret how hard I made that decision for you. I'm sorry.

La Juve is coming to the States on tour in two weeks. We're facing the MLS All-Stars in Utah, of all places. No offense, but we intend to obliterate them.

I know you're in the middle of your season, but if you have some time, I'd love to see you. You still owe me some shots, after all. I think I can beat you to ten.

The ball is on your half, Furia.
Always yours,
Diego

No more lying, no more running. No more regretting things I never said.

I press Diego's number on the screen. It rings once, then his voice travels over the ocean, the sorrow, the months apart.

"Camila?"

"The one and only," I say, and he laughs.

Author's Note

Furia isn't an autobiographical story. However, like Camila, I come from a multicultural and multiracial family, was raised in barrio 7 de Septiembre, have always been obsessed and in love with fútbol, and my nickname has always been either Negra (because of the color of my skin, much darker than anyone else's in my family) or Turca (because of my Syrian-Palestinian ancestry).

In Argentina, nicknames are given according to appearance, country of origin, or any other distinctive personal feature or attribute. Many times, the names (like Gorda, Negra, Chinita, etc.) would be considered offensive to an American, but the level of offensiveness to an Argentine can vary depending on the intention or tone of voice. So, while the nicknames can be endearments that wouldn't be considered microaggressions, they can also be flung as insults.

I debated whether or not to write the more palatable version of how Camila would react to being called Negra or Negrita by eliminating the instances completely or having her call them out, and I ultimately decided that doing either one of these would have been unrealistic for her character. In a situation in which her life is at risk every day just for being a woman—a woman who wants to play fútbol professionally, no less—she wouldn't have the emotional energy to notice or address the nickname, much less call it out. Sometimes, she would even use the words herself.

Argentina, my birthplace, my home even after all the time away from it, has a complicated relationship with race. From president Domingo Faustino Sarmiento (1868–1874), whose legacy was to replace the undesirable gaucho, indigenous, and Black population with the more "desirable" Western European immigrants, to president Julio Argentino Roca (1898–1904), who commandeered la Campaña del Desierto to eradicate indigenous nations, the history of our country since its colonization has been riddled with struggle when it comes to race, education, and social class. The struggle continues to this day.

Although in some respects our society has become more inclusive and tolerant, there is still a lot of work to do to eradicate injustices. I deliberately included this dilemma in Camila's life to open up the conversation about race, colorism, and discrimination in Argentina and how the racial conflicts of our society differ from those in the United States. At the same time, I'm writing from my own lived experience and perspective, which by no means represent those of the rest of the Argentine people, including my own family.

Acknowledgments

I'm a blessed person. This book wouldn't have been possible without the following people. Thank you to all.

Kari Vidal, my alpha reader, for the daily emails asking what happened next.

The Sharks and Pebbles: Scott Rhoades, Julie, Daines, Jaime Theler, and Taffy Lovell.

The writing communities at Vermont College of Fine Arts (especially the Harried Plotters), VONA, WIFYR, Storymakers, SCBWI, Pitchwars, and Las Musas.

My mentors: Cynthia Leitich-Smith, Mary Quattlebaum, Jane Kurtz, An Na, Daniel José Older, Martine Leavitt, Carol Lynch Williams, and Ann Dee Ellis.

The retreat that changed my life: Diane Telgen, Katie Bayerl, Mary-Walker Wright, Anna Waggener, and especially Suma Subramaniam.

Nova Ren Suma, for believing in me.

My amazing editors. Elise Howard, working with you is a dream come true, and sometimes I still pinch myself to see if this is my real life. Sarah Alpert, your expertise and guidance helped me shed the extra words to let my story breathe.

The Algonquin Young Readers team: Ashley Mason, Laura Williams, Megan Harley, Stephanie Mendoza, Caitlin Rubinstein, Randall Lotowycz, Alison Cherry, and Nell Ovitt.

Rachelle Baker. I will never forget the moment I saw Camila's expression for the first time.

Linda Camacho, and the Gallt and Zacker Literary family.

Amigas: Yuli Castañeda Smothers, Veeda Bybee, Karina Rivera, Anedia Wright, Romy Goldberg, Olivia Abtahi, and Courtney Alameda.

Iris Valcarcel. I'll miss you forever.

Adriana Jaussi, Becca Lima, Jennie Perry, Chloe Turner, Kassidy Barrus, and Natalie Mickelson, for loving my kids!

Verónica Muñoz and Rachel Seegmiller, for everything!

Jefferson and Paola Savarino, for answering all my questions about a young couple in the world of professional fútbol.

Ruby Cochran-Simms, my real-life Coach Alicia.

Familia Saied y Stofler. La casa de mi infancia no está más, pero siempre tengo un hogar con ustedes.

Mis hermanos Damián, María Belén, y Gonzalo y sus familias.

Mi mamá, Beatriz Aurora López. Mami, you broke the cycle.

Las mamás de Auxiliadora por el partido de fútbol.

Las familias del 7 de Septiembre.

Las chicas de la promoción Bachiller 1995 del colegio Nuestra Señora de Guadalupe: Natalia Bernardini, Sabrina Bizzoto, Verónica Luna, y Carolina Cip.

My fútbol idols and teams: Pablo Aimar, Diego Ordoñez, Paulo Dybala, Martín Palermo, Paulo Ferrari, Lionel Messi, Marta, Alex Morgan, Mia Hamm, Abby Wambach, el equipo Argentino de Francia 2018, and the USWNT! Rosario Central, Utah Royals, RSL, Barcelona, Juventus, and Argentina. I love you even when you make me suffer so much.

The Power Zone Pack: Matt Wilpers, Denis Morton, Christine D'Ercole, Olivia Amato, and Angie VerBeck. The Boocrew and Cody Rigsby.

My husband, Jeff, for never asking me to choose. My children, Julián, Magalí, Joaquín, Areli, and Valentino. We all grew up together. Here's the fruit of our labors.

The Méndez family in the US and Puerto Rico.

Las futboleras who paved the way.

The girls and women lost to violence, and those who live in dire circumstances and still make the world a better place. This book is for you. ¡Ni una menos! ¡Vivas nos queremos!